THE FOUR GRACES

D. E. Stevenson

sourcebooks
landmark

Published by Sourcebooks Landmark, an imprint of Sourcebooks, Inc.
P.O. Box 4410, Naperville, Illinois 60567-4410
(630) 961-3900
Fax: (630) 961-2168
www.sourcebooks.com

Originally published in 1946. This edition is based on the second impression paperback edition published in 1974 in Great Britain by Fontana, an imprint of HarperCollins Publishers.

Library of Congress Cataloging-in-Publication data is on file with the publisher.

Printed and bound in the United States of America.
VP 10 9 8 7 6 5 4

To the March Hare
with much love

Author's Preface

T he author has been asked whether this is a funny book or true to life and has some difficulty in answering the question, for life is a funny business altogether (both funny peculiar and funny ha-ha, as Elizabeth would say). The story covers less than a year in the life of a family, and during this comparatively short period many things happen, some serious and important, others cheerful and gay. It is summertime—a summer during the greatest and most terrible of wars—but the author felt disinclined to bring such a grave and desperate matter into a lighthearted tale; here, then, are to be found only the lighter side and the small inconveniences of Total War; the larger issues are ignored. The people in the story are imaginary and bear no resemblance whatsoever to anybody the author has met, but they *are* intended to represent human beings; if they fail in this, they fail in everything. The Graces are unusual, perhaps, but surely not incredible. They talk a good deal of nonsense and a certain amount of sense; they disagree violently on occasion and sometimes are extremely rude to one another, but they are also extremely loyal and show a united front to the outside world. It may be that the Graces will be criticized for levity upon important matters, or, on the other hand, for taking trifles au grand sêrieux, but the author is of the opinion that life is bearable only if it be leavened with humor, and that a spice of humor is not out of place even in the most solemn and weighty affairs. When we find Sarah taking to heart the slight misunderstanding with Miss Bodkin, and Elizabeth "laughing wild amid severest woe," we need not conclude that the former is too anxious-minded, nor the latter too frivolous to be true to life...for life is like that (so the author has found) and all the best people have at least one bat in the belfry.

Chapter One

"The voice that breathed o'er Eden,
That earliest wedding day,
The primal marriage blessing,
It hath not passed away."

Matilda Grace was humming the words to herself as she played it on the organ. She enjoyed playing the organ in her father's church—firstly, because she knew the instrument so well (it was a very old friend and possessed the faults and failings of an artistic temperament); secondly, because making any sort of music gave her pleasure; and thirdly (why not admit it?), because it really *was* rather amusing to see everybody without being seen. This godlike condition was due to the fact that the organ gallery was raised and shut off from the rest of the church by a wrought iron grille; not a very convenient arrangement, perhaps, but the grille was of such fine workmanship—adorned with vine leaves and delicately curling tendrils—that nobody had the heart to demand its removal. Matilda Grace liked the grille; being naturally shy, she would have felt most uncomfortable perched up at the organ in full view of the congregation. The grille gave her confidence, she was unseen; she could almost imagine herself unheard (almost but not quite) and this was the more important because Matilda was now the official organist at St. James's in the absence of Mr. Carruthers who was serving with His Majesty's Forces in the Far East. Matilda had felt very nervous about this wedding; indeed this morning when she got out of bed she had suddenly decided that she could not do it...but then it had seemed even more impossible not to do it, for there was nobody else in the village who could, or would, make the attempt...and of course it was so very important that everything should go off with a swing. Now, thank goodness, her nervousness had vanished and she was managing it all quite nicely.

In the intervals of the service Tilly could peer through the grille and see everything that was happening—could see far better than if she had been sitting with her sisters in the Vicarage pew—and this wedding was a particularly interesting one; the bridegroom was interesting to Tilly because she had known him for years, and the bride because Tilly had never seen her before. Tilly gazed down upon the happy pair, standing at the altar steps. They certainly *looked* happy. They looked well matched. She felt very glad about it. When Tilly was fifteen she had imagined herself in love with Archie Cobbe, for he was exactly the sort of young man to awaken a romantic attachment. He was so big and so good-looking and people said he was wild. You met him sometimes, riding about Chevis Green on a prancing horse and he always waved his cap and shouted "Hallo!" Then old Lady Chevis had died and left him Chevis Place, and Archie had taken the name of "Chevis" and settled down into a model squire. A good many young women in the neighborhood had hoped to marry Archie...and then people had begun to say he would never marry...and now, here he was at the altar with a completely strange young woman, a young woman out of the blue, of whom nobody in Chevis Green had ever heard. Jane Watt.

It wasn't a very romantic name, but Tilly thought she looked romantic. She was small—or at any rate she looked small beside Archie—she was graceful and elegant, and the beam of clear light that shone upon her from the south window showed that she had a beautiful complexion, good features, and fair curly hair, cut rather short. Not young, exactly, thought Tilly, but Archie wasn't exactly young. In the early thirties, perhaps.

Most brides arrange to be married in their own neighborhoods but Jane Watt had defied this time-honored convention. Perhaps she had no home. It would matter tremendously to the village what sort of person she was. It would matter tremendously to the Vicar's daughters. Tilly hoped she was capable—but not too managing, not the sort of person who would want to change everything and turn everything upside down. Perhaps she would take over the Women's Institute...was it too much to hope that she would help with the Girl Guides?

Mr. Grace was talking now. His clear voice rose and fell as he delivered his homily. Tilly was free to have a good look around. She looked first at the Vicarage pew and saw her sisters—Elizabeth, Sarah, and Adeline. How pretty they were! Nobody would suspect for a moment that Liz had made her own frock, or that Sal's coat had been turned inside out by the little dressmaker in the village. It was because they wore their clothes with an air, thought Tilly, because they were unconscious of their appearance. Addie was in uniform of course. (She was the youngest Miss Grace and had joined the Women's Auxiliary Air Force. Having just received her commission her uniform was brand-new and exceedingly smart, but she looked no nicer than the others.) Seeing her sisters like this, without being seen, was rather a startling experience. Tilly was seeing them as other people saw them, people who knew only their outsides, the front they chose to show. This was how they appeared to strangers. There was a young man sitting behind and a little to the left of the Vicarage pew (probably he had come over from the camp at Ganthorne) with a very brown face and smooth brown hair. This individual was looking at the three Miss Graces with interest and admiration—with so much interest and admiration that Tilly felt quite annoyed with him.

The church was full. All the villagers were here, and there were quite a number of strangers as well; there were officers from the camp and people from Wandlebury and Popham Magna; people from Gostown, too, though how they had managed to get over (in wartime, without gas) Tilly could not imagine. The bridegroom's sister lived at Ganthorne Lodge, which was quite near the camp. There she was in the front pew, Mrs. Sam Abbott was her name...and beside her were the other Abbotts, who lived in Wandlebury: Mr. and Mrs. Abbott and their small boy, Simon (he looked a perfect angel, Tilly thought). Beyond Simon was an elderly lady in an old-fashioned hat with white flowers—perhaps an aunt. These were the bridegroom's relations, of course. On the bride's side there seemed to be no relations at all, for Colonel Melton was sitting in the front pew with his pretty daughter beside him—Colonel Melton was in command of the camp at Ganthorne.

But now the homily was over and Tilly remembered her duties and returned to them (feeling more than a little ashamed of herself for not having listened to a word), and there was no further opportunity for "peeping" until the end.

"Tum, tum te tum tum tum tum, *tum*, tum te te tum..." The Wedding March, of course; it was all over and Tilly was letting herself go and the congregation was streaming out, first two by two and then in a flood as if a dam had burst. Tilly could hear the chatter of voices outside the church door where people were standing about in the bright spring sunshine waiting for each other. It was not far from the church to Chevis Place, and most of the guests would walk because there was no transport for them. They would walk through the woods; it was shorter that way and much more pleasant. Tilly could not make up her mind whether to go to the reception or not. She had been asked, of course, but she found crowds of people rather alarming; crowds of strangers being introduced to her and expecting her to produce small talk! But perhaps she had better go. She had no excuse for not going...it seemed silly...

She was about to close the organ when she noticed a horrid smear of dirt upon her pale-gray skirt. (Dash! said Tilly to herself. I should have dusted the organ.) It certainly was rather a nuisance, for of course it was her best frock, but, on the other hand, this decided the matter. She would not go to the reception. She would go home and make herself a cup of tea—it would be much more comfortable. Having decided this, Tilly played on for a little, amusing herself with variations upon the Wedding March, undreamed of by its composer. Then she closed the organ, ran down the little side stair and so out into the churchyard.

Just at that very moment somebody emerged from the main door of the church. This was unexpected because Tilly thought everyone had gone long ago. Tilly hesitated, looking back. It was a woman in a long black coat and a round hat with white flowers in it—the woman who had been sitting beside little Simon Abbott in the front pew. What was she doing here, wondered Tilly. Why hadn't she gone on to Chevis Place with the rest of her party?

The woman came out into the sunshine and stood there, as if dazed by the sudden brilliant light; then she sat down, suddenly, in the porch. Tilly went back, stepping lightly over the grass, and as she drew near she was horrified to find that the woman looked ill. Her eyes were shut and she was leaning back against the porch in an attitude of exhaustion.

"Are you—are you feeling all right?" inquired Tilly anxiously.

There was no reply.

"Can I do anything for you?" asked Tilly in a louder voice.

The woman looked up. "I am a little tired," she said, adding almost immediately, "There is no need to be alarmed."

"A glass of water?" suggested Tilly with solicitude. She had to repeat her offer twice and now she realized that the woman was hard of hearing.

"Please—if it is not a bother," was the reply.

When Tilly returned from the vestry with a glass of water she was glad to see that her patient was looking a good deal better.

"Thank you very much," she said, accepting it gratefully. "I think you must be Miss Grace. I saw you in church, did I not? My name is Miss Marks."

"Yes—no," said Tilly loudly. "As a matter of fact, you didn't see me, but you probably saw my sisters. We're rather alike in a way—to people who don't know us. You were sitting with Mrs. Abbott, weren't you?"

"Yes," nodded Miss Marks. "But if you were not in church, how did you see me?"

"I *was* in church. I was playing the organ."

"How clever of you!" exclaimed Miss Marks.

Tilly was often praised for her ability to play the organ and such praise usually irritated her, but today she did not feel annoyed for Miss Marks was perfectly sincere.

"It isn't clever," said Tilly. "The organ is easy when you get into the way of it—just at first it seems a bit complicated, of course."

"I never could manage it," said Miss Marks regretfully. "And the fact is all the more deplorable because it would have been an extremely useful accomplishment." She sipped the water and looked sadly into her past. Tilly was silent, wondering about her. A blackbird, sitting on an adjacent tombstone, burst into song.

"My father was a Presbyterian minister," continued Miss

Marks. "We lived in Fife. It was a small parish and—but that will not interest you."

"It interests me a lot," declared Tilly, smiling.

"Ancient history," said Miss Marks, returning the smile.

Her smile was very sweet and lighted up her rather heavy face in the most remarkable fashion. She's a dear, thought Tilly, and impulsively said, "Would you like to come over to the Vicarage? It isn't far—but perhaps you feel well enough, now, to go to the reception."

"The Vicarage, please—if it would not trouble you. The fact is I have recently undergone an operation and, although it was by no means serious, I have not yet recovered my strength. I shall not be missed at the reception," continued Miss Marks somewhat grimly. "Archie and I have never managed to see eye to eye." She rose as she spoke and leaned upon her umbrella, which was long and thin and had a sharply pointed furrule. For some reason Tilly received a strong impression that the umbrella was a symbol—perhaps even a weapon—rather than a means of keeping its owner dry. This impression was intensified (as they walked across the little churchyard toward the Vicarage) by the manner in which Miss Marks used her umbrella to give point to her remarks. Not that her remarks needed point, for Tilly found them most intriguing.

The worn and weathered stone that commemorated the victims of the Black Death caught her attention. "Ah!" she exclaimed. "A memorial to a very grim war!"

"Worse than war," agreed Tilly. "Though of course David did not think so."

"He chose pestilence, but only three days of it, remember," returned Miss Marks, who was quite as well grounded as Tilly in scriptural history.

There were forty names upon the memorial. Miss Marks read out some of them in ruminative voice. "Josiah Barefoot, Karen

Toop, Johanna Element, Aaron Aleman, Sarah Bouse, John Bodkin, Reuben Trod, Hannah Search…"

"Queer names," said Tilly. "But there are still people with those names living in the parish. Jos Barefoot is our gardener, and our maid is called Joan Aleman—at least she *was*. She's married now, and her name is Mrs. Robinson, isn't it a pity? The butcher is Toop and the man at the garage is Element. Liz says it's a good name for a person who has to do with electric irons."

Miss Marks was an unusual sort of person. She herself was pedantic in speech but she was quite undismayed by Tilly's babble, and this was just as well, because now that Tilly had recovered from the shyness that afflicted her in the presence of strangers, she continued to babble in the most cheerful manner imaginable.

The Vicarage was an old house with small-paned windows, pointed gables, and tall brick chimneys. It was surrounded by very tall trees so that you came upon it suddenly and if you were appreciative of Elizabethan architecture—as Miss Marks was—it was a little apt to take your breath away. Tilly gave her new friend time to recover breath and then led her through the cobbled yard, which was shaded by an elm, and so by the back door into the kitchen. (This was an unconscious tribute to her new friend's personality. If Tilly had not liked Miss Marks she would have conducted her into the drawing room by the front entrance.) It was cool and dim in the stone-paved passage and the kitchen was a pleasant room, airy and comfortably furnished.

"This is nice of you, my dear," said Miss Marks, recognizing the compliment that had been paid her. She laid her umbrella upon the dresser and sat down near the fire.

"We'll have tea," said Tilly happily. "We'll have it here—unless you'd rather have it in the drawing room."

"Certainly not. This seems to me a charming place for tea."

"Good," said Tilly, throwing off her hat and coat. "We'll

have tea here. I'm glad I didn't go to the party. It's funny, you know. I *would* have gone if I hadn't dirtied my skirt. If I'd dusted the organ—as I ought to have done if I'd had any sense—I shouldn't have met you, should I?"

"*Le nez de Cléopâtre,*" said Miss Marks, smiling.

"Cleopatra's nose?" asked Tilly in a bewildered voice.

"'*Le nez de Cléopâtre: s'il eut été plus court, toute la face de la terre aurait changé.*'"

"Oh!" said Tilly, hesitating with the kettle in her hand. "Oh, yes…yes, I see. The duster that I didn't use is like Cleopatra's nose. I mean if I'd *used* it, Cleopatra's nose would have been shorter and we shouldn't have met."

"Exactly," said Miss Marks, without batting an eyelid. She really was a very remarkable woman.

"Well, I'm glad her nose wasn't shorter. I hate parties, you know. One person is much more interesting than a lot of people…and it will be lovely for Liz and Sal to tell me about it when they come home. You saw them in church, didn't you?"

"Very good-looking young women," said Miss Marks, nodding.

"Darlings," said Tilly, as she shook out a clean tablecloth and spread it on the table. "Liz and Sal are older than me and Addie is younger. She's just here for forty-eight hours, and she has to go back to London tonight. Liz works on the farm at Chevis Place—Archie's farm, you know—Sal and I keep house and help father. We arranged it like that," said Tilly, as she gathered cups and saucers and plates and spoons from the cupboard and laid them on the table. "Because Sal isn't terribly strong and I can play the organ…and of course Joan stays with her mother now and only comes to us for the day. She has a baby… I told you she was married, didn't I?"

Tilly paused, aware that she had been babbling, but her new friend was not only perfectly calm but appeared to be following with interest. "Mrs. Robinson," said Miss Marks, nodding.

"You're interested in people!" said Tilly, surprised at this feat of memory.

"What could be more interesting?"

"Some people like books better, or—or *things*."

"Books are people," smiled Miss Marks. "In every book worth reading, the author is there to meet you, to establish contact with you. He takes you into his confidence and reveals his thoughts to you."

Tilly nodded thoughtfully. "Are you Archie's aunt?" she inquired.

"I am no relation, but I have lived with young Mrs. Abbott for years. I was her governess at one time. Now I run the house and do the cooking. I like it," she added defiantly.

"Yes—well—it's useful," said Tilly, a trifle taken aback.

Tea was ready now so they sat down at the table, and Miss Marks took off her gloves.

"I thought the bride looked nice," said Tilly suddenly.

"Jane is a very pleasant young woman," said Miss Marks, sipping her tea with great satisfaction. "She has been staying at Ganthorne Lodge for some months, so I can speak with authority. Jane has a sweet nature."

This encomium might have sounded halfhearted (as a matter of fact, Tilly was usually "put off" by the report that so-and-so had a sweet nature, for she had found that, more often than not, it meant that so-and-so was rather wet), but already she had weighed up Miss Marks and realized her habit of understatement.

"I'm glad she's nice," said Tilly. "It'll make a lot of difference to us—I mean, in the parish. People are so touchy in Chevis Green."

"Not only in Chevis Green—but you need have no fears on that score. Jane is essentially kind."

"Oh, good!" said Tilly.

Chapter Two

Miss Marks had gone and supper was almost ready when the merrymakers began to return. Sal was the first to reach home. She walked into the kitchen and smiled at Tilly. "Cinderella," she said in a teasing voice.

"Not really," replied Tilly, shoving a tray of bread under the grill. "Cinderella wanted to go to the party, and I didn't…but, anyhow, I've had a fairy godmother to keep me company."

"So I see. She's left her broomstick," said Sal, pointing to the dresser upon which lay, forlorn and forgotten, Miss Marks's umbrella.

"Oh!" cried Tilly in dismay.

"Why worry?" asked Sal, sinking into a comfortable chair. "It hasn't rained for a fortnight and probably won't rain for another three weeks. Why did she bring it, I wonder."

"I don't think she ever goes anywhere without it," replied Tilly seriously.

Sal was silent. She talked less than the others and, perhaps, thought more. Tilly, looking at her as she lay back in the chair, thought how peaceful she was. Liz or Addie would have been full of questions—not so Sal. Sal would listen if you wanted to tell her something, but she never probed.

"Was it a nice party?" asked Tilly, turning the toast. "Did you talk to anyone interesting? What did you think of *her*?"

"Rather a dear," replied Sal, answering the last question.

She might have gone on to answer the others but she had no chance, for the door burst open and Liz appeared on the scene. Liz took off her hat and shook out her curls. "Oh, you've managed everything," said Liz. "I rushed home to help you. Why didn't you come? You'd have liked it. I looked for you everywhere. There was champagne cup and ices. Lovely party! Poor Addie had to leave early to catch her train, but one of the officers took her straight to the station in his jeep."

"With a brown face?" inquired Tilly, remembering the one who had stared so hard in church.

"No, pink," replied Liz. "Tall and pink with fair hair."

"Jimmy Howe," said Sal.

"Very new," added Liz. "And as a matter of fact, you needn't try to scent a romance. It was me he liked in spite of the fact that I'm old enough to be his grandmother. I asked him to take Addie to the station…Oh, Tilly, *not* macaroni and cheese! Father had awful dreams last time."

"There wasn't anything else," said Tilly. "And you needn't worry because this is macaroni and cheese with a difference."

"I didn't know there could be much difference. Hallo, where's the umbrella come from?"

"It's hers," said Tilly, whisking around the kitchen and piling the dishes onto a tray. "I mean she showed me. She said it couldn't give anyone awful dreams if you made it like this— beautifully creamy—"

Sal laughed. "Did she stir it with her broomstick, Tilly? Is it fairy food?"

"Real silk!" murmured Liz, fingering it reverently. "Somehow it seems—*more* than just an umbrella—"

"Oh, it *is!*" cried Tilly.

Mr. Grace was the last to arrive. He came in smiling; although he was always reluctant to attend social functions, he enjoyed them tremendously when he got there.

"It went off very well, I think," said Mr. Grace. "In spite of the heat everyone seemed to be enjoying it, and the bride looked charming."

"It always does, and *she* always does," declared Liz. "I mean I've never *heard* of a wedding that didn't go off well, have you, darling? Can you imagine anyone saying, 'It didn't go off very well, did it? And wasn't the bride plain?'"

Mr. Grace was so used to the imbecility of his oldest daughter that it did not worry him. "I'll just go and wash," he said.

They had their supper in the kitchen because Joan had gone home and it was easier, and if anyone had seen the Graces sitting around the kitchen table, enjoying their evening meal, he would have seen a pleasant sight. The girls talked about the wedding, of course, but their conversation wandered about a good deal and veered to and fro in a manner a stranger would have found perfectly natural. Sometimes they disagreed with each other and said so, making no bones about it, but they were so much in tune and so fully in accord upon essentials that it did not matter how violently they disagreed upon nonessentials. In fact a good hearty disagreement was welcome, adding spice to their talk. Now and then Liz would emit her sudden explosive snort of laughter, and Sal would chuckle delightedly.

"I met a young man at the reception," said Mr. Grace.

"And you asked him to lunch," added Liz reproachfully.

"How did you know?" inquired her father in amazement.

"I know *you*, darling."

Mr. Grace sighed. He was of a hospitable nature and the

straitness of war rationing was a burden to him. "I keep on forgetting," he explained.

"We could kill Pedro," soothed Tilly. "We've always meant to, haven't we?"

"Yes," agreed Mr. Grace, comforted. "Yes, kill Pedro by all means. We must give the young man a good lunch."

"Is he an officer?" asked Liz.

"Yes, from the camp at Ganthorne. I have no idea of his rank, but I should think he is too young to be a major."

"Too old to be a lieutenant?"

"Don't pull his leg," said Tilly quickly.

"He likes it," declared Liz. "It's good for him to have his leg pulled."

"Your uncouth idiom revolts me," said Mr. Grace, who, when he liked, was perfectly capable of holding his own. "I suppose you will know what his rank is when you see him. You can count the buttons on his shoulder strap. To me his rank is immaterial—"

"'Tis but the guinea stamp," murmured Sal.

"Quite so. His name is Roderick Herd and he is coming to see the rose window."

"Interested in rose windows," said Liz regretfully.

Mr. Grace let that pass. He was aware that his daughters did not appreciate rose windows—not as much as they should—and his thoughts were busy in a different direction for he was remembering his conversation with Roderick Herd. (If Mr. Grace had been an habitué of the local picture house, he would have recognized this "remembering" as a "flashback.") It had happened as follows: Mr. Grace, slightly dazed by the babble of talk, had withdrawn to the edge of the human whirlpool when suddenly a very brown young man (brown face, brown hair, brown eyes) had accosted him in a respectful manner. "Excuse me, sir. You are Mr. Grace, aren't you? May I ask if you are any relation to W.G.?" This was a question often put to Mr. Grace (though not as often now as formerly, for the present generation is lamentably indifferent to the giants of the past), and he always made the same answer: "No, but I have four daughters." It was a "mad hatter" reply, but Mr. Grace found it a useful test of character. Some people said, "Oh, had *he* four daughters?" Others abandoned W.G. and inquired about the daughters; others looked puzzled, mystified, or merely stupid. Time was when Mr. Grace had replied, "No, but I'm very keen on cricket." But the daughters were better. This particular young man, Roderick Herd, had taken the daughters without flinching. "Yes," he had said (almost as if he had known). "Yes, you can't have everything, can you, sir?" And one had to admit that, as a response, it was pretty hard to beat.

You can't have everything, thought Mr. Grace, looking around the table with satisfaction. He was of the opinion that his daughters were beautiful. He knew they were good. Liz was the most attractive, perhaps, she was so full of life, vital and glowing and eager for any adventure that might come her way. She was tall and slim, her hair was golden and full of deep waves, her complexion was milk and roses. Tilly was nearly as tall, but not so slim; her cheeks were rounded and dimpling. Her head was like the head of a bird (an English thrush, thought Mr. Grace, waxing poetical); it was smooth and broad and her brown hair swept back from her forehead, thick as feathers. Sal's hair was darker, with reddish lights; it was softer hair, little tendrils curled about her forehead and her ears. She had a fragile look but there was resilience there, an unexpected toughness and spring. Less taking than the others, perhaps, but with a charm of her own, with well-molded bone beneath the softness of her smooth white skin and rather a wide mouth with a gracious curve.

Mr. Grace liked to think of his daughters as "children" (about ten years old), but sometimes they alarmed him because suddenly they seemed older than himself, and wiser, and because he had discovered that they understood him too well and occasionally "managed" him tactfully. At other times, they alarmed him by their foolishness. What mysterious creatures they were! Was it because they were motherless? If Mary had lived...but Mary had died and left him to deal with the daughters as best he could. His sister had offered to help him, but he had decided against the plan, for the daughters were his responsibility and nobody else's. Mary helped. He was often conscious of her guidance. It had worked out pretty well, really. There had been anxious times, of course, but—yes—it had worked out pretty well. Mr. Grace looked at them again, and his heart warmed toward them. I love them all alike, thought Mr. Grace. But although this was his honest conviction, it was not quite true, for Sal had a special place in his heart. He had been frightened of his first child, for he knew nothing about babies, and he had scarcely dared to touch the fragile morsel of humanity that was Liz, but when his second child arrived, he was "broken in" and was able to enjoy her from the first. He had bathed Sal and put her to bed, he had sung to her and told her stories. Sal was delicate when she was a child and had had to rest, lying for long hours on her back. She had been too delicate to go to school so he had taught her himself and taken pleasure in it. Together they had explored the highways and byways of knowledge.

They have taught me a lot, thought Mr. Grace humbly. I am a more useful servant of God for having four daughters.

Chapter Three

The Graces had evolved an elaborate technique for dealing with visitors, and especially with their father's "finds." His swans were often geese, of course, but even geese have their feelings and the Graces were kindhearted young women. To a stranger visiting the Vicarage for the first time and entering the drawing room in the wake of his host, the sight of four young women all at once was overpowering (the Graces knew this from experience, for they had beheld many a poor goose lose his composure and his power of speech and blush to the roots of his hair at the unexpected sight); to a stranger, sitting in the study and chatting quietly to his host, the entrance of four young women was even more alarming. They had talked it over seriously. "It's because we're all rather big," said Liz. "And rather beautiful," said Addie. "'A bevy of beautiful maidens,'" said Sal, obviously quoting.

"It wouldn't be so bad if we weren't so alike," said Tilly thoughtfully. This raised a storm of protest from the other three and a good many remarks of a "personal" nature, but Tilly stuck to her guns. "We *are* alike to strangers," she declared. "Not to ourselves or each other, but to strangers who see us for the first time." "I don't agree," said Liz, "but that doesn't matter, really. Something has got to be done." So, after several unfortunate experiences, the Graces had formulated a plan to meet the case…one at a time was the rule.

"But we needn't bother today," said Liz. "Addie isn't here, so there are only three."

"Too many," said Tilly firmly. "Besides, I shall be busy with Pedro. I *do* want Pedro to be a success."

Liz took the point. In life Pedro had been a failure; he was a cock without a crow.

"I can't leave him to Joan," continued Tilly. "She's apt to lose her head when anyone is here for lunch, and the rhubarb tart—no, I *must* be in the kitchen. You and Sal can entertain father's young man."

"I'm going to cook Pedro," said Sal firmly.

"Oh, well…" said Tilly, giving in, for after all, nobody had a better right. Sal was the hen-woman. She had brought up Pedro from egg-hood.

Tilly opened the front door to Roderick Herd. She saw at once that it was the young man who had stared so hard in church. (Rose windows, indeed! said Tilly to herself.) Aloud she said, "How do you do? I'm Tilly Grace. My father said I was to take you over to church to meet him."

"Oh, thank you," said Roderick Herd, smiling at her and disclosing very white teeth, which looked all the whiter in contrast with his very brown face.

Three pips on his shoulder proclaimed him a captain to Tilly's experienced eye, and she was able to address him as Captain Herd when necessary. They walked across the church-yard together chatting of this and that, of the weather, and the state of the roads, and whether Captain Herd had taken the shortest route from Ganthorne to Chevis Green, but Tilly's thoughts were a good deal more interesting than her conversation. Definitely not a goose, thought Tilly, as she described the crossroads before you got to Wandlebury where Captain Herd should have turned to the left, but not a swan, either…more like an eagle…and I don't believe he knows the first thing about glass. Will he be able to get away with it or will Father find out?

She put a blue silk handkerchief over her head and tied it beneath her chin. It matched her eyes exactly.

"St. Paul?" asked Captain Herd, looking at her. "But I thought they had washed that out?"

"We've always done it," said Tilly. "It would feel rather funny not to—custom dies hard, as Father would say."

They stepped out of the bright sunshine into the dim and shadowy church.

"It's beautiful," said Captain Herd impulsively. "It's much more beautiful than it was yesterday…"

Tilly thought so, too. She liked the old church best when it was empty, shadowy, and peaceful. You could see it better when your eyes were not distracted by people, nor your ears by sounds.

Captain Herd was now admiring the font. "For christening babies," he said in a thoughtful voice, not really proffering this unnecessary piece of information, but trying to show an intelligent interest in all he saw.

"Yes," agreed Tilly.

"That reading desk isn't very pretty," said Captain Herd.

"The lectern," said Tilly. "No, we don't like it much, either. We hope to get a new one some day—after the war, perhaps." She hesitated and then added, "And that's the rose window, of course," pointing to it as she spoke, for by this time she felt doubtful whether Captain Herd would know, and it seemed better for everyone's sake that Captain Herd should not put his foot in it too badly, at the very start.

"Yes," said Captain Herd. "It's shaped like a rose, of course… I like *that* window, too."

"Oh, you mustn't," said Tilly quickly. "You must be

absolutely horrified at Joseph and his Brethren. Old Lady Chevis gave it in memory of her husband so they can't take it down, but it's terribly, terribly bad."

"Thank you," said Captain Herd, with a little smile (he certainly wasn't a goose).

"You may admire the south window, of course," she continued. "Lots of people do. The glass is modern but good— look at the shafts of sunlight streaming through the panes."

"One might say one admired the richness of coloring," suggested Captain Herd.

"Oh, definitely," said Tilly. "But as a matter of fact one would be better not to say too much—"

"Oh, definitely," agreed Captain Herd quickly.

Mr. Grace was in the vestry. He came out when he heard their voices and welcomed his visitor cordially, so Tilly abandoned the eagle to his fate and went home to peel the vegetables.

⌒∞⌒

"Pedro was very tender," announced Tilly, as she entered the kitchen with a trayload of china.

"I'm glad," said Sal. "I thought it was safer to do him in a casserole. I had him in soon after eleven and did him slowly. Put those in the scullery—Joan's there."

Tilly carried the tray through the kitchen, noticing as she went that everything was tidy. Sal was that sort of person, she cleared as she went along. If Liz had cooked the lunch, the whole place would have been piled up with bowls and dishes of every description.

Joan was clattering about in the scullery and singing tunefully, but she stopped to smile at Tilly. "Did I do all right?" she inquired. "I didn't 'and the plates the wrong side or anything, did I?"

"I thought you did splendidly," replied Tilly.

"Miss Sal said I can go early," continued Joan, seizing this favorable moment for her announcement. "It's because m' uncle's 'ere. 'E's 'aving 'is 'olidays now. So m' mother said, come 'ome early, she said, if ther's nothing special on. I don't need to, if you want me special."

"Of course you must go," said Tilly. (She was aware that a visit from Joan's uncle was an important event.)

"M' uncle's still at Brighton," said Joan, plunging about at the sink. "'E still runs that garage. Of course there ain't much doing in the gas line, but 'e does munitions now—does them in 'is own workshop, like. Little bits of shells and things. People come in an 'elp. It's a pity we ain't got munitions at Chevis Green. There's plenty of people could spare 'alf a day to make them…don't you bother drying those dishes, Miss Tilly, you'll muss up your nice frock. I'll do them in 'alf a jiff."

"What about tea?" inquired Sal, looking in. "It's disgusting to think of tea when we've just finished lunch, but if that young man is staying I'll have to make a cake or something—"

"He isn't," said Tilly. "In fact he's just going—he seemed sort of restless, I thought."

"Restless?"

"It may have been the rose window. He knew nothing about it, of course."

"Nothing at all?" asked Sal in alarm. "Then Father—"

"Oh, he got through," declared Tilly. "Father was calling him 'Roderick' so it must have been all right. He asked for Addie's address."

"Did you give it to him?"

"Why not?" said Tilly. "Addie's quite capable of dealing out raspberries if she feels that way."

The old house settled down to a peaceful afternoon. Tilly was weeding in the garden, Liz had gone back to the farm, and Joan had finished her work in record time and vanished. Sal fetched a book and sat down in the rocking chair near the kitchen window. She had done a good job of work and earned her leisure, and she intended to enjoy it to the full. She was rereading *Emma*: it was one of her favorite books, partly because she felt that Chevis Green was a modern version of Highbury. There was a "Miss Bates" in Chevis Green—or at least a lady who resembled her closely—and a "Mr. Woodhouse" too: perhaps these characters are to be found in most English villages. It was very quiet, and Sal was sure that this was the sort of afternoon the old house enjoyed. Old gentlemen enjoy being at rest during the hottest time of the day, and the old house was very like an old gentleman. The clock ticked stolidly and the fire crackled and Sal "read in her book."

Suddenly Sal heard a sound—it was the creak of the back door opening—and a moment later there were footsteps in the passage; footsteps that sounded furtive and hesitating. Sal raised her head and listened. She was alarmed. There were dozens of people who had right of access to the back premises of the Vicarage, but any of these would have walked in confidently, sure of a welcome, sure of sympathy or of help in any trouble that had brought them here. Who could this be? Sal half rose—and then hesitated and sat down again; it was too late for flight.

The kitchen door was opening now, and the intruder looked in…he was an officer in battle dress.

"Oh!" he exclaimed. "I didn't know anyone was here," and then he stopped and looked at Sal. "But—they said you were in London!" he cried.

Sal had never seen the man before. "They said I was in London?" she repeated.

"Yes," he declared, coming nearer and gazing at her. "Yes, that's what they said. Why did they?"

"I don't know what you mean," said Sal in alarm, for it seemed to her that the young man was behaving in a very odd manner.

"It doesn't matter," he declared. "I've found you, that's the main thing."

"But I don't know you."

"You're Addie, aren't you?"

"No, I'm not," replied Sal firmly. "And I'm not the least *like* Addie."

"You aren't the least like anybody," he agreed, smiling at her and perching himself on the edge of the table.

Sal did not return the smile. She assumed a dignified air. "I don't know you," said Sal. "If you want something you had better say so—"

"It's all right," he interrupted. "Honestly it is. I ought to have explained before, but it gave me a sort of shock meeting you like this. They said you were in London, so I managed to get your address and I was going to call on you at your flat. I thought you were Addie, of course."

"I've told you I'm not Addie."

"I know," said the young man. "I'd forgotten there were four."

Sal heaved an elaborate sigh.

"I'm muddling it all frightfully," said the young man in self-reproach. "It's all so clear to me that I keep on forgetting to explain. I'll tell you exactly what happened. I've been having lunch here, and then I said good-bye and Mr. Grace saw me off. Well, when I was about halfway to Wandlebury I remembered about the umbrella. Miss Marks left it here yesterday, didn't she?"

"Yes," said Sal, who was beginning to see light.

"She said she left on the dresser in the kitchen...yes, there it is!"

"Yes," said Sal.

"I didn't know what to do, really," declared Captain Herd, frowning. "I'd said good-bye and all that. I didn't want to barge in and disturb Mr. Grace…so I thought I'd just nip in by the back door and see if I could find the gamp myself. It was lucky, really."

They were silent for a few minutes. Captain Herd took the umbrella and put it beside him on the table. Then his eyes came back to Sal. "You aren't angry with me, are you?" he inquired.

"Not now," said Sal, smiling.

"Why do you ask me what I meant? Most people would have said, 'Why was it lucky?' or something."

Sal laughed. "Because you'll tell me if you want to. People do. If they want to tell you a thing, they tell you, and if not…"

"I do," he said earnestly. "I saw you in church yesterday at the wedding and I wanted to meet you properly."

"This isn't properly," Sal pointed out.

"Markie's umbrella has introduced us," declared Roderick Herd. "If it hadn't been for Markie's umbrella, I shouldn't have met you. Odd, isn't it?"

Sal looked thoughtful. She might have looked even more thoughtful if she realized that the umbrella was only a link in the chain—the chain stretching back to Tilly's duster and Cleopatra's nose.

"Markie is rather a wonderful person," continued Roderick Herd. "We see quite a lot of her, of course, because Ganthorne Lodge is so near the camp and the men are allowed the use of the kitchen premises—it's like a club, really. Miss Marks is always about, cooking or washing or something, and the men simply adore her. She helps them to write their letters and shows them how to mend their socks." He laughed softly and added, "When word went forth that Miss Marks had lost her umbrella, the whole battalion volunteered to come over to Chevis Green and fetch it—but of course I was coming, anyhow."

"To see the rose window," put in Sal.

"Yes," agreed Captain Herd, looking at her doubtfully. "Yes—it's—as a matter of fact, I've learned a good deal about ecclesiastical architecture today. And you needn't think—"

"Oh, I didn't!" said Sal quickly.

There was a little silence; quite a comfortable sort of silence. The clock was still ticking away industriously.

"What a quiet house it is!" said Roderick Herd, lowering his voice to match the quietness.

"It's so old," explained Sal. "Old people like being peaceful, so do old houses—at least that's what I think."

"What do you do?" he asked.

"I've been exempted—if that's what you mean. I do the shopping, and cook—all that sort of thing."

"Do you shop in Wandlebury?"

"Once a week," said Sal. "We get most of our rations in Chevis Green because we like dealing with our friends."

"I suppose you go to Wandlebury on Mondays," said Captain Herd in a casual sort of tone.

"No," replied Sal gravely. "I'm much too busy on Monday mornings."

"Are you busy on Tuesdays?" he inquired. "I mean we might have coffee together at the Apollo and Boot."

"Yes—no," said Sal. "I go on Thursdays, but there's no time for coffee. It takes ages, standing in the queue for fish and things." She hesitated, wondering whether to ask him to come here to tea. Liz would have asked him. Liz would have said, "Come over and see us; come whenever you like," but Sal couldn't—the words wouldn't come.

He sighed and stood up. "I must go," he said. "I ought to have been back before this. What a life!"

She went with him to the door. His motorbike was in the yard, leaning against the wall.

"I shall have to whizz," he said, smiling at her.

"Don't whizz too fast," said Sal anxiously.

He was not tall. In fact, he was just about her own height—so the very brown eyes were on a level with her own—but he was tremendously strong. You could see how strong he was by the way he wheeled out the heavy motorbike. He was tremendously self-confident, too. His brown face and his white teeth were rather an intriguing contrast. Sal watched him "whizz" down the road and then went back to the kitchen. She found Miss Marks's umbrella lying on the table.

Chapter Four

S al was laying tea in the schoolroom. When no outsider was expected, the Graces always had tea in the schoolroom; it was comfortable and informal, it encouraged comfortable, informal conversation (you could eat more and let your hair down, as Liz put it). The schoolroom was a very pleasant place; it was a long-shaped room, low-ceilinged, with windows facing south and west. The carpet was very shabby, so was the furniture, but the Graces had seen these things from infancy so the shabbiness did not worry them. Here were old-fashioned armchairs (in which Victorian ladies had sat, embroidering petticoats, or sewing lace collars onto their dresses), and a large sofa, shaped like a half-moon, which fitted into a corner; there were also a gate-legged table and a battered Sheraton bureau, and several bookcases, full of shabby books. The only modern note was struck by the electric kettle that stood in the grate…it was beginning to sing cheerfully as Sal chose the cups and plates from the cupboard in the wall. She chose them carefully for each one was different—they were, in fact, survivors of many different sets that had belonged to members of the Grace family in bygone days. The Coleport cup and saucer had come from old Mrs. Thynne—Sal's maternal grandmother—and the Dresden had belonged to Mr. Grace's aunt and had been bestowed upon Liz for her seventh birthday. There were two cups and several saucers and plates of the Limoges set, very fine and fluted and decorated with sprays of autumn leaves, which had been a wedding present to Mr. and Mrs. Grace—Sal remembered the days when this set had been complete. Other cups and saucers were souvenirs of visits to Bath and to Brighton and bore the heraldic devices of these towns. The remainder of the china reposing in the schoolroom cupboard had been discovered in a box in the attic. Some of it was good and some without intrinsic value, but the Graces found it interesting to speculate and to discuss where it had come from, and which of their ancestors had chosen and used it. The silver teapot was old and dented, but very bright, for Sal loved it and liked to see it shining. She warmed it carefully and measured out the tea—the kettle was boiling now.

"Joan doesn't mind when she has her holiday," said Tilly, coming in.

"Oh, good," said Sal, without enthusiasm. Liz came in after Tilly and shut the door. She sat down on a Victorian chair and stretched out her long legs before her; they looked longer and slimmer in the closely fitting breeches and heavy stockings and thick brown shoes she wore for her work on the farm. "Joan's going to Mant for her holiday," said Liz in a casual voice.

"To Mant?" inquired Sal with interest. "I thought she was going to her uncle at Brighton."

"Mant is a person, not a place," explained Liz.

"A man or a woman?"

"A woman," said Liz firmly. "She said, 'I'll go to Mant. She can have me anytime so it doesn't matter when I get my holiday,' or words to that effect."

"Mant!" said Sal, savoring the word thoughtfully. "Mrs. Mant, I suppose."

"Miss Mant, perhaps."

"Short for Mantalini?"

"Who knows?" said Liz, leaning back and cocking one leg over the other.

Tilly had taken no part in the discussion; she had begun to giggle. "Tilly knows," said Sal, looking at her.

"I'm sorry, but you're both wrong," declared Tilly. "Mant is m' uncle's wife."

"What a *pity!*" said Sal regretfully. She took up the teapot and announced, "You can't have sugar because I want it for jam, and Joan forgot the saccharines."

"Hell," said Liz without rancor.

"If Father heard you—"

"But he can't, the darling," reasoned Liz. "And anyhow, I only mean that place in Sweden—or is it Norway? Father wouldn't mind a bit if I said Birmingham."

"It's those men—" began Sal.

"Not on your life," interrupted Liz. "*Those men* are scared stiff when I'm anywhere about. I think they're afraid I'd tell Father if they said damn. It cramps their style a lot. Can't we have jam?"

"Not today," said Sal.

"You can have jam yesterday and tomorrow," said Tilly solemnly as she helped herself to a cress sandwich and handed the plate to Liz.

"I don't mind much," declared Liz. "I look forward to this all day—sprawling and drinking tea and saying whatever happens to come into my head. Heaven will be like this—not golden gates and harps."

"Some people want harps," objected Sal.

They were silent for a few minutes, munching cress.

"And anyhow," said Sal at last. "You wouldn't appreciate doing as you like if you could do it all the time...like the people in the Abbey of Thélème. They were *obliged* to do what they liked all the time. It was a punishment."

"Makes one believe in astrology—almost," said Liz thoughtfully.

"What does?"

"People's lives. What you want in Heaven depends entirely upon what you've got here, and what you've got here depends upon Fate. Some people's lives are so dull and others' are so interesting."

"It's you, really," objected Sal. "Your life is what you make it."

"Yes, it is. Some people would find it frightfully dull to be the daughter of the parson at Chevis Green."

"But *we* don't," cried Liz. "That's exactly what I mean. It's in you from the beginning. Either there's this mysterious thing in you that makes you happy—that makes you interested in everything and interesting to yourself—or else there isn't, and you're dull and dreary and discontented."

"Who is dull and dreary and discontented?" inquired Mr. Grace, appearing suddenly in the doorway.

"Nobody, darling," replied Liz. "Your daughters are quite contented with their lot. Isn't that nice for you?"

"Liz was saying we might have been, if we'd been born under different stars," explained Tilly.

Mr. Grace sat down and accepted a cup of tea.

"Not really stars—it's just a way of putting it. Some people are born bored," said Liz.

"Born bored!" echoed Mr. Grace. "I can't think of anything worse. Born with a soul blind to the beauties of nature and the peculiarities of one's fellow man."

"Some people are," said Liz. "If you don't understand people you aren't interested in them."

"Solomon asked for an understanding heart."

"Oh, but he had one already!" declared Sal. "I mean he wouldn't have asked for it if he hadn't got it."

"Of course," agreed Tilly. "People who are born bored don't want to understand."

There was a short silence.

"I suppose we can offer a bed to William Single," said Mr. Grace suddenly.

Three faces turned toward him with identical expressions of dismay, but Mr. Grace had rather expected this reaction, so he was not surprised. He stirred his tea and waited.

"William Single?" asked Sal, who was the first to find her voice.

"You may have heard me speak of him."

"Never," said Liz firmly.

"I scarcely know him, of course, but we cannot condemn him to the Whistling Man."

"Must he come to Chevis Green?" inquired Tilly anxiously. "I mean why—"

"There's a good deal to do, one way and another," began Sal.

"He will be no trouble in the house," declared Mr. Grace with his usual optimism.

"How do you know?" inquired Liz. "I mean if you scarcely know the man, you can't possibly know his habits."

"He will require a bed," said Mr. Grace firmly. "A bed and a seat at our board. I have no doubt he will bring—er—food tickets."

"He must!" cried Sal in alarm.

"Why is he coming?" asked Liz. "When is he coming…and for how long?"

"What is he going to do?" asked Tilly.

"He is one of the greatest living authorities upon Roman Britain," said Mr. Grace as if that explained everything, which perhaps it did.

"Birmingham!" exclaimed Liz emphatically.

"No, Oxford," said Mr. Grace. "He has rooms in the High. He is coming to Chevis Green to examine some Roman remains. I am looking forward to his visit with keen interest."

There was a short silence, broken by Tilly. "He certainly won't remember to bring his ration book," she said.

Chapter Five

It was Thursday morning, Sal's day for shopping in Wandlebury, and as it was fine and windless, she had bicycled the three miles instead of taking the bus. Now she was standing in the queue at the fishmonger's, pressed closely between Joan's mother and a fat man with a very bald head. Mrs. Aleman had come in the bus, of course, and the bus had been late. It usually was late on a Thursday morning. They stood in the queue for half an hour, and during that time Sal learned quite a lot about Joan, things she had not known before. It was odd, thought Sal, that you could know a person very well—as she knew Joan—and yet learn so much about her from another person. Joan came to the Vicarage every day, but she had a separate life at home...you might almost say Joan led a double life, thought Sal.

"Fretting, that's what she is," said Mrs. Aleman. "Bob's a good 'usband to 'er in a way, but 'e don't write as often as 'e might, an' the days go by so quick. If she don't get a letter once a week she begins to think something's wrong. You'll 'ear soon enough, I said to 'er. You'll 'ear if anything's wrong. No news is good news, that's what I tell 'er."

"Yes," agreed Sal. "I didn't know she was so worried. Bob is in Shetland, isn't he?"

"Some such place," agreed Mrs. Aleman. "It's the sharks

she's worrying about—and them nasty little Japs. You read such awful things in the papers about them."

"She needn't worry about sharks—or Japs," declared Sal. "As a matter of fact— "

"That's what I tell 'er, Miss Sal. Don't you worry, I said. If Bob's going to be bitten by a shark, 'e'll *be* bitten an' no amount of worrying will 'elp 'im."

"I don't think there are any sharks in Shetland."

"You tell 'er, Miss Sal. She'll listen to you. Lor', I 'ope there'll be a few 'addocks left. Mr. Aleman's sick of that Icelandic cod."

"If you soak it—" began another woman.

"I know," interrupted Mrs. Aleman. "It tells you on the wireless. You soak it till you're tired of seeing it lying in the bowl an' then you cook it, an' then it looks like a piece of white flannel that's been used for a poultice."

"Tastes like it, too," said the fat man in front.

Sal felt quite as strongly about Icelandic cod (it was food, and that was all you could say in its favor), so she was enchanted to find that there were a few haddocks upon the slab when her turn came to be served. Half a dozen haddocks were weighed out and rolled loosely in a sheet of yesterday's *Times*, which she had brought with her for this purpose. She clasped the parcel with both hands and wriggled out through the crowd. Several people near the end of the queue stopped her and inquired anxiously if there was any chance for them, and Sal was obliged to dash their hopes. She felt extremely greedy, of course, but if she had done as her better nature directed and bestowed her fish upon Mrs. Bouse, who had a delicate child, or upon Mrs. Feather, whose mother had just undergone an operation, her own father and sisters would have had to go supperless. I was early, thought Sal, trying to drown the voice of conscience. They could have come early, couldn't they? I've stood in the blinking queue for forty minutes, so there...

but perhaps they couldn't come early, said conscience in a still, small voice.

Sal ignored conscience. She crossed the road to her bicycle, which was leaning against a wall, and was just stretching out her hand toward it when something soft and heavy struck her in the middle of the back. It was such a powerful blow that Sal lost her balance and fell forward against the handlebars…the bicycle slid from the wall (Sal clinging to it desperately the while) and the pedal caught her ankle with a vicious kick. Meanwhile, the haddocks burst through their inadequate wrapping and scattered themselves all over the pavement in a silvery shower. Sal lay there for a moment because she could not move, she was sprawling full length over the bicycle.

"I *beg* your pardon," exclaimed a strong deep voice, a voice full of the most intense anxiety and solicitude. "I can't tell you how sorry—this is terrible. Are you seriously injured?"

"Help me up," said Sal, who was beginning to realize what she must look like to the gathering crowd.

A strong hand immediately appeared under each of her elbows and she was lifted bodily from the bicycle and set upon her feet.

"There," said her rescuer. "There now. How do you feel? Not—er—injured in any way? No bones—er—broken?"

"No-o," said Sal, looking at him. He was an enormous man, clad in a somewhat shapeless tweed suit; his head was bare, and his thick brown wavy hair was floating in the breeze.

"Dreadful," he said. "Dreadful! I really can't begin to tell you how sorry I am." And he took a large silk handkerchief out of his pocket and began to dust Sal's skirt very carefully, as if he were dusting a Dresden china figurine.

Sal let him. She was still feeling a bit dazed.

"And now the fish," he said, bending and beginning to gather them into his hands. But this was not so easy for their slippery bodies eluded him, sliding from his grasp and leaping into the air as if they were alive.

Sal leaned against the wall and began to laugh and with that he laughed too, deeply and heartily, his whole immense body heaving with the uncontrollable spasms.

"So good of you—to take it like this," he panted. "It was a terrible thing to do. I just stepped back—to allow one lady to pass—and in so doing—upset another." He stepped back as he spoke and knocked another passerby off the pavement.

Sal saw it was time to intervene. She seized his arm and drew him into the doorway of the baker's shop. "There," she said, holding him. "There, now."

He still shook. He was like a volcano gradually settling down after an eruption. "So clumsy," he murmured, mopping his eyes with the handkerchief he had used to dust Sal. "So dreadfully clumsy. I beg your pardon a thousand times. What more can I say?"

"You can't," said Sal. "I mean you've said more than enough already."

"And your fish," he lamented. "Your—er—whitings. What *can* we do?"

"I'll pick them up in a minute," said Sal, giggling feebly.

"No!" he cried, struck by a sudden brilliant idea. "No, they are uneatable—I shall buy you some more fish. Why didn't I think of it before?"

"You can't—" began Sal.

"Of course I can! Whiting, turbot, sole—whatever you like. You have only to say the word."

Sal gazed at him. Here was a creature from another world! Here was a man who (obviously) did not know there was war! Here was somebody who (most probably) had never heard of Icelandic cod. She was speechless. She was paralyzed.

Already he had crossed the road to the fishmonger's and

was shouldering his way gently but firmly through the waiting queue. He's never seen a queue, either, thought Sal in dismay, and she abandoned bicycle and fish to rush after him and rescue him again. But this time he had reached the door, and oddly enough nobody was offering any resistance. "Pardon me," she heard him say as he pushed Mrs. Toop aside—Mrs. Toop, the wife of the butcher at Chevis Green, a virago if ever there was one—and Mrs. Toop moved and allowed him to pass. He was now inside the shop. Sal peered through the window and saw his huge form making its way down the aisle between the empty marble slabs.

"*Well*," said Sal to herself. She could say no more.

Sal returned to her bicycle and found that some good Samaritan had dealt with the situation, propping the bicycle against the wall and filling the basket with fish. There was no paper around them, of course, and they looked a trifle the worse of their experience—a little dusty and just a trifle mangled. Should one take them home, wondered Sal, looking at them with aversion. Could one wash them thoroughly and skin them, and make them into a fish pie? Was it possible that people who did not know their past might eat them in a fish pie and relish them?

He came toward her across the street, looking like a god (Zeus, thought Sal—or, no, it's Jove) with his eyes shining and the sun in his hair. "Salmon!" he cried, holding out a neat brown paper package. "Salmon from the Tay! You like salmon, I hope."

"But how—" cried Sal. "And, goodness, you must have paid a fortune for it."

He was immediately crestfallen. All the godliness seeped away. Sal's heart was melted within her.

"Salmon," he repeated, holding it out to her pleadingly.

Sal took it. "But he hadn't any—" she began.

"It arrived in a box straight from the Tay."

"Straight from Heaven," murmured Sal. "Or Olympia," she amended, remembering she had thought him like Jove.

"There were other people in the shop," he continued. "One or two of them seemed a trifle disagreeable. The war," he added, nodding his head. "Yes, that's the explanation. People are feeling a bit strained and their manners suffer."

"So you know about the war," said Sal gravely.

"They wouldn't have me," he said, shaking his head. "I'm over forty and in a reserved occupation. They took the younger men—weeds compared with me. It seems strange that they didn't take me, doesn't it?"

It was just as well, thought Sal. They were well advised not to have him, for he would have spoiled the symmetry of any regiment. He might easily have knocked the colonel off his horse, thought Sal, looking at him. He would almost certainly have trodden upon a mine or shot one of his comrades by mistake. Give him a grenade to throw, and ten to one he would have dropped it…no, he was better at home.

She found, somewhat to her embarrassment, that he had attached himself to her, following her from shop to shop and holding her bicycle while she went in and bought sugar and hen food and soap. It was embarrassing because he was so large, because he was constantly getting in people's way, stopping to apologize and, in so doing, blocking the pavement. It was like having an enormous dog, thought Sal. One felt responsible for his behavior. Though why one should feel responsible for him when one had only just met him, and would never see him again, it was difficult to say. She was further embarrassed by the notion that they might meet Captain Herd, for although she had told him definitely that there would be no time for "elevenses" at the Apollo and Boot, it was quite possible that he would ignore the warning—he had seemed that sort of person. If he met them, what was she to do? She could not introduce her new acquisition because she did not know his name. Liz could have carried off the whole adventure; in fact, Liz would have enjoyed it. By this time she would have found out the man's name and most of his history, or, if necessary, she would have shaken him off politely and gone on her way unencumbered. However, there was no sign at all of Captain Herd and the moment was approaching when he must get rid of her companion and ride home.

"That's all," said Sal at last. "Thank you very much for carrying the parcels, and thank you again for the salmon. Good-bye."

"Good-bye," he said vaguely and somewhat forlornly.

Sal hesitated. "Where are you going?" she asked. "I mean do you know your way?"

"I can find out," he replied. "It's a place called Chevis Green."

"Chevis Green! That's where I live," cried Sal in surprise.

"You live there? How very strange," said her new friend happily. "Perhaps you know Mr. Grace. I'm going to stay with him."

"You're going to stay with him!" echoed Sal incredulously.

The big man nodded.

"Does he—does he *know*?" asked Sal. And then, suddenly, light broke. "Goodness, you must be William Single!" she exclaimed.

Mr. Single admitted that he was.

Sal was gazing at him. I might have guessed, she thought. Yet how could she? An authority upon Roman Britain sounded old and dried up. Sal had envisaged their prospective guest as bald and bearded, pedantic in the extreme. She had envisaged him as vague and unpractical—and of course he was—but—

Mr. Single waited for a few moments and then he said, "I don't think Mr. Grace is actually expecting me today, but I got away sooner than I expected. Do you think he'll mind?"

"*He* won't mind," said Sal, trying to think whether there

was enough food in the house, and if not how she could obtain more.

"You know Mr. Grace," said her new friend. "Perhaps you know his children. He has four little girls."

"I am one of them," said Sal dramatically.

Chapter Six

Mr. Grace was hoeing the front drive when his daughter arrived back from Wandlebury with William Single in tow. "This is delightful," declared Mr. Grace, shaking his guest's hand. "This really is a most delightful surprise. You met Sal in the village, I suppose."

"In Wandlebury," said Sal. "We bicycled back—ride and tie—but Mr. Single wouldn't play fair so I did most of the riding. I expect he could do with a drink. Will you get him one, Father."

"Of course, of course," cried Mr. Grace, throwing down his hoe and taking his guest by the arm. "Come into my study and I'll get you a glass of lemonade or something."

"Beer," said Sal firmly.

"Yes, yes, of course," said Mr. Grace. "Come along, my dear fellow…"

Having made certain of her protégé's comfort, Sal hurried away to find Tilly and see about domestic affairs. She found Tilly in the dining room, told her the news, rearranged the table, and laid an extra place.

Tilly disliked being fussed. "Goodness!" she exclaimed. "Couldn't the man let us know? I meant to give the spare room a thorough cleaning."

"He won't notice," declared Sal. "We'll make the bed—it always looks better when the bed is made—and Joan can give it a dust over."

They hastened upstairs to the front spare room, a large pleasant room looking out onto the garden.

"It's fusty," said Tilly, wrinkling her nose. "It smells unaired. Why can't people stick to their plans? Did you meet him in Wandlebury or what?"

Sal threw open the window. "In Wandlebury," she said.

"How did he know you?"

"He didn't know me."

"Just picked you up?"

"First he knocked me down and then he picked me up," said Sal gravely.

"He knocked you down!" cried Tilly, in horror-stricken tones.

"And then," said Sal, continuing her story, "and then he walked straight through the fish queue and bought me a piece of salmon; three pounds of salmon if I'm any judge of weight."

"Three pounds of salmon!" exclaimed Tilly, aghast.

"Darling, do help," said Sal reproachfully. "We'll never get the bed made if you stand there with your mouth open. Tuck in the sheet."

Tilly tucked it in obediently. She said, "Why are you giving him these twill sheets? The hemstitched ones are ever so much nicer."

"He would tear them to ribbons," said Sal firmly.

Tilly's eyes were almost popping out of her head, but she could not demand an explanation, for Joan had appeared with a duster and had begun to dust the dressing table.

"Where is his suitcase?" asked Tilly, as she spread the counterpane.

"I don't think he has one," said Sal, wrinkling her brows and trying to think back. "He may have left it in the fishmonger's, of course, but I can't remember seeing a suitcase."

"'E's big, isn't 'e?" said Joan, pausing to shake her duster out of the window. "I saw 'im coming up the garden with the master. 'E's as big as m' uncle, very nearly. These big fellows eat a lot," added Joan, with a little sigh.

"About his suitcase," said Tilly anxiously. "Oughtn't we to find out—"

"Perhaps he hasn't one," said Sal. "His pockets are very large, so I expect he's got a toothbrush in one of them. He's got a doll."

"A doll!" cried Tilly.

"For us," explained Sal. "If you and Liz don't want it, I'd like it immensely. It's a very nice doll."

William Single was certainly outsize, thought Tilly, as she shook hands with him in her father's study. He made the large, well-proportioned room look quite small, but unlike Joan's uncle (that legendary figure who was also of gigantic stature), William Single did not eat very much. In fact, he seemed uninterested in food. During the first part of lunch the conversation was entirely concerned with Roman Britain and was so technical and erudite and so full of references to various authorities upon the subject that Tilly and Sal ceased to listen and exchanged remarks in an undertone about the fish pie Sal was proposing to make. Then Liz arrived—in her working clothes, of course—and with her arrival the atmosphere changed. The talk became general, or perhaps it would be more exact to say that the Graces talked more and their guest less. After lunch Mr. Grace was about to lead the way to his study but William Single demurred.

"I should like to help," he said, looking at the girls, who had begun to clear the table. He took a plate in each hand and hesitated.

Liz was making for the door with a piled-up tray of dishes. "Come on," she said. "You can open the doors for me. I'll show you the way."

Mr. Grace followed the little procession to the scullery. He was anxious to rescue his guest and enjoy some more conversation. He wanted to show him an old book he had picked up at the library in Wandlebury. "You need not bother about this, Single," said Mr. Grace. "The girls will finish it in half no time."

"I like to help," replied Mr. Single, taking up a wet plate and drying it with meticulous care. "I'm very slow, of course, but I daresay I shall improve."

"Of course you will," declared Liz, smiling at him dazzlingly.

"Oh!" exclaimed Mr. Single, and with that the plate slid out of his hands and crashed onto the stone floor, where it disintegrated.

"Oh!" exclaimed Liz in horrified tones. She might have said more, for it was a valuable plate, belonging to the best dinner service, but Mr. Grace intervened.

"'Mistress of herself though China fall,'" said Mr. Grace, laughing.

It was a command—or at least an exhortation—and Liz recognized it as such. She drew a deep breath and assured Mr. Single that it did not matter.

"Matter!" cried Mr. Single in agonized tones. "Of course it matters. It's dreadful! It's the most appalling catastrophe! I can't think how it happened. It just slid—"

"It was slippery," said Liz.

"No, not really. It was already dry…" He was kneeling at her feet now, gathering up the pieces and trying vainly to fit them together, lamenting over them.

"Don't worry," said Liz. "Really and truly it doesn't matter." And this time she meant it, for only a very hardhearted person could have gone on being angry in the face of such abject remorse.

None of the girls had looked forward with pleasure to Mr. Single's visit, Tilly least of all. She was conservative by nature and enjoyed the company of her family. A man in the house would change everything; he would make more work, they wouldn't be able to talk properly, they couldn't have tea in the schoolroom. But somehow or other William Single did not disturb the balance at all and nobody suggested that they should alter their habits on his account. That very first afternoon Sal set tea as usual in the familiar place—quite without thinking—and here they were. It was odd how well he fitted in, thought Tilly, looking at him. He was sitting near the window in a very large, old-fashioned chair with a straight back and projecting ears. Sometimes he looked out of the window and you could see his profile, which was strong and blunt, like the profile of a lion, and sometimes he turned his head and looked at you squarely. He was benevolent, thought Tilly—rather pleased with herself for finding the exact word—yes, he was benevolent. Already she had discovered that there was no need to talk to him. He did not want that; nor did he want to talk. But although he rarely contributed to the conversation, he was sympathetic and his presence was by no means cramping to one's style.

The schoolroom was full of sunshine. Sal had made the tea. Liz came in from her work and flung herself into her usual chair with her usual careless abandon.

"It's full of hay," she said, sweeping her hair back from her forehead with both hands.

"A cap is the answer," said Sal, pouring out tea as she spoke.

"Or a poke bonnet," suggested Tilly.

"I'm tired," said Liz. "Why is it that when you're tired you see things differently—more distinctly, I mean?"

"Like fasting," said Tilly nodding. "Colors and smells, too."

"Fasting weakens the body and strengthens the spirit," said Sal. "There's jam today. It's the last pot so go easy with it."

"It isn't spirit," declared Liz, helping herself to jam. "That isn't what I mean. It's—something else. You see things differently when you're tired. I'm no better; in fact, I'm worse when I'm tired and hungry—it makes me cross and irritable—but I see things in a brighter sort of light and with more meaning to them. That teapot, for instance," added Liz as Sal moved the teapot and the sunshine caught it in a dazzling ray.

"It always means things to me," said Sal, stroking it affectionately.

"Everything means something to me," declared Tilly, looking around. "Nothing is just itself in a person's mind, because it gets all mixed up with memories…and of course the same object means something quite different to different people…even a frying pan."

"What do you see when you look at a frying pan?" wondered Sal.

"Not consciously," objected Tilly. "But it *is* connected with all sorts of different things that have happened, and you remember them subconsciously when you look at a frying pan and that makes you see it differently."

"I just smell bacon," said Liz.

"A frying pan isn't a good example," declared Sal. "But I know what Tilly means. For instance, when I'm lying in bed in a dark room and the door opens slowly and a slice of light appears on the wall, it takes me straight back to being a child and having measles."

"Oh, yes!" cried Tilly. "Father coming in with a night-light to see how we were! Oh, yes, I *am* a child again!"

"All spotty," added Liz, *sotto voce*.

"You might be, if you had enough imagination," said Sal thoughtfully.

"Stigmata?" wondered Tilly, stirring her tea.

One would think this sort of conversation was liable to bamboozle an antiquarian, used to the measured logic of his kind, but William Single seemed perfectly at ease. Obviously this was not because he was the same sort of person as the Graces. He was totally different. He was like a person from a foreign country—from a different planet—who found the inhabitants of the Vicarage utterly incomprehensible, strange in habit, language, and mentality. He sat and listened to their conversation and drank his tea. Presently he asked if he might smoke his pipe and was immediately granted permission. Sitting and smoking and listening—occasionally smiling sympathetically—William Single seemed completely happy in his own quiet way.

The talk flowed on until it was interrupted by the noise of a powerful motor bicycle coming into the yard.

"Who on earth is that?" asked Tilly indignantly.

Liz was already hanging out of the side window with her long legs waving in the air, for it had been discovered, long ago, that by performing this somewhat dangerous acrobatic feat, one could get a glimpse of the yard.

"It's that man," said Liz, a trifle breathlessly. "The one who came to lunch when we had Pedro."

"Oh, *him*!" said Tilly, with more emphasis than grammar.

"I expect he's come back for the umbrella," said Sal. She half rose as she spoke and then sat down again.

"Shall I go?" asked Mr. Single. "Shall I ask him to come upstairs?"

"I suppose we shall have to give him tea," said Tilly inhospitably.

Mr. Single was away for some time and presently returned with Roderick Herd. Roderick was a living example of the matter that had been under discussion before his arrival, for each of the Graces thought about him in a different way. Tilly thought of him principally as the man who had stared so hard in church, and the rose window was mixed up with him, too. Liz obviously thought of him as fellow devourer of Pedro. Sal's idea of him was much more complicated.

Roderick looked small beside Mr. Single; you could hardly hope to find two men more different in appearance, manner, and personality. A St. Bernard dog and a terrier was the nearest comparison Tilly could find...and as a matter of fact Roderick was much more like a terrier than an eagle. Could you have brown terriers, wondered Tilly, as she shook hands with him. He sat down and accepted a cup of tea and explained at some length that he happened to be coming in this direction and remembered that he had forgotten the umbrella. William Single had not disturbed the atmosphere of the room, but this man did. There was a sort of electricity in him, thought Tilly.

Liz was talking to the man, chatting gaily about her work on the farm. Sal was saying nothing. Mr. Single was looking out of the window. I don't like the man, thought Tilly. She was, in fact, a little frightened of him.

Chapter Seven

The site William Single had come to examine was on the shoulder of a hill not far from Chevis Place. It was downland country in that direction, high grassy hills, rolling southward toward the sea. Mr. Single had obtained permission from Archie Chevis-Cobbe to do whatever he liked on the site. Nobody would interfere with him except perhaps the sheep. In normal times William Single would have brought a team of trained excavators to help him, but this was impossible in wartime. He did not intend to dig seriously, but merely to measure and take notes for future use. Even for this job it would have been easier to have some help, but he had decided to do the job alone. It was better to work alone than have inexperienced men muddling around; as a matter of fact, William Single enjoyed being alone, and as this was really his holiday, he need not feel he was wasting time, either his own time or other people's.

He explained all this to Archie Cobbe who had walked up to meet him on the site. The two men stood on the hill together, smoking their pipes and talking. They were both big, but William Single was the bigger. His clothes were loose and clumsy, which made him look even more gigantic than he actually was.

"It doesn't look much of a place," said Archie Chevis-Cobbe, surveying the tumbled heaps of stones in some surprise. "I've often been up here before, of course, but I never took much notice of the stones. Are you sure it's the site of a Roman Camp?"

"Yes," said Mr. Single simply.

"Well, you ought to know," said its owner. "Do what you like. Sure you wouldn't like the loan of a man to dig?"

"Yes," said Mr. Single. "It's very kind of you, but I shouldn't dream of allowing you to lend me a man."

"Isn't it Emerson who says, 'A man of thought should not dig ditches'?"

"Yes," said Mr. Single again. He smiled and added, "But I don't intend to dig ditches. I shall make a trench here and there, just to confirm my measurements. I'm perfectly capable of that."

"You look it, I must say. Well...good luck. I hope you'll find—er—whatever it is you're looking for. Pottery, I suppose?"

"No," said Mr. Single. "Not anything like that." He hesitated and looked at his companion. Did Chevis-Cobbe want an explanation? Was he interested? No, obviously not, for he was holding out his hand to say good-bye. "Good-bye. And thank you again, very much indeed," said Mr. Single politely.

William Single was alone now, and, as has been said before, he enjoyed being alone. He relighted his pipe, which had gone out during his conversation with Chevis-Cobbe, and sat down on the close-cropped turf. Soon he would begin his work; he would drive in his pegs and take his measurements, but there was no hurry. He had the whole summer vacation before him. He sat in his favorite position, leaning forward, his great shoulders hunched, his hands between his raised knees, and as he sat there he looked around and noticed various details of the site. It was an extremely commanding site, with a view that embraced several valleys, yet it was sheltered from the east. There was a stream not far away—William Single was pretty sure he would discover a lead from the stream to the camp. He nodded to himself. All he saw was confirming his opinion that this particular camp was an important one—not just a station upon the military road. He allowed his thoughts to drift; he began to absorb the atmosphere of the place. It was quiet and peaceful now; the place belonged to the sheep, to the rabbits and the birds, but it had not been always thus. It had been the scene of martial force…it had been peopled with Roman soldiers…the hillside had echoed to their shouts, to the rattle of their armor and the tramp of their feet…

William Single was hundreds of years away in time when he heard the rumble of iron-shod wheels upon the stony track. This did not surprise him, nor did it draw him back to the present year of grace (for, of course, the Roman garrison had chariots at their beck and call), but when he raised his eyes, half-expecting to see a chariot descending the hill, he saw instead a farm cart, piled with marigolds, driven by a young woman with curly, golden hair.

"Liz!" exclaimed Mr. Single, leaping two thousand years or thereabouts in a second of time.

"Yes, it's me," said Liz, smiling down at him. "I suppose you thought it was a Roman girl or something."

"Er—not exactly," he replied, rising and holding out his hand to help her down.

"You were dreaming about the Romans, weren't you?"

"Er—yes. Roman legionaries. There were not many Roman girls in this part of the world."

"And they didn't drive chariots, I suppose?"

"No," said William Single.

"Dull for them," said Liz, putting her hand in his and leaping to the ground. "Very dull for them. I suppose they did embroidery while their knights fought duels in the lists—or am I muddling it up with *Ivanhoe?'*

"I think you are," said William Single gravely.

"Archie told me you were here," said Liz, as she took a rope and tied up her horse. "I had to go up to the seven-acre field for marigolds, so I thought I'd come back this way and have lunch with you. Have you had lunch yet?"

"Lunch?" he said in surprise.

"Yes, lunch. You'll find some sandwiches in your pocket. Sal put them there this morning."

He searched his pockets and found the little parcel. "How kind of her!" he said.

Liz was looking around. "You haven't started yet, or have you? Are you going to dig holes? Will there be gold coins buried here? I suppose they'll belong to you if you find them, won't they? How do you know where to look?"

"No—yes—no," said William Single breathlessly.

Liz gave a little snort of laughter. "Oh, poor William!" she said. "It will take you some time to get used to the Graces, won't it? By the way, I suppose I can call you William as you've started calling me Liz?"

"It was a mistake," said William hastily. "It was just—seeing you suddenly—it came out without thinking."

"That's the best way," Liz told him. "I mean it's much more natural that way than somebody you don't like at all saying, call me Maureen."

William began to laugh.

"Yes, it *is* funny," agreed Liz, smiling gently. "Call me Maureen, she says, and of course you simply can't, because you only think of her as Mrs. Snooks, so you avoid calling her anything at all or you address her as 'Er—I say.'"

"'She would answer to "Hie" or to any loud cry,'" said William, shaking and mopping his eyes.

"Oh," cried Liz in delight. "Oh, of course... *The Hunting of the Snark.*"

"Ha-ha-ha!" laughed William.

"'His intimate friends called him Candle-Ends.' I shall call you Candle-Ends, William," said Liz gravely.

"As long as—you don't call me—Toasted Cheese," agreed William, gasping and shaking and rocking to and fro with uncontrollable mirth.

When William had recovered a little, they sat down together and ate their lunch, and Liz was surprised to find that William could talk quite reasonably. So far she had only heard him talking to her father about Roman Britain; he had been dumb in the company of herself and her sisters. He explained this by saying he was not used to the society of girls, nor had he ever had the opportunity to enjoy family life. He was an only child and had gone to school when he was eight years old, after which time his life had been spent at schools and colleges.

"Always with clever people!" exclaimed Liz, much impressed.

William was a little surprised at this point of view. "Clever in their own way, of course," he said doubtfully. "But clever in their own way *only*. Somewhat circumscribed in their outlook and—"

"No wonder you think we're silly!" cried Liz, interrupting him.

"I don't," declared William. "I don't think so at all. I'm tremendously interested. The fact is I had no idea…" He stopped. What he had intended to say suddenly seemed a little rude.

"You had no idea people like us existed," said Liz, nodding understandingly.

Chapter Eight

It was Sunday. The day had been wet and the evening was dark with thunder clouds, so they were obliged to have lights in the church for evensong. It was not yet "blackout time" so it did not matter. Tilly was playing the organ, and the congregation was singing "Nearer, My God, to Thee," which was the favorite hymn of Edward VII—and also of Tilly Grace. It was sad, of course, thought Tilly as she played the last few bars very softly, but all the best hymns were sad...

The music died away and Mr. Element, the verger, who was of an economical turn of mind, extinguished all the lights except the light in the pulpit where Mr. Grace was standing. The church was very dim now, and very still. The faces of the people shone white, as though with an inward rather than a reflected light. A band of ruby light from the west window caught old Jos Barefoot and turned his wizened little face into the face of a demon. Amber radiance haloed the head of Cynthia Bouse who served in the bar at the Whistling Man. Addie had come home for the weekend so there were three Graces in the Vicarage pew—and William Single, of course—and behind them, a little to the left near the pillar, sat Roderick Herd. Here again! said Tilly to herself, looking at him. He was here, in Chevis Green, much too often in Tilly's opinion.

Mr. Grace was talking about gardens; he liked to talk about simple things on Sunday evenings, about fields and trees and the homes of his people, and his people liked it, too, for they were realistic and could understand things of the spirit so much better if these were related to the things they could see. "England has been called a garden," said Mr. Grace. "But gardens don't grow by themselves without being tended. This country we love so much didn't grow by itself to beauty. Geology played its part by providing suitable soil, and our climate provided the necessary moisture, but it was our ancestors who made the England we know. About two hundred years ago people became land-conscious. Landowners improved their estates, farmers enclosed their fields and planted woods and coppices. Roads were made and beautified and villages were remodeled. We talk of town planning today as if it were a new thing, but our ancestors planned the countryside; they loved beauty, they understood the art of landscape, they planted trees and opened vistas and changed the face of the land. These people made their improvements with two objects in mind, beauty and utility; not incompatible objects (as is sometimes thought) but married and existing together in unity. These people planned for future generations—for us—so it is our duty to look ahead and to plan for our children's children. The Englishman's natural taste for beauty in landscape is not dead, it is alive today in his passion for gardens; every cottager loves his garden and likes to see it full of bright flowers…but perhaps the best time of all in a garden is the planning time, when the gardener sees it bare and empty and plans the arrangement of his flowers, for it is then he is using his imagination and looking forward to the summer flowering."

Mr. Grace leaned upon the edge of his pulpit and continued in a lower voice, an intimate, conversational tone. "But it wouldn't be much good for a man to plan his garden, to say to himself, 'It would be nice to have hollyhocks in that corner,

and lupins in front, and a trellis with sweet peas over there...
and it would be a good idea to plant stock near the sitting room
window so that we can smell their sweetness on a summer
evening.' *No*, he's got to sow his seeds and water them. He's
got to keep the beds weeded and free from slugs. Life is like
that, too. We need faith—just as a gardener needs faith when
he plans his garden and sows his seeds—and we need work. We
can all do our part to make our little patch in the garden of life
gay with flowers. Let's plant happiness in our little patch; it has
such a sweet smell on a summer evening. Yes, but how can I
plant it, you'll say. The best way to plant happiness is to do at
least one thing every day to make one person happier, and to
do it for God. That shouldn't be difficult. We can all do that.
Happiness grows best that way, and it's a plant that seeds itself
in the right kind of soil. We shall find it growing in our own
hearts if we sow it freely—growing and flowering not only in
the summer, but all through the year..."

Mr. Grace had chosen a very simple hymn to close the service.
Hymn no. 573. "All Things Bright and Beautiful." Everybody
knew it so everybody sang. Tilly felt the comradeship, the
"oneness" of the little congregation. She was moved, almost
to tears. She did not want to meet anyone, nor talk, so she ran
quickly down the little stair and home across the churchyard.

The dining room table was already laid for supper and there
was nothing to do except to heat the coffee and the milk and
take the vegetable pie out of the oven. It was a very large pie,
savory and appetizing, for there would be six people to eat
it tonight. Six at least—perhaps more—for Mr. Grace often
asked somebody to come in and share the Vicarage supper on a
Sunday evening. It was always vegetable pie (a dinner of herbs)
so one need not worry about rationing. But perhaps he won't
tonight, thought Tilly hopefully as she carried the tray into the
dining room and gave the last-minute touches to the table.

Her hopes were almost immediately dashed by the appearance in the garden of Liz and Roderick Herd. They were standing beside the lily pool, talking to each other, and their figures were reflected in the still pool with curiously faithful accuracy.

At this moment Sal came in. She said, "Oh, you've got everything! I must lay another place. Captain Herd is coming."

"I know," said Tilly, pointing to the window. "He's there—with Liz. Oh, Sal!"

"What's the matter?" asked Sal sharply.

It was so unlike Sal to be sharp that Tilly was taken aback.

"It's just—" she began. "I mean—he—frightens me rather."

"How absurd!" exclaimed Sal.

There was no time for more. The others arrived and soon the whole party was seated around the table. At first Tilly was busy seeing that everyone was served, but once that was accomplished, she began to listen to the conversation.

"Yes, I know that, sir," Roderick was saying. "But why don't the different churches amalgamate? From a layman's point of view, it's—well—muddling to have so many different religions all calling themselves Christians."

"It may seem so," agreed Mr. Grace. "And indeed many people hold that view."

"You don't, sir?"

Mr. Grace hesitated. "I feel a universal religion would have to be so very cut and dried that one would lose all one's freedom of belief. Religion is a kind of scientific research and every faith and creed is a part of the truth. 'No creed does more than shadow imperfectly forth some one side of the truth.' I can't remember who said that, but it was well said."

"Father Hall in *John Inglesant*," said Sal in a low voice.

"I can always depend on Sal," said Mr. Grace, smiling at his second daughter.

"Because I never went to school," explained Sal. She was

alarmed at the trend of the conversation (for it was impossible to foretell what Roderick would say next), but it was pretty certain that Addie would rise to that bait.

Addie did. "Oh, what rot!" exclaimed Addie. "You're always down on schools because you didn't go to one yourself. School taught Tilly and I all sorts of important things we couldn't have learned at home."

"What a pity it didn't teach you grammar," said Sal, smiling.

"We *did* learn grammar—parsing and all that," declared Addie indignantly. "I must say none of us were very keen on parsing. What use is it?"

"Apparently none," said Mr. Grace dryly.

William laughed.

"I suppose it's a funny joke, but I didn't see it," said Tilly with regret.

"Sal only meant she had more time for reading," observed Liz. "And of course that's true. I think it depends what sort of person you are whether school is the right thing for you. I was terribly happy at Hill House School."

"I wasn't," said Tilly, with a sigh.

Roderick had not seen the joke either. He returned to the attack. He was evidently of a persistent nature.

"But, sir," said Roderick. "If every creed is part of the truth, why not put them all together and make a whole truth?"

"Who could do that?" asked Mr. Grace, smiling at him. "Who could make a path broad enough and narrow enough for every man who calls himself a Christian?"

Addie was talking to Liz, who was sitting next her. "It doesn't suit me," she was saying earnestly. "Some girls look their best in uniform but not me. I *must* have another frock—honestly—something decent to wear. So I thought perhaps if you could spare a few coupons—I mean you can't want many clothes *here*. You wear breeches most of the time, don't you?"

"I'll see," said Liz vaguely.

Tilly was talking to William—they all called him William now—she was saying: "If you really like sardine sandwiches that's too easy. We've got lots of tinned sardines in the store cupboard because we laid in a stock of them when it said on the wireless that everyone was to lay in a store of food in case of invasion…and then, of course, it changed its mind and said people who stored food were food hoarders and ought to be shot, but by that time the deed was done."

"You weren't shot," said William.

"Nobody knew," replied Tilly, dimpling.

Supper was over now and the party was breaking up. Roderick was saying good-bye for he had to be back in camp at nine o'clock.

"I'll wash the dishes," said Sal.

"It's Tilly and me tonight," declared Liz, gathering the dishes onto her tray. "Come on, Tilly—our turn."

Tilly was nothing loath, for it was fun washing up with Liz. She did it, as she did everything, with tremendous gusto; she flung herself into the job with zest, clearing the table, piling the dishes in the sink, turning on the taps full cock so that the water gushed out and the steam rose and enveloped her.

"Ha-ha!" she cried, rolling up her sleeves and plunging her arms into the sink. "Ha-ha! I love hot water. It's one of the pleasures of life!"

Everything in life was a pleasure to Liz—hot water, cold water, sunshine, even rain—she loved everything. She was like a goddess, a Brunhilde, muscular, vital, energizing. Her hair glittered like spun gold under the harsh light that hung, unshaded, over the scullery sink…but the clean dishes had begun to pile up on the draining board, and Tilly was obliged to take her eyes off Brunhilde and get on with her job.

Chapter Nine

A ddie was not a good correspondent. She wrote only when she wished to inform her family of an important fact, or to warn them that she was coming on leave and must be met at the station, so it was with some surprise that Tilly received Addie's letter from the postman and took it into the kitchen where she was peeling potatoes. It can't be leave again, thought Tilly as she slit the letter open with the potato peeler and ran her eyes hastily down the closely written page. The letter didn't seem to be very interesting and, as usual, was liberally scattered with the pronoun "I." Sal had once remarked that it was a pity Addie used such a very ornate letter to denote herself. The ornate letter drew one's attention to the extraordinary number of times it appeared in her correspondence…and yet, how could she help it? wondered Tilly. How can you help using "I" when you're writing about yourself?

"Letters?" asked Sal, coming into the kitchen.

"One from Addie," replied Tilly. "'I's' all over the place as usual."

"Eyes all over the places?" inquired Sal, with mild surprise.

"Here, take it," said Tilly. "My hands are all wet."

Sal took it. "Oh, I see what you mean!" she said.

"Tell me what she wants."

"I can tell you that before I read it. She wants clothes coupons, of course. She screwed some out of Liz when she was here, and she's got most of Father's already. I had to use some of mine to buy him a new shirt."

"I might let her have four," said Tilly thoughtfully, rubbing her nose with the back of her hand, which was the only dry part of it.

Sal was reading the letter and now she began to expound its contents. "Addie is busy," announced Sal. "Addie was kept late at the office making out returns. There's a new girl in the office and Addie doesn't like her. Addie met Aunt Rona in Debenham's buying a smart hat—"

"Who is Aunt Rona?" asked Tilly.

"Aunt Rona…" said Sal thoughtfully. "Yes, the name seems to ring a bell. Aunt Rona…Let me see. A woman with dark hair and a big nose. Why do I think of her like that?"

"Because that's what she's like, I suppose," suggested Tilly sensibly.

"And a loud voice," continued Sal. "Ugly but smart."

"Where did you see her, Sal?"

"Where *could* I have seen her?"

"D'you know who she is?" asked Tilly, dropping the potatoes into the pan.

"I believe I do," said Sal, delving into her memory. "I have a feeling she's mother's brother's widow, and after Uncle Jack died she married someone else. It's ages ago, of course. You would be too young to remember…Yes, I'm almost sure that's who she is. Don't ask me how Addie managed to get to know her," added Sal, and she seized the two pails of hen food and was gone.

Mr. Grace, when tackled upon the subject, could do little but corroborate the facts already known. "Very dressy," he said. "Rona spent a great deal of money on her clothes, but I must admit they became her. I haven't seen poor Rona for at least twelve years."

"Poor Rona?" asked Tilly.

"Your Uncle Jack died," explained Mr. Grace.

"But she married someone else. Who did she marry, Father?"

"Mapleton was his name. He died, too, some time ago. I remember seeing his death in *The Times*."

Addie's next letter was full of Aunt Rona. Aunt Rona had asked Addie to lunch at her flat. Aunt Rona had called at the office, looking terribly smart. Aunt Rona had taken Addie to see a play, introduced Addie to her hairdresser, and bought her a new hat.

The others were amused at this sudden infatuation, but Sal was not. Sal had delved more deeply into her memory and discovered bits and pieces of Aunt Rona, which, put together, made an unpleasant sort of picture. A picture that was all the more disturbing because it was so vague. She had a curious feeling of unease when Aunt Rona's name was mentioned.

This being so, Sal was not really surprised when one fine morning the station taxi (from Wandlebury, of course) drew up at the Vicarage and deposited Aunt Rona on the doorstep.

"Aunt Rona has come!" cried Sal, putting her head around the kitchen door.

"Aunt Rona!" exclaimed Tilly in amazement.

"Has come," said Sal, and with that she smoothed her hair with both hands, tucked her pullover neatly into her waistband, and sallied forth to meet the guest.

Aunt Rona was standing on the step beside her extremely handsome pigskin suitcase. She was saying in a loud firm voice, "I have been here before, my man, and the fare is seven and sixpence." Then she turned and saw Sal and held out both hands. "Ah, Sarah!" she exclaimed. "It *is* Sarah, isn't it?"

"Yes," said Sal, taking her hands and shaking them, and hoping that Aunt Rona would not expect to be kissed.

"We know each other, don't we?" said Aunt Rona gaily.

"Yes," said Sal.

Aunt Rona *was* ugly. She was very dark, with a big mouth, full of very white teeth; her eyes were large and deeply set; her nose was unusually prominent, but she knew how to dress, thought Sal, noticing the neat black coat and skirt, the crimson scarf and hat to match, the elegant patent leather shoes and fine silk stockings. Sal remembered now exactly when and where she had seen Aunt Rona.

"I have been bombed," declared Aunt Rona. "I have had all my windows broken. You see before you a refugee. Yes, refugee—I had absolutely no idea where to go or what to do until dear little Adeline suggested Chevis Green."

"I'm sure Father will be very pleased," said Sal, trying to make her voice sound reasonably convincing.

"I shall pull my weight, of course," said Aunt Rona, sailing into the hall and leaving Sal to follow with the pigskin suitcase. "I am no passenger, Sarah. It is wartime and we must all do our bit. Only the other day I was saying to Sir Teal Mallard—a very dear friend of mine—we must all do what we can to win this war. Where is your father, Sarah?"

"He's busy," said Sal a trifle breathlessly, for the case was heavy. "We never disturb Father in the morning unless it's something important—" She hesitated and stopped, aware that this might have been put in a more felicitous way.

"Of course," agreed Aunt Rona. "I used to stay with the Goslings. I daresay you know his books. Highly improper, of course, but most diverting. Egbert Gosling always shut himself up every morning from nine to one and nobody dared to go near him. On one occasion when the drawing room curtains caught on fire, poor Alice rushed into the study and Egbert threw the ink pot at her."

"Like Luther," said Sal, in a dazed voice. It was a foolish thing to say, but she had so much on her mind. She must find Tilly and arrange about food. Cheese and eggs for lunch—would that do, or would they have to open a tin of Spam? Why didn't Tilly come and help? Tilly was probably in the linen cupboard looking out sheets for Aunt Rona's bed—hemstitched sheets of course—and (Goodness! thought Sal) Aunt Rona must have the back room, because William couldn't possibly be turned out of the front room now that he had settled down with all his drawings and measurements. These disjointed ideas sped through Sal's mind as she led Aunt Rona into the drawing room and asked if she would like a cup of tea.

"I can wait until lunch," replied Aunt Rona, looking around and selecting the most comfortable chair. "I don't want to be the least trouble to anyone. You mustn't look upon me as a guest, Sarah."

"No," said Sal doubtfully.

"Do you remember me?"

Sal nodded. "I met you in London with Mother."

"You were very small," said Aunt Rona, with the flash of white teeth that did duty for a smile. "But people *do* remember me. I have often been surprised to find that people remember me when I have no recollection of them."

"Yes," said Sal, unsurprised at the news.

"Of course this doesn't apply to you, Sarah," continued Aunt Rona, gazing at her critically. "I shouldn't have known you in the street, but meeting you here it was obvious you were Sarah. You were always pale and thin."

"Yes," said Sal.

"I met you at Parkinson's Hotel," said Aunt Rona. "It was when poor Jack was with me—we called at the hotel because he wanted to see your mother. You had been to the dentist that afternoon."

"To the doctor," said Sal.

"Of course. Your mother had brought you to London to see a specialist about your back."

Sal wished Aunt Rona would talk of something else. It had been so frightful. The doctor had said she must lie perfectly flat on her back for six months…Mother had tried to be cheerful about it—both of them had tried to be cheerful.

"Poor Mary," said Aunt Rona, with a sigh. "What an anxiety you were! What an expense!"

"Yes," said Sal. "I must have been, I suppose."

"Mary had a very unfortunate life—four daughters and no son."

Sal was about to agree again, and then she changed her mind. Why should I? she thought. It isn't *her* business…how does *she* know Mother wanted a boy? Mother never said so to *her*, that's certain.

"You must let me do the flowers," Aunt Rona was saying. "That shall be my job, Sarah. It's astonishing what a difference flowers can make to a room—even to a dull, shabby room—if they're really well arranged. One has to love flowers and understand them to get the best effect."

"Yes," said Sal. "Well, if you'll excuse me, I'll go and see about—about some things."

Sal had said that Father must not be disturbed, but now she had changed her mind. She would have to tell Father that Aunt Rona was here; she must break it gently to him so that he might get used to the idea before lunchtime. With this end in view she opened the study door and went in. He was writing.

"It's Aunt Rona," said Sal in a low voice. "She's had all her windows broken."

"Poor soul!" said Mr. Grace vaguely, without looking up.

"Father—"

"I'm busy, Sal. We'll talk about it at lunch. She isn't seriously injured, is she?"

"She isn't injured at all."

"I thought you said she had broken something."

"Her windows," said Sal urgently.

Mr. Grace looked at Sal over his spectacles. "She must have them mended," he said.

"She can't, Father. Everyone's windows are broken. There isn't enough glass—"

"Not everyone's," interrupted Mr. Grace, glancing at his own.

"In London, Father."

"Yes, yes. But I'm not a glazier. What can I do about it? Really, Sal—"

"Addie told her to come here."

"*Here!*" exclaimed Mr. Grace. "No, no. That would never do. Rona was always a trifle—er—difficult. Even Mary found her a little—er—difficult, and Mary was extraordinarily easy herself. So you see—"

"Yes, Father, but—"

"No," said Mr. Grace with unusual vigor. "No, Sal. The desire to have her here does great credit to your heart, but you don't quite understand."

"She is here," said Sal.

"She is here!" cried Mr. Grace in—yes, in *alarm*, and he half rose from his chair and looked toward the windows as if (Sal thought afterward, though at the time she was too distracted to formulate the idea) he actually contemplated escape in that direction.

"It's all right," declared Sal, assuming the role of comforter. "We'll look after her—Tilly and I—and Liz of course. You needn't bother about her at all."

"But Sal—"

"But, Father, how *can* we refuse to have her? She's brought her suitcase."

"A big one?" asked Mr. Grace, speaking in a whisper and glancing at the door.

"Not *very*," replied Sal unconvincingly.

꧁

Tilly was in the back bedroom flicking about with a duster in a desultory way. It was obvious that Tilly was feeling a bit ruffled. She would be more ruffled, thought Sal, when she had had the opportunity to converse with Aunt Rona.

"Have you told Father?" asked Tilly, flicking the mirror contemptuously.

"Poor Father," said Sal. "He isn't at all pleased. I believe he would have liked to say damn."

"Liz will say it for him when she gets home. It's perfectly frightful *cheek*. That's what it is. Why should we have her? She isn't even related to us."

"Because she hasn't anywhere else to go."

A silence ensued, a very lugubrious silence. It was broken by the entrance of Aunt Rona.

"Ah, here you are!" she exclaimed. "I wondered where you had gotten to."

"This is Tilly," said Sal, introducing them.

Aunt Rona advanced upon Tilly and kissed her in a pecking manner on the cheek. "There," she said. "Now I know you all—except Elizabeth, of course."

"Yes," said Sal. "Yes, you'll see Liz at teatime."

Aunt Rona looked around. "This is a very small room," she said. "I should prefer the front bedroom. I looked in as I passed and saw some—er—garments there, lying about. A friend of your father's, I suppose."

"Yes," said Sal, nodding.

"He won't mind moving in here," said Aunt Rona cheerfully.

"We can't move him," said Tilly, opening her mouth for the first time.

"No," said Sal, backing her up. "He uses the table for his

work. It would be too cramped to bring the table in here. No, I'm afraid we can't ask Mr. Single to move."

"So perhaps you'd rather not stay," mumbled Tilly, her face very red with embarrassment.

Sal looked at Tilly in amazement (it *did* seem odd that Tilly, the shy one of the family, had managed to utter these words, but, like many shy people, Tilly sometimes burst forth with startling utterances, astonishing herself no less than her friends).

"I mean," continued Tilly, floundering in a morass of silence. "I mean this isn't a very nice room, it's rather dark—it faces north, too—but it's the only room we've got for you, so if you don't like it—"

"No, no, you mustn't worry," said Aunt Rona, finding her voice and speaking in the most friendly manner imaginable. "Of course I *quite* understand, Matilda. It doesn't matter in the least. I'm sure I shall be most comfortable here."

It was fortunate that Joan appeared at this moment, carrying the pigskin suitcase. She dumped it down on the floor and stood back, breathing heavily (perhaps a trifle more heavily than was actually necessary, thought Sal, looking at her in some alarm).

"Oh, thank you," said Aunt Rona in a curiously high-pitched voice, quite different from her normal manner of speaking. "Thank you. If you will just move it a little…No, over here…or perhaps I could have it on the ottoman…and please undo the straps."

"This is Joan," said Sal, trying to make things easier.

Aunt Rona took no notice; she had moved over to the dressing table and was using her lipstick with a practiced hand.

"Is there anything else, Miss Sal?" inquired Joan.

"No, thank you, Joan," said Sal.

"Oh, wait a moment, please," said Aunt Rona, still speaking in that extraordinary voice. "I will give you my hot water bottles. I have two. I should like one put in now and the other at nine o'clock. Fill them with hot—but not boiling—water, please."

Chapter Ten

S al knew that she would not sleep so she took *Emma* to bed with her, hoping that the well-known story would soothe her troubled spirit and dissipate her worried thoughts, but it was no use at all; the worries kept flooding in and she found herself reading whole pages without taking in the sense. She put down the book in despair and allowed her thoughts full rein. What a frightful day it had been! Aunt Rona had arrived only this morning, yet it felt like a month at least. I shouldn't have let her stay, thought Sal, but how could I help it? I couldn't turn her away from the door, could I? All the same, thought Sal, if I had known what she was like, I believe I could have tried...

Sal thought of the day in detail. Lunch first. Liz had not come home to lunch, for they were busy at the farm, and William had taken sandwiches with him, so he was not home, either. Four of them sat down to lunch, a very small party, and Aunt Rona talked the whole time, with Father answering politely. Sal had done her best but she was not good at small talk—none of the Graces was—and Tilly had been absolutely dumb. Aunt Rona had rested in the afternoon, to recuperate after her journey, and had come down to eat (in the drawing room, of course) with renewed vitality brimming over with conversation. Roderick had come over from Ganthorne on his motorbike, then Liz had arrived—and William—and to each one, Aunt Rona's presence had to be explained, and each one had seemed less pleased to make her acquaintance. Fortunately (or was it unfortunately?) Aunt Rona seemed oblivious of the fact that her presence was resented. She had chatted brightly, leaving no gaps at all in the conversation, and everyone had sat around eating and drinking and saying "yes" or "no." She must think we're awful, thought Sal. Perhaps we *are* awful. Perhaps if we tried to love her… but how could you love a person who bored you to death, a person who made interesting conversation impossible by talking banalities all the time? Liz had been the first to lose patience. She rose and said, "I'll feed the hens for you, Sal." And Sal, who had been looking forward to feeding the hens herself and so escaping from the room, had been obliged to thank Liz for undertaking the task. "Ah, hens!" said Aunt Rona. "One of the little daily tasks! And I daresay Captain Herd will go on with you and help you to carry the heavy pails." "Er—oh, yes, of course," said Roderick.

Liz and Roderick! Well, Sal had known before, hadn't she? She hadn't needed Aunt Rona's arch look as the two left the room together to tell her what she had known before.

Then after supper Aunt Rona had gotten hold of Father (who had been out all the afternoon visiting his parishioners and wanted—as Sal well knew—to be left in peace to read his book), and the two of them had walked up and down the terrace together, Aunt Rona talking interminably in her penetrating voice. Sal had made up her mind that Father must be protected from Aunt Rona, and yet, the very first day of her visit, Aunt Rona had gotten him like this, had carried him off beneath Sal's very nose…and Sal could do nothing about it, nothing at all except watch them from the window and worry and fret. I'm no use, thought Sal. I'm no match for her—none of us is. She can do what she likes with us.

The following day was wet; Tilly took the key of the side door of the church and went off to play the organ. The churchyard was dismal, the grass sodden, the tombstones black and dripping. Water poured off the roof of the church, gurgled down the pipes, and splashed into the gratings. Tilly opened the side door and went up the short flight of steps to the organ. She did not start practicing at once but took her seat and leaned back against the grille. It was quiet and peaceful here. There was no peace at home. Presently she would begin to practice the voluntary that she intended to play next Sunday—it was Handel's "Water Music"—but for the moment she only wanted silence.

Suddenly she heard steps on the little stair and William's head appeared. He hesitated there and looked at her. "I followed you," he said.

"Why did you?" asked Tilly crossly.

"Do you and Sal want me to move?"

"Move?"

"From my bedroom," explained William. "Mrs. Mapleton asked me to change with her, and of course I can—easily—it would be no bother at all."

"If you move, I shall never speak to you again," cried Tilly hysterically.

William seemed undaunted by the threat. He said, "That's all I wanted to know. It seems rather unchivalrous but my shoulders are fairly broad." He gave a deep chuckle and turned to descend the stairs.

"Don't go," said Tilly imperiously.

"I thought you didn't feel like talking," said William.

"I didn't, but now I do," she replied.

William sat down on the top step and waited patiently.

"Everything is horrible," said Tilly at last. "Everyone is upset—Father, Liz, Sal, everyone. It isn't *all* Aunt Rona's fault, either."

"Most of it is, but not all," agreed William.

"You notice things, don't you?" said Tilly, looking at him curiously.

"I'm learning," said William, with a sigh.

"You aren't happy, either."

"Not very," agreed William.

There was a little silence.

"I expect things will come right," said William at last.

"I don't," declared Tilly. "I think everything is going wronger and wronger every day—every hour, really. I don't want Liz to marry Roderick."

"You can't do anything to stop it."

"And what's the matter with Sal?" continued Tilly in an unsteady voice. "Sal is always so—so dependable, so peaceful and—and understanding—but now—"

"Sal is very worried," said William.

"I'm a beast," said Tilly miserably. "I *feel* all beastly inside... as if there was a devil inside me. It's because I hate Aunt Rona, that's what it is. I hate everything about her...the way she talks to Joan...it makes me feel quite sick to hear her talk to Joan."

"I don't suppose Sal likes it either," said William thoughtfully.

"You think I'm a beast, don't you?"

"I think you could—help—more," said William cautiously.

❦

Sal and Joan were in the kitchen, making jam. It was a good employment for such a wet morning, and a very companionable sort of employment. Sal heard all the gossip of the village. She heard that Cynthia Bouse (from the Whistling Man) was walking out with Jim Feather, and his father wasn't half mad about it, neither: and she heard that young Mrs. Foley was "having another," the third in two years, and she heard that

Mrs. Toop had fallen out with Miss Bodkin, and they were not on speaking terms.

There never was such a fiery-tempered woman as Mrs. Toop, thought Sal, with a sigh. Practically all the trouble in the village could be traced back to Mrs. Toop; she had a perfect genius for saying the wrong thing at the wrong moment, and in the wrong way…and little Mr. Toop was such a kindly, sociable man.

"It was at Elsie Trod's," said Joan, with relish. "Maria Toop was there, and in comes Miss Bodkin. They were 'aving a cup of tea and Elsie was giving a drop to 'ar baby. 'You didn't ought to do that,' says Miss Bodkin. 'Tea's bad for 'is stummick.' With that Maria goes off the deep end and says, 'What do *you* know about babies, any'ow?' And that was 'ow it began."

"Miss Bodkin was right," said Sal. "I'll stir for a bit, shall I?"

"If you don't mind," agreed Joan, surrendering the wooden spoon. "It's pretty 'ot 'anging over the fire for long. That's 'ow it *began*," continued Joan. "It went on for hours—so Elsie says—she says they'd both forgotten 'ow it began before they got to the end of calling each other names."

Sal nodded. She could well believe it.

"The new people at The Beeches 'ave moved in," continued Joan. "Lovely furniture they've got. It's Empire, Mrs. Feather says. She's doing a bit of cleaning till they find a cook. Fancing getting furniture all the way from New Zealand, Miss Sal!"

"From New Zealand?" asked Sal in surprise.

"Empire," explained Joan. "New Zealand would be Empire."

"It means French Empire," said Sal.

"French Empire! Well, Mrs. Feather didn't know *that*."

Sal smiled. It was obvious that Mrs. Feather's ignorance would soon be remedied.

"Mrs. Feather says they're queer sort of people," continued Joan. "They don't 'old with church, Mrs. Feather says, and they're always 'aving rows together."

This was getting a bit too gossipy so Sal changed the subject. "How is your father?" she asked.

"Better," said Joan. "You let me stir, Miss Sal, your face is like a beetroot. You can get out the pots if you like; they'll warm nicely on the cool part of the stove."

"I'm glad he's better," said Sal, counting out the pots. "Does the doctor think he'll be able to get up soon?"

"Sunday," replied Joan. "It's a great 'elp to m' mother, me getting 'ome early. She said I was to thank you, Miss Sal. That Mrs. Mapleton thinks I get out too much."

"Oh, I don't think so!"

"She said to me this morning, you've got a very good place 'ere, 'aven't you? That's what she said."

"Well," began Sal.

"Oh, yes," agreed Joan. "I know I'm well off compared to some, but she didn't mean it like that. It wasn't so much what she said as 'ow she said it. She meant it spiteful."

"Hasn't it boiled long enough?" inquired Sal, knowing quite well it hadn't.

"Five minutes more," replied Joan, glancing at the clock. "Oh, Miss Sal, I almost forgot. Did you 'ear about the Fate?"

"The Fate?" asked Sal.

"Sports and that," said Joan. "It's going to be at Chevis Place. Mr. Feather told me when he brought the letters this morning. Tea and ices and Aunt Sallies, and all that—a proper first-rate Fate."

"No!" exclaimed Sal. This was news indeed.

"Yes." Joan nodded. "Quite soon, too. I was just wondering 'ow I could freshen up my best dress a bit. P'r'aps I could get a new collar or something."

There was a little silence, filled with the bubbling of the jam. Sal was reflecting philosophically upon values, upon the shifting values of material things. The value of a possession depends upon whether or not you really need it, thought Sal. If a woman has six pairs of stockings, the value of one pair is not very high, but if she has only two pairs, the value of one pair is far more than three times as much. This was too muddling for Sal so she abandoned that line of thought and came down to brass tacks. A frock hanging in your wardrobe (a frock you wore only very occasionally) was not really of very much value to you, but if you gave it to Joan and Joan could wear it at the fete and enjoy it…and it really would suit her, thought Sal, looking at Joan and envisaging her attired in it.

Joan was even more enchanted with the offer than Sal had expected.

Chapter Eleven

It was still raining in the afternoon. Sal had hoped Aunt Rona would retire to bed but, instead, she seated herself in the drawing room and indicated that she wished Sal to keep her company.

"We can do some mending," said Aunt Rona. "I expect you have quite a lot of mending to do."

For a moment Sal thought Aunt Rona intended to help her with her task and was about to accept gratefully, but even as the words formed themselves upon her lips, Aunt Rona produced a silk stocking from her work basket and surveyed it with a worried frown.

"So annoying," said Aunt Rona. "One can't get silk stockings in England, and of course I can't wear anything else. I have them sent over from America—it's the only way."

She took out a little hook and began to pick up the stitches of a ladder, one by one.

Sal's basket of household mending was bulging with garments requiring attention. She always intended to keep the mending down but it piled up too quickly. The linen was old and needed constant patching and Father was terribly hard on socks.

"You see," said Aunt Rona, displaying her work. "You see, it scarcely shows. Of course it takes a long time to do, but it's worth the trouble. If you do a thing at all, you should do it with all your might," added Aunt Rona complacently.

"Yes. It's very neat," said Sal. She chose a piece of gray wool and began to fill in an enormous hole in the heel of Father's sock.

A few moments later Tilly came in and sat down. "Shall I put a patch in this towel?" she inquired, holding up the article in question.

Sal looked at her in amazement. It was not Tilly's job to help with the mending. She did other things, of course, knitting, or ironing or anything else that needed to be done; mending was Tilly's pet aversion.

"Shall I?" repeated Tilly. "It needs a patch, doesn't it? I can take a bit off this old towel to patch it with."

"Oh, yes! Yes, thank you," said Sal gratefully.

There was silence. Tilly tried to think of something to say, something bright and cheerful, or amusing, but she couldn't think of anything at all. How queer it was! She and Sal and Liz could talk all day without stopping, but now, with Aunt Rona sitting there, her mind was an absolute blank. It seemed odd that Aunt Rona wasn't talking—but perhaps Aunt Rona felt the same, or perhaps Aunt Rona thought it was not worth while making conversation for girls. Yes, that must be the reason, thought Tilly, glancing in Sal's direction. Was Sal trying to think of something to say? Sal's head was bent over the sock. She was darning as if her life depended upon it.

I must say *something*, thought Tilly, so she opened her mouth and said, "I wish it would stop raining."

"The farmers need rain," said Sal.

There was another silence.

"You must find it dull here, Aunt Rona," said Tilly.

"Not at all," replied Aunt Rona brightly. "As a matter of fact, I'm very fond of the country. Of course one would have to run up to town occasionally."

Tilly pondered these words, and the more she pondered them, the more ominous they seemed: "One would have to run up to town occasionally." That meant—well, obviously that meant...if one lived here...always. Tilly glanced at Sal to see if she had heard and, hearing, understood the implication, but Sal was darning assiduously.

The silence that followed Aunt Rona's statement became unbearable. Tilly wanted to scream. She was just wondering what would happen if she screamed when the back door bell rang.

"That's the back door," said Sal, rising.

"Doesn't Joan answer the bell?" inquired Aunt Rona.

"Joan's out," replied Sal.

"Again!" exclaimed Aunt Rona.

Sal was glad to escape. It was a bit mean to leave Tilly there alone, especially when Tilly had been so decent, but Sal *had* to escape. If she hadn't been able to escape, something appalling might have happened. Sal could not have borne it another minute. She ran through the kitchen and opened the back door and found Mrs. Element on the step; a wet bedraggled figure in a very long, brown waterproof and a shapeless felt hat. Mrs. Element was thin and angular with large feet that flapped as she walked; her face was pale and freckled; her forehead was bumpy; her hair had been sandy, it was now faded to the color of old hay, but these misfortunes were redeemed by a pair of really beautiful brown eyes, clear as crystal and full of human kindness.

"Oh, Mrs. Element!" cried Sal in dismay. "Oh goodness, how wet you are! Your rheumatism—"

"I won't come in," said Mrs. Element. "It'll muss up your floor."

"Of course you must come in! Let me take your coat. I'll get you a cup of tea in half no time."

"It's reel good of you, Miss Sal," said Mrs. Element, coming in with a show of reluctance, though of course she had intended to come in all the time and would have been surprised beyond measure if she had not been offered tea.

"I knew Joan was out," continued Mrs. Element, taking off her felt hat and placing it on the draining board of the sink. "So I just thought I'd come up and see you. It's about Bertie. Bertie Pike—*you* know. I've 'ad 'im all the war."

"I know," nodded Sal. "You've been most awfully good to him."

"Yes," agreed Mrs. Element. "Yes, that's right. Jim and me, not 'aving children of our own (through no fault of ours, Miss Sal, though there's people who throw it in our faces), we took a fancy to the little chap. Just like our own 'e is."

"Yes, I know."

"Well, Miss Sal, 'is mother's wrote to Jim saying as 'ow the bombs are over and she wants 'im back. That's the *position*, Miss Sal," added Mrs. Element, obviously pleased with the word.

"Oh, Mrs. Element!"

"That's the *position*," repeated Mrs. Element. "Bertie don't want to go back and we don't want 'im to go back. There it is."

There it was. Mrs. Element was sitting back in the chair with her hands folded, waiting confidently for the verdict, quite certain it would be a favorable verdict, too. What was Sal to say? Solomon had ordered the child to be cut in half, thought Sal distractedly.

"I'm afraid," began Sal. "I'm afraid his mother has a legal right—"

"Oh, Miss Sal!" cried Mrs. Element reproachfully. "Oh, Miss Sal, 'ow *can* you! We've 'ad 'im four years come October—and *you* know what 'e was like when we got 'im. Thin and miserable and 'alf starved—neglected, that's what 'e was—nobody 'adn't bothered their 'eads about the pore lamb, nobody 'adn't even taught 'im to be good. What sort of a mother is that, Miss Sal?"

Sal was silent. She agreed with Mrs. Element wholeheartedly.

"You'd 'ardly believe it," continued Mrs. Element. "You'd 'ardly believe it, but when Bertie came to us 'e didn't even know about Jesus. 'Oo's Jesus?' 'e said to me. You'd 'ardly believe it, but it's true. You ask Jim. Seven years old, 'e was, and knew nothing more than a black 'eathen…and now," continued Mrs. Element earnestly. "Look at 'im now, Miss Sal; as nice a little chap as anyone would want to see, a reel little gentleman and clever as paint. Doing well at school and winning prizes for arithmetic…Look at 'im now, Miss Sal!"

Sal knew it was all true—all and more—the Elements had made a splendid job of Bertie.

"I thought you might write to Mrs. Pike," said Mrs. Element, after a short silence.

"She wouldn't take any notice of what I said."

"You could tell 'er the *position*," declared Mrs. Element. "You could put it nicer than Jim and me. It was Jim's ideer really. Ask Miss Sal, 'e said. You go up and ask Miss Sal, she'll put it right. You will, won't you, miss?"

"I'll try," said Sal reluctantly. "I'll write to her if you want me to, but I'm afraid if his mother wants him, he'll have to go back."

"You write," said Mrs. Element, smiling for the first time. "It'll be all right if you tell 'er. Jim said so. Jim said, 'It'll be all right if Miss Sal writes 'er a letter. Remember that beautiful letter Miss Sal wrote when Mother died?' A beautiful letter it was," said Mrs. Element reminiscently. "Jim and me 'ad gone to Bristol for the funeral, and you wrote to us, Miss Sal. I 'adn't never got on very well with Jim's mother, but when I read that letter, I cried and cried—*beautiful*, it was."

Sal was so full of conflicting emotions that she was speechless. She poured out a cup of tea for Mrs. Element and handed her the sugar bowl.

"Not for me, thank you," said Mrs. Element. "It ain't right to take people's sugar. If you 'appen to 'ave a sack-reen 'andy

83

I'll 'ave one. Useful stuff, ain't it? I don't know 'ow I'd get on without sack-reen. I use it for rhubarb—sweetens it lovely—makes a nice tart, rhubarb does, if you can spare the fat."

Sal agreed. She was glad to change the subject—cooking was always a nice safe subject and practically inexhaustible. She sat down and poured out a cup of tea for herself and they proceeded to exchange recipes. But Mrs. Element had not forgotten and as she was going away, with Sal's pet recipe for a ginger sponge tucked into her handbag, she paused on the step and said, "Oh, it's stopped raining, that's nice. You'll write and tell 'er the *position*, won't you, Miss Sal?"

When Sal returned to the drawing room, Aunt Rona had vanished and Tilly was sitting alone on the sofa staring in front of her in a dejected sort of way.

"Where *have* you been!" she exclaimed. "I thought you were never coming back…I was rude to her, Sal."

"You weren't!" cried Sal incredulously.

"I was—really—about Joan. She's such a pig about Joan, isn't she? And I just couldn't stand it any longer. I was definitely rude," declared Tilly emphatically.

"How did she take it?" inquired Sal.

"That was the queer thing. She didn't seem to notice. Do you think she's very stupid?"

Sal sat down beside Tilly on the sofa so that they could talk in whispers. (Odd that one should have to talk in whispers in one's own drawing room; odd, but necessary, for Aunt Rona had a way of appearing suddenly and silently when one least expected her.)

"Do you think she's stupid?" repeated Tilly.

"No," said Sal. "No, she's rather clever in her own way. Stupid in some ways, perhaps…"

"You never know what she's thinking," complained Tilly.

It was true, of course, and to Sal's mind this was the most

unbearable trait in Aunt Rona's personality. You never knew what she was thinking. Her eyes were opaque, and unchanging, they gave no clue to her thoughts; her tongue, instead of revealing her thoughts, obscured them still further. Her armor had no chinks—or none that Sal could find—and you could not offend her for she never took offense. She was always bright and pleasant and often smiling, but her smile was not a proper smile for it never reached her eyes.

"She's made us all horrid," said Tilly miserably.

"There's frightfully dangerous poison in her," said Sal.

They were silent for a few minutes, their heads close together, and Tilly began to feel comforted, for she and Sal were in tune again (it was wretched to be out of tune with Sal). Sal understood about it now, she understood that Tilly was sorry for being "difficult" and the blame had been laid upon Aunt Rona and her poisonous influence; so *that* was all right.

"Sal," said Tilly in a threadlike whisper. "Have you noticed Aunt Rona talks as if she intended to stay here—always?"

"Yes," said Sal.

"It couldn't be—I mean do you think she has designs on—on Father?"

"Yes," said Sal.

"You've noticed it!" exclaimed Tilly in dismay. "I was just hoping it was imagination!"

"No," said Sal. "No, it isn't imagination. That's why I try to—to keep track of her. Father is terrified of her, I'm certain of it."

"What are we to do?" cried Tilly. "What *are* we to do? If she has made up her mind to marry him, he hasn't a chance!"

"I don't know about *that*," said Sal thoughtfully.

They were silent again.

"Perhaps William could do something about it," said Tilly at last.

"William!"

"Yes, William is rather—deep. I don't mean deep in a horrid way, of course, but he sees a good deal more than you would think."

"I don't believe William could help much."

"I shall talk to him anyhow," declared Tilly.

Chapter Twelve

Yesterday had been wet, but today it had cleared up and the sun was shining brightly. Sal walked down the garden with a bucket in each hand; she was going to feed the hens. The henhouse was at the end of the garden near the stream; it was the same stream that flowed between the cottages at Chevis Green and, later, joined the Wandle and flowed through the square at Wandlebury. Here, in the Vicarage garden, the stream was in its infancy, smiling and chuckling like a happy baby. Watercress grew in the shallows in the curve of the bank, and willows flourished beside it. Quite near, and casting a shade on the water, was a weeping elm and, back from the henhouse, there was a wild piece of ground, gay with rose-red willow herb that Jos Barefoot treasured for his bees. Jos loved his bees. He was like a bee himself; small and brown and wizened. His eyes were brown like chestnuts and his voice was high-pitched. Bees crawled over his arms but never stung him. "They knows old Jos," he would say. He was too old to do much work, but he pottered around and kept the garden from becoming a wilderness.

Sal called the ducks and fed them; the hens came scurrying after her; she had one hen sitting on a clutch of eggs and another with a brood of young chickens. Usually this work made her happy but today it had no power to cheer or soothe her. She was so worried and miserable. It had been hard for Sal to grow up, she had gone through a difficult time, she had felt discontented and unhappy...then that phase had passed or been overcome and for a long time she had felt serene and at peace with the world, wanting nothing more of life than her father, her sisters, her books, people to help, and enough to do. Now the old turmoil had returned and she felt that life was rushing on and she was standing still. It was a horrible feeling. Liz and Tilly were so different, thought Sal. They had few problems. Tilly was still a child for all her twenty-three years. She was shy and retiring; she did not lay herself open to the hurts of life, she sought no adventures. Tilly lived in her "little wooden hut," content and happy. Liz took life as it came, enjoying it, living in the present. Sometimes she got hurt, of course, but she did not learn to be careful. She gathered herself up and rushed on. Gay, golden, brilliant Liz! She was a year older than Sal, but Sal had always felt herself to be the elder. Liz would never grow up; nothing would teach her to be cautious. It was natural that men should fall in love with Liz, she was so friendly and unselfconscious, so vital. Sal paused in her work and thought of Eric Coleridge. He had come to Chevis Green as Mr. Grace's curate, a delicate creature with a thin, eager face and soft, brown eyes, which followed Liz like the eyes of a faithful spaniel. He had loved Liz to distraction—there was no doubt of that—he had loved Liz and won her heart and then he had gone away to succor the heathen. He had received a call, and because he did not want to answer the call, he had answered it. Eric was that sort of man, conscience-ridden, ultrasensitive, fanatical. Sal had been very angry with Eric, for it seemed to her that Eric had a duty to Liz, and surely Liz was just as important as the heathen? But she was glad afterward when she thought about the matter in cold blood, for a fanatic does not make a comfortable husband. Liz had been badly hurt, but she had faced it bravely, so bravely that nobody had known—not even Father, thought Sal—and after a little while, there was no need to be brave. Liz was whole again, breasting the world with her usual zest and confidence… And now there was Roderick. (Well, of course. Who could help falling in love with Liz?) And Roderick was a real man, a proper man, the sort of man who would know exactly what he wanted and go all out to get it…and Liz was more than half in love with him already.

So I ought to be glad, thought Sal. She was trying very hard to be glad when Jos Barefoot came around the side of the henhouse with a large rake in his hand.

"Them chickens is growing well," said Jos in his thin high voice. "They be pecking already. You give 'em a 'andful of grit, Miss Sal. Chickens be like 'umans; they needs grit."

That's what I need, thought Sal, looking at him. She was very fond of Jos and she respected him. Like Tilly he was content and happy in his little hut.

"Were you at the wedding, Jos?" she asked.

"I don't 'old with weddings," declared Jos, sitting down upon an upturned barrow and beginning to fill his pipe. "Too much fuss, to my mind. Weddings is nothing to make a fuss about. Weddings is lotteries, that's what."

"You never took a ticket, Jos."

"Not me," said Jos. "I never 'ad a woman—never wanted one. Weddings is lotteries; they may be all right an' they may be all wrong. You'm not thinkin' of gettin' married, Miss Sal?"

"No," said Sal, smiling.

"That's right. You be better as you are. Passon couldn't do without you neither. You be better as you are."

"It's a good thing everybody doesn't think so."

Jos shook his head. "Ar," he said gravely. "There's Toop. Toop would 'ave been better without that woman. You can't deny it, Miss Sal."

Sal could not, so she was silent.

"It 'appened when Toop was in Lunnon," said Jos, striking a match and lighting his pipe. "'E met Maria at a party—fish an' chips it was—an' Maria looked reel smart in a blue dress an' 'er 'air done up to kill. Toop was took with 'er but 'e wouldn't never 'ave 'ad 'er if 'e 'adn't 'appened to see it wrote up on the Albert 'All."

"Wrote up on the Albert Hall!" exclaimed Sal, repeating the statement word for word in her amazement.

"'Ave Maria," nodded Jos. "That's what it said—'Ave Maria. It give Toop quite a turn…wrote up on the Albert 'All in letters a foot 'igh…so 'e 'ad 'er."

Sal knew the Toops well, of course, and she had often wondered what had induced the cheerful, friendly little man to marry Maria. Now she had been told the reason and she saw no reason to disbelieve it. The story was too circumstantial; neither Toop nor Jos could have made it up.

Jos was now talking about his bees. He always came back to his bees if you listened to him long enough and Sal was glad to listen. Already she felt a good deal better about things. Jos was so friendly and good, and (in spite of his eighty-odd years) so innocent. The world could not be such a bad place, after all, when it contained people like Jos. She was still standing there, enthralled, when she heard her father calling her. Jos heard him too, for his hearing was extraordinarily keen.

"There's Passon," said Jos, motioning with his thumb. "Sounds to me as if something's up, Miss Sal."

"Yes," said Sal, her eyes widening with anxiety. "Yes, I'd better fly—"

"I'll finish 'ere," said Jos, nodding.

Mr. Grace was coming to meet Sal; they met halfway down the garden. He took her arm and led her to a seat.

"What is it?" asked Sal. "Aunt Rona—"

"No, no, it isn't anything serious."

"Nothing serious?"

"Just a little—er—misunderstanding with Miss Bodkin," said Mr. Grace.

"Miss Bodkin! Oh, dear!" said Sal. "What *has* Miss Bodkin been doing now?"

"Nothing," replied Mr. Grace. "She seems a little put out, that's all. I think perhaps you might be able to—er—clear up the matter."

Sal looked at her father. He had a slightly guilty air, the air of a small boy who has been discovered stealing the jam. "What have you been doing to Miss Bodkin?" Sal inquired sternly.

"Er," said Mr. Grace. "The fact is Mrs. Chevis-Cobbe brought some flowers to church on Sunday morning and put them into the altar vases."

"Oh, Father, how awful! Miss Bodkin always does the flowers on the first Sunday in the month."

"I know," agreed Mr. Grace. "Miss Bodkin had them. They were all white—rather uninteresting—and then Mrs. Chevis-Cobbe arrived with some lovely pale blue delphiniums."

"Oh, Father! You don't mean to say she put them in!"

"Er—yes. As a matter of fact—"

"You let her!"

"I helped her," said Mr. Grace in defiant tones. "I held them for her and handed them to her, and she put them in. It was a great improvement."

"How *could* you!" cried Sal in horror-stricken tones.

"Really, Sal—"

"It's serious," declared Sal. "It's very, *very* serious. I don't know *what* we can do about it."

"Serious?" said Mr. Grace. "The whole thing is absolutely childish. Miss Bodkin ought to know better."

"Yes, but she doesn't," said Sal.

"You can go and see her," said Mr. Grace, who was feeling more cheerful now that he had confessed his sin. "You'll be able to make it all right. You could take her a few flowers, perhaps." (He stopped. Sal was looking at him.) "Oh, well, perhaps not—flowers," said Mr. Grace doubtfully. "Perhaps—er—eggs. We want to make things right. It would be a pity if Mrs. Chevis-Cobbe were to fall foul of Miss Bodkin."

It had happened already, thought Sal—and yes, it was a thousand pities. Miss Bodkin, though extremely trying and touchy, was kindhearted *au fond* and wielded a good deal of influence in Chevis Green. She was a prominent member of the Women's Institute; she was an authority upon knitting and jam and invalid food. The village laughed at Miss Bodkin behind her back, of course, but it was kindly laughter for she was well liked and always ready to help when there was trouble in the house.

"I'll go now," said Sal, rising. "I'll go to the village first and see what I can do. It's *most* unfortunate. I *did* want Archie's wife to start off well. She could do such a lot for the village if she liked people—and people liked her."

"Yes," said Mr. Grace thoughtfully. "Yes, Sal. You're right and I'm wrong. It isn't a small thing. I am extremely sorry about it."

⁘

The village of Chevis Green had been altered and remodeled by an ancestor of old Lady Chevis. The cottages, separated from each other by little gardens, were disposed upon two sides of a large triangular patch of bright green grass; the few shops, the garage, and the inn were built along the third side. There were trees on the green, mostly large beeches, which threw a pleasant shade. At one end of the green was the War Memorial and beside it a comfortable wooden seat that had been gifted to the village by Archie Chevis-Cobbe on his accession to the property. There had been a large German gun beside the seat, but it had been removed for salvage during the Chevis Green salvage drive.

Mrs. Element, emerging from her cottage to pick some mint, happened to glance in the direction of the War Memorial and saw two figures sitting upon the seat in earnest conclave. She called to Mrs. Bouse, who lived next door, and Mrs. Bouse popped out.

"Miss Sal talking to Mrs. Chevis-Cobbe," said Mrs. Element, pointing.

"Lor'!" exclaimed Mrs. Bouse. "Fancy that, now! They don't 'alf look friendly—fancy Miss Sal takin' up with '*er*. Interferin', Emma Bodkin says."

"Yes," agreed Mrs. Element doubtfully. "Yes, Emma Bodkin seems to 'ave got 'er knife into 'er for some reason."

"Emma Bodkin says she's goin' to turn the village upside down."

Mrs. Element seemed wonderfully calm in the face of this frightful prospect. Her eyes strayed to the two ladies on the seat and at this moment the two ladies laughed very heartily indeed—even at this distance one could hear them laughing. "Miss Sal won't let 'er," said Mrs. Element firmly.

There was a short silence and then Mrs. Bouse said, "I'll send Clarer along to Mary Feather."

"Tell 'er to look in at the Alemans on the way," suggested Mrs. Element.

Clara did her errand thoroughly, and ten minutes later, the whole population of Chevis Green—or at least the female half of it—was peeping out of its windows at the two ladies and discussing the implications of their meeting.

Sal had run Mrs. Chevis-Cobbe to earth at the garage and had led her gently but firmly to the seat. She had found it quite easy to explain the position to Mrs. Chevis-Cobbe; that lady had "caught on" at once and expressed her contrition in suitable terms.

"Well, there it is," said Sal. "Awfully silly, of course, but people are like that—especially Miss Bodkin—you've got to walk like Agag in a village like Chevis Green."

"I'm terribly sorry about it," repeated Mrs. Chevis-Cobbe. "I never thought—but of course that's no excuse—I *should* have thought...only, you see, I've never lived in a village before. Tell me about Miss Bodkin."

"Her father used to be the vet. He sent Emma to school in Wandlebury when she was young, which wasn't yesterday, and Emma came back with big ideas. There isn't anybody in Chevis Green with whom she has much in common—that's the trouble."

"She's a cut above the village women, you mean?"

"Yes. She wants to be friends with them, but friends on her own terms—slightly patronizing terms. She's always willing to help them when they're in any sort of trouble but she won't accept help in return."

"Not a true daughter of the horse leech?"

"No," said Sal, smiling.

"I wonder why they were singled out as being so frightfully rapacious," said Mrs. Chevis-Cobbe thoughtfully. "It seems a little unfair. Thousands of years pass and the daughters of the horse leech are still a byword."

"It's most unfair in this instance, at any rate," declared Sal. "Miss Bodkin is a nuisance, admittedly, but she's frightfully generous and kind. As a matter of fact, I'm sorry for Miss Bodkin; she's lonely, you see, and lonely people are apt to be prickly."

"I feel an absolute beast," said Mrs. Chevis-Cobbe. "Do tell me, what can I do about it?"

"It won't be easy," Sal warned her.

"No," agreed Mrs. Chevis-Cobbe. "No, I daresay it won't. What can you suggest?"

"Well," said Sal. "Well, I'm afraid there's only one thing for it; I'm dreadfully afraid you'll have to go and see Miss Bodkin and ask her to tea."

Mrs. Chevis-Cobbe began to chuckle and then she threw back her head and laughed heartily, so heartily that Sal was forced to join in.

"But, honestly, it *will* be rather awful for you," declared Sal. "Miss Bodkin is—well, Father calls her an estimable woman…"

"Don't," said Mrs. Chevis-Cobbe, mopping her eyes.

"She's *very* kind, of course," continued Sal. "I don't know what the village would do without her, really, but she isn't—awfully—interesting."

"It doesn't matter," said Mrs. Chevis-Cobbe in a trembling voice. "Just tell me what to say. Do I apologize about the delphiniums?"

"Heavens, no!" cried Sal in alarm. "You don't mention delphiniums."

"I see," nodded Mrs. Chevis-Cobbe. "I just ask her to tea and show her around the garden—or no, perhaps that would be a mistake. The garden is full of delphiniums."

It was Sal's turn to lead the laughter this time.

"Tell me," said Mrs. Chevis-Cobbe, blowing her nose. "Tell me, will Miss Bodkin be very—er—"

"I don't think so," replied Sal. "She may be a tiny bit sticky at first, but she'll simply love being asked to tea at Chevis Place."

Mrs. Chevis-Cobbe rose. She said, "I know how busy you are so I won't keep you. Thank you *very* much. I do hope you'll go on looking after me. It looks as if I shall need a good deal of looking after."

"Don't go," said Sal. "I mean unless you have to, of course."

"Don't go?"

"No," said Sal, patting the seat with her hand. "Sit down for another—well, say for another ten minutes."

Mrs. Chevis-Cobbe sat down. "Why?" she asked.

"Because they're all looking at us," said Sal. "I didn't tell you before, because it's rather a horrid feeling. Do you hate it?"

"No, not really," replied Mrs. Chevis-Cobbe. "But why— oh, yes, I see! It's very nice of you, Miss Grace."

They were silent for a few moments. Sal felt the eyes of the village boring into her (but I must bear it, she thought). She could not see the audience, but she knew it was there.

"It really is *very* kind of you," reiterated Mrs. Chevis-Cobbe.

"Not particularly," said Sal, smiling. "Not entirely altruistic, I'm afraid. You see we want you to help us. There are all sorts of things you could do; for instance, the Women's Institute."

"Of course. Perhaps they would like a talk," said Mrs. Chevis-Cobbe with alacrity.

Sal was pleased, but also surprised. Most people had to be pressed to talk to the Women's Institute, persuaded and encouraged, assured that the audience would be small, uncritical, and appreciative of the simplest peroration; here was somebody actually offering to talk as if talking was the most natural thing in the world.

"A talk! Oh, yes," said Sal.

"About books, I suppose?"

"Ye-es, but not too literary. They would like a talk about the sort of books they read themselves."

"What do they read?"

"Light novels, mostly. Janetta Walters's books—that sort of thing."

Mrs. Chevis-Cobbe was silent.

"I know Janetta Walters isn't exactly literature," continued Sal, smiling. "But Chevis Green loves her books, and to tell you the truth I rather enjoy them myself. You must admit there's something rather nice about them."

Mrs. Chevis-Cobbe admitted nothing.

"Perhaps you don't read them," ventured Sal.

"I used to," said Mrs. Chevis-Cobbe.

Sal glanced at her companion and saw that she was staring at the War Memorial in a very odd way; staring through it, really.

"Archie likes them," said Sal. "He's got a whole set of them."

"I know," replied Archie's wife.

It was distinctly intriguing, but it was not Sal's way to probe into affairs that did not concern her, so she decided to change the subject.

"About the fete—" she began.

"Oh, yes," interrupted Mrs. Chevis-Cobbe, looking very much relieved. "I wanted to talk to you about that, but Miss Bodkin put it out of my head. I'm running the flower stall, and I wondered if you could possibly take it over for about an hour in the afternoon to give me a chance of having tea. I don't really mind about tea, but Archie seems to think I shall die if I don't have some refreshment."

Sal agreed at once. "Of course," she said. "Archie's quite right. When shall I come?"

They made the necessary arrangements and rose to go. The ten minutes had extended itself to nearly twenty.

"I wonder," said Mrs. Chevis-Cobbe, hesitating before saying good-bye. "Would it be a good thing to ask Miss Bodkin to help me at the flower stall—or not?"

Sal looked thoughtful. "Rather—daring," she said, "but—yes—I think you might. As a matter of fact, I don't believe Miss Bodkin could *resist* it."

"I shall put my fate to the test," declared Mrs. Chevis-Cobbe.

Sal watched her walk across the green toward Miss Bodkin's cottage. She's going to get it over at once, thought Sal. It's what I should do myself…

Chapter Thirteen

After Sal had departed to clear up the Bodkin imbroglio, Mr. Grace remained sitting upon the seat. It was an iron seat, not nearly such a comfortable seat as the one near the War Memorial on Chevis Green, but Mr. Grace did not notice the outward discomfort, his inward discomfort was so acute. He had said to Sal that the matter was childish—and so it was—but the fact did not absolve him from blame. He had caused offense to a woman; a lonely woman, defenseless, one of his own flock. Thinking of Miss Bodkin as a sheep made his behavior seem a good deal worse, made it seem unreasonable. He had said Miss Bodkin ought to know better, but does a sheep know better? Does any sane person expect a sheep to know better? Isn't it the very essence of sheephood to be foolish, easily led, to rush madly from one end of the field to the other for no reasonable cause? And poor Miss Bodkin *had* reasonable cause, thought Mr. Grace, pondering the matter gravely. Here was a woman who had done her best to beautify the altar of her church, had picked flowers from her garden and brought them to God's House…and he had allowed, nay, he had helped to "improve" her handiwork. It was natural that she should be hurt by the implication that her work was not good enough. Mr. Grace beat his breast—figuratively speaking, of course—thoughtless in the extreme, inconsiderate, lacking in understanding, deficient in charity. Sal had been right to take a grave view of the matter; he had been lamentably wrong to treat it as of no account.

Mr. Grace was so busy reproaching himself that he did not perceive the approach of his sister-in-law. It was not until Rona was within a few yards of him that his danger became apparent, and by that time, it was too late to escape.

"Ah, George!" exclaimed Rona in her usual penetrating voice. "I saw you from the window and I thought you looked a little depressed."

Mr. Grace said nothing. He had no intention of taking Rona into his confidence, neither did he intend to lie.

"And it is *such* a beautiful day," continued Rona, sitting down beside him. "The sunshine, the flowers, the birds singing in the trees…all sent for our benefit, George, to cheer us and to uplift our spirits."

"Yes," said Mr. Grace shortly. It was, to a large extent, his own attitude to Nature, but oddly enough the sentiments coming from Rona's lips annoyed him profoundly. If only she would go away, thought Mr. Grace, with (it is to be feared) a deplorable lack of Christian charity and hospitality.

"So beautiful," added Rona, with a sigh.

"Yes," said Mr. Grace again. "Yes, but I can't help feeling you must find it dull here after London."

"Never feel that, George," said Rona earnestly. "I am exceedingly happy at Chevis Green. I have lived in London for years, of course, but the country is my spiritual home. I should like to settle down in the country; in fact I am thinking of selling my flat."

"I shouldn't do that," said Mr. Grace quickly. "It would be *most* unwise."

Rona was silent for a moment or two and then she said, "You have a very interesting family, George."

"They are good girls," agreed Mr. Grace.

"And most attractive."

"Yes. Yes, I think they are."

"They need a woman, George."

"A woman!" exclaimed Mr. Grace in amazement. "They've got Joan. They seem to manage all right. It's extremely difficult to get any sort of domestic help at the moment."

"Not *that* sort of woman," exclaimed Rona. "They need a gentlewoman, a kind, wise, experienced friend to turn to in all their little difficulties. They are standing at the threshold of life—one false step might ruin their whole future."

"They're very sensible girls—" began Mr. Grace.

"They lack experience, George. They lack guidance. I feel a want of stability in their natures."

"They are young, Rona."

"Exactly," she replied. "They are very young. They need an older woman to guide them. Take Adeline, for instance. I saw quite a lot of Adeline when I was in town and I was able to help her in all sorts of little ways—little tactful hints, George, mere suggestions—and I could see that Adeline welcomed them and acted upon them. Yes, there was definite improvement there. Adeline has a flair for clothes," added Rona, nodding thoughtfully.

Mr. Grace was silent. A flair for clothes seemed unimportant to him.

"Then there's Elizabeth," continued Rona, counting off Elizabeth on her fingers. "Elizabeth is a very pretty girl but she does not make the best of herself. A trifle hoydenish, I think. Of course some men admire that boyish manner. I suppose you've noticed that Roderick is very *épris*?"

"He comes over pretty frequently," said Mr. Grace. "But I think he's Addie's friend. I heard him ask Tilly for her address."

"Oh, George!" exclaimed Rona. "How can you be so blind!

The man is head over heels in love with Elizabeth. What have you done about it?"

"I don't believe in interfering."

"I'm afraid you're inclined to let things drift. We must find out all about Roderick," said Rona thoughtfully. She let that sink in, and then continued, "Now we come to Matilda."

"Tilly is very well as she is," said her father hastily.

"No, George. Matilda is *not* very well. That *farouche* manner of hers is the outcome of inhibitions and complexes. Of course the child has attraction and, if she were taken in hand by someone who understood her condition, something might be made of her. She ought to go about more, she ought to meet interesting people."

"She's shy, that's all."

"Ah, George, you are being a little selfish, I think. Just a teeny bit selfish," declared Rona, tapping him lightly on the knee. "You are keeping Matilda at home and giving her no chance to develop her personality. You want her to marry, I suppose?"

"She's much too young!"

"Not at all. She's just the right age. You don't want her to grow up into a sour old maid."

"There is no need for her to be sour," objected Mr. Grace.

"An old maid then," pursued Rona, pushing him into a corner.

"No," said Mr. Grace. "No, I must say I hope all the girls will marry—eventually."

"Sarah will never marry," declared Rona. "Sarah is quite different from the others. I don't think we could make much of Sarah."

"Sal is a very fine character," said Mr. Grace, his thoughts flying to the daughter who, even at this moment, was spending herself ungrudgingly in his service.

"She is capable, of course," admitted Rona. "But there is a curious hardness there. She isn't the type that appeals to men at all. We might think of a career for Sarah; some sort of training—"

"Sal will do exactly as she wants," said Mr. Grace stoutly. "I would rather you didn't interfere. We've all been very happy together."

"Oh, George!" cried Rona. "Of course not. I shouldn't *dream* of interfering. I was trying to offer a few teeny weeny suggestions, that's all. I know how difficult it is for a lonely man to understand these young creatures and give them what they need. I just want to help you, George."

Mr. Grace was getting very nervous indeed; he was more relieved and delighted than words could tell when he saw the burly form of William advancing toward him across the lawn. In fact, to the eyes of Mr. Grace, the burly form of William took on a positively angelic guise. William was an answer to a prayer.

"How very annoying!" exclaimed Rona. "Can't he see we don't want to be disturbed!"

"He has a note for me," said Mr. Grace.

William had an envelope in his hand. He held it out to Mr. Grace, who took it and opened it, and unfolded the piece of paper it contained. The message was terse and to the point; it read as follows: YOU CAN MAKE THIS AN EXCUSE IF YOU WANT TO ESCAPE.

"Oh!" exclaimed Mr. Grace in surprise. "Oh, yes—er— please excuse me, Rona." He rose as he spoke and hurried into the house.

"What was it?" asked Rona.

"I didn't open it," replied William. (This was perfectly true, for he and Tilly had composed the missive together and sealed it up.)

"It's most aggravating," said Rona, with a sigh. "Most aggravating. One can never have a consecutive conversation in this house. We were talking about something *very* important."

"I was afraid you were," said William gravely.

Mr. Grace did not slacken pace until he had gained the sanctuary of his study. He locked the door behind him and sank into a chair. He discovered that his forehead was quite wet—and the palms of his hands—so he took out his handkerchief and wiped them. He was not pleased with himself. He had behaved like an arrant coward. He had behaved deceitfully. Why? Simply because he was terrified of Rona. And why be terrified of Rona? Rona couldn't marry him without his consent, could she? Rona couldn't drag him to the altar against his will. Mr. Grace's mind said, "No, of course not," but *in his bones* he was not so sure. Rona was so managing, that was the trouble. Already she was managing—or mismanaging—the whole house. It was extraordinarily difficult to stand up to Rona, for if you stood up to her, she immediately retired and came at you from a different angle. I *did* stand up to her, thought Mr. Grace. I said I would rather she didn't interfere. Most people would have taken the hint—but not Rona. Rona had merely carried out her usual tactics, giving way at once ("I shouldn't dream of interfering!" she had cried), and immediately returned to the attack. If William hadn't appeared at the psychological moment, anything might have happened. Mr. Grace's forehead was wet again; he wiped it and sighed wearily. Of course some of the things she had said were true. Mr. Grace couldn't deny it. He *was* inclined to drift. He was inclined to let things take their course and trust that all would be well. Perhaps he ought to have done something about Roderick—but what? Fathers didn't tackle young men, nowadays, and ask them their intentions. Mr. Grace had no idea what fathers did nowadays. He sighed again. Then Tilly. It was true that Tilly had not been quite so cheerful lately. Perhaps Rona was right (not about the inhibitions, of course, that was nonsense); perhaps Tilly should be poked out of her shell and made to go about even if she didn't want to. He might arrange for Tilly to go to Bournemouth, to her cousin's, for a long visit. That could be done. Rona was quite wrong about Sal—absolutely and entirely wrong. Sal wasn't hard. Everyone loved Sal, except (apparently) Rona. Sal might not be the marrying type (Mr. Grace didn't feel able to judge of that); in his heart of hearts he rather hoped she wasn't. What on earth would he do without Sal? His thoughts moved on, his optimistic temperament reasserting itself, things would sort themselves out. Once Rona was gone and Liz was married (if Liz intended to get married), and Tilly had been sent off to enjoy herself at Bournemouth, he and Sal would settle down happily and comfortably. He envisaged all this vaguely, his thoughts moving without volition in a sort of dreamlike trance. He saw himself and Sal walking up and down the terrace, arm in arm. This was a favorite exercise of theirs—or had been, before Rona's arrival—it had been a favorite exercise of Mary's, and Sal was like Mary, more and more like Mary every day.

But all this was getting him nowhere. Here he was, drifting again, and indulging in daydreams. This was no time for daydreams, there were things to be done, and the first thing to be done was to tackle Rona, thought Mr. Grace, nerving himself to the task. This state of affairs could not continue. It was an unbearable state of affairs...No peace for anyone, no comfort, everyone at loose ends...and his work was suffering. How could he think out a sermon when his whole being was constantly upset (*like this*, thought Mr. Grace). He must tackle Rona firmly. The next time she sought a private conversation, he must pull himself together and take the bull by the horns. Mr. Grace sat there for a long time, trying to decide what he would say to Rona next time.

Rona was washing for supper. She was thinking about George and trying to decide what she would say to him next time. George was very slow. It was extremely hard to bring him to the point. The worst of it was there was so little opportunity for private conversation. People came and went. You started to talk and then you were interrupted. There were far too many people in the house. The mornings were quiet, of course, but George was shut up in his study the whole morning and even Rona had not dared to disturb his seclusion. In the afternoon he was usually out, visiting his parishioners or distributing books to the patients in the local hospital; people called frequently at the Vicarage and George interviewed them all. It really was a revelation to Rona to see how busy George was; she had always thought a country parson had a pretty easy life. I must take a firm line, thought Rona. I must keep them all under my eye. She finished her ablutions and watched the water gurgling away through the plug hole; then she dried her hands with quick, competent movements and hung up the towel. No more nonsense, said Rona to herself. Her reflections looked back at her from the bathroom mirror (the round, beveled mirror in which Mr. Grace saw his round, ruddy face every morning when he shaved), and she touched her hair lightly, arranging it, turning her head from side to side. She powdered her face and reddened her lips, carrying out the familiar ritual with intense concentration…then she noticed there was a frown between her brows and smoothed it out hastily. She was aware that frowns beget wrinkles.

The evenings at the Vicarage were usually the most pleasant part of the day, for the day's duties were over and there was a feeling of relaxation in the air. Mr. Grace smoked his pipe and read; the girls sewed and talked. Sometimes Mr. Grace would look up from his book and would remark in pathetic tones, "These Graces chatter so!" and Liz would kiss her hand to him in an airy way and reply, "We've heard that before, darling, and it isn't even original. It was Sir Timothy O'Brien who thought of it first, wasn't it?" But in spite of this "cheek"—which of course was very reprehensible—the chatter would cease, or perhaps continue in low tones that did not disturb the reader. William's advent had made no difference to the evenings at the Vicarage. He usually read, though sometimes his book would be put aside and he would listen to the chattering of the Graces. But the coming of Aunt Rona had changed everything and, instead of being the most pleasant part of the day, the evening was the worst. Her idea of a pleasant evening was conversation, with herself as chief performer. Indeed one could hardly call it conversation for it developed into a monologue. She talked without ceasing in her clear penetrating tones, which precluded all idea of "not listening." She talked about people—people the Graces didn't know and didn't want to know; people she had met before the war, staying in hotels in Switzerland; people she had met in London, or Paris, or country houses, where, according to herself, she was always a welcome guest.

She would start by saying, "You know Lord Wetheringham, George…Oh, *don't* you? I thought you might know him, such a very cultured man. His daughter married a Bull—not one of the Bulls of Nether Astwick, of course. These Bulls live near Newmarket. Henry is a delightful creature and tremendously artistic, so their house is quite a gem—not large, of course, there are only twelve bedrooms—but so well planned and comfortable. Fixed basins in *every* bedroom, and any amount of bathrooms."

"How nice!" Mr. Grace would say.

"A very large connection," Rona would continue. "Mavis Bull married three times and her first husband was a Paggleton-Smythe. I met *his* brother Frederick at a hotel in Cannes. He was staying at Cannes when I was there, just after poor Gerald passed on. Gerald was my second husband, of course. I don't think you ever met him. Of course I knew exactly who the Paggleton-Smythes *were*, so I spoke to them in the lounge and we became very intimate. They used to take me over to Monte in their Rolls. Then, when I was at Biarritz, I met Crispin Paggleton-Smythe—Frederick's cousin—so of course I made my number to him. He was quite the most handsome man I ever saw and all the women in the hotel were mad about him. His mother was an American, of course. A lovely woman. I was devoted to Sadie Paggleton-Smythe, and his sister—Crispin's sister, I mean—has a delightful little service flat in Palace Gate and writes for all the society papers. I met her at a wedding and I went straight up to her and told her I knew her mother. We had a most interesting little chat. Then, of course, there's Walter. He went out to South Africa and built a bridge—quite wonderful, it was—they gave him the O.B.E. I expect you know Walter."

"I don't know any of them," Mr. Grace would say.

"You must have *heard* of Walter."

"No," Mr. Grace would reply, stifling a yawn.

"You'd like him, I'm sure. He's quite charming, so friendly and unspoiled by his success. Unfortunately he got in tow with a most extraordinary woman, definitely *not* out of the top drawer. It was a great shock to the family. Clarence (that's Walter's half brother, of course) was *very* naughty about poor Robina. He used to say, 'The only excuse for Robina is her children.' They have three sweet children—or is it four? I can't remember at the moment..."

The Graces—and William—were obliged to sit and listen while Aunt Rona racked her brains (aloud of course) trying to remember whether or not a woman in whom they had not the slightest interest had three or four children.

It was impossible for anybody else to talk while this was going on; equally impossible to read. They had tried turning on the wireless but Aunt Rona talked it down without the slightest difficulty (music, plays, Brains Trust, Aunt Rona talked them all down) and the resulting noise was simply unbearable. The Graces—and William—had no option but to sit and listen to Aunt Rona until they could, with decency, rise and go to bed.

Tonight Aunt Rona settled herself in her usual chair and asked Liz (as usual) to get her a footstool and suggested that the window should be shut. This having been done she opened her mouth and said, "George, have you ever met—" But she got no further.

"Let's do a crossword!" said William loudly, and he opened the paper and folded it carefully into a little square.

Liz was surprised at the suggestion coming from William, for William was not good at this particular form of mental sport. They had tried him before and had given him up as hopeless, his brain was much too orderly and literal; he could not even see the point when it was explained to him. You need a special sort of brain to be good at crosswords, a mad-hatter type of brain, quick, intuitive, and slightly illogical—in short just the sort of brain the Graces possessed.

Liz was about to say, "But, William, you don't like cross-words," when she encountered William's eye and received a forbidding look. "But, William, you—haven't got a pencil," said Liz, changing her remark in midair.

"A pencil! Oh, yes, I have," declared William, producing it from one of his capacious pockets.

Sal smiled to herself. It was rather clever of William. Of course he might be wrong, Aunt Rona might be terribly good at crosswords, but, somehow, Sal thought not.

"I'll read out the clues," continued William. "It won't bother you, will it, Mr. Grace?"

"Not at all, William," replied Mr. Grace in cheerful tones.

"Er," said William, gazing at the paper. "Um—let's see now. She enables an ally to unite the Poles. Five letters."

There was a short silence, and then Liz said, "Susan."

"Susan!" exclaimed Aunt Rona. "Who is Susan? It doesn't sound like a Polish name."

"Oh, very neat," said Tilly, smiling.

William wrote it down. He had no idea at all why it should be Susan but he was willing to takes the Graces' word for it... not so Aunt Rona.

"I think it must be Vashinska," declared Aunt Rona. "I remember reading about her in the papers. She's a captain in the Russian Army, and Russia is our ally, of course."

"Five letters," William objected.

"Susan is right," declared Liz. "It has nothing to do with Russia or Poland."

Aunt Rona was unconvinced. "It *must* have, Elizabeth," she objected. "The clue is perfectly clear. She enables an ally to unite the Poles. I can't see how you make it Susan."

"South and north with America in between," explained Tilly, in the patient voice one might use to a very stupid child.

William cleared his throat. "The candidate seems to have been elected by a narrow majority. Six letters and the third is S."

"Ah, that must be Sir Lancelot Twigton-Malling," announced Aunt Rona. "I know him well. He stood for Pestlethorpe in 1924, and was only elected by three votes. They had a recount, of course, and I remember—"

"Justin," cried Tilly.

"Oh, good!" exclaimed her sisters with one accord.

"Why Justin?" asked Aunt Rona.

"Just in," said Liz. "Go on, William."

"Gloating insect. Six letters."

"Mosquito—that's obvious," said Aunt Rona quickly.

"Six letters," William reminded her.

"It must be a mistake—a misprint," said Aunt Rona. "I'm sure it's mosquito—or gnat, perhaps."

"Why gloating?" inquired Liz. "Mosquitos don't gloat, do they?"

"When they sting you," explained Aunt Rona kindly.

"It's Beetle," said Sal.

"Beetles don't sting," objected Aunt Rona.

"Sal knows," declared Liz. "If Sal says beetle—beetle it is. Write it down, William."

Sal laughed and waved her arms. "'*Je vais gloater*,'" she chanted. "'*Je vais gloater tout le* blessed afternoon. *Jamais j'ai gloaté comme je gloaterai aujourd'hui*!'"

"Stalky's Beetle, of course!" cried William in delighted accents. He was delighted not only with the neatness of the clue, but also with himself for understanding it.

"Congratulations, William," said Liz, smiling.

Aunt Rona was tired of this game. She began to talk...but, alas, nobody listened; the Graces with their teeth into a crossword puzzle had no ears for anything else. Mr. Grace, lured from his book, joined in the fray. William's idea was successful beyond his wildest dreams. Tonight it was Aunt Rona who hid a yawn—not very thoroughly—and suggested bed.

"But it's only just after ten!" cried Tilly.

"And we *must* finish the puzzle," added Liz.

Chapter Fourteen

Sal was in Wandlebury for her usual weekly shopping (it was Thursday morning, of course); she was tired and hungry and her basket was full, and she was on her way to catch the bus to Chevis Green. The shopping had been more difficult than usual today, the queues seemed longer than ever, the supplies shorter. I wish we could live on grass or something, like Nebuchadnezzar, thought Sal, as she hurried across the square.

"Hallo, Sal!" exclaimed Roderick Herd, rushing after her and catching her by the arm. "Hold on a minute, Sal, I want to talk to you. I've been chasing you around the square. Every blinking shop I went into said you'd just gone."

"I'm in a hurry," said Sal. "Honestly, Roderick—"

"I want to talk to you."

"The bus won't wait."

"It needn't wait. Come and have lunch with me at the Apollo and Boot."

"No," said Sal quickly. "I mean it's very kind of you, Roderick, but I—"

"It isn't the least kind. Look here, Sal, I must talk to you."

"I must go home. I've simply *got* to catch the bus, because—"

"You can't catch the bus," said Roderick, pointing.

Sure enough the bus had begun to move. Sal ran a few steps

and then stopped. It was no use. The bus was gathering speed…
already it had reached the corner…now it had vanished. She
found to her amazement that her eyes were pricking with tears.

Roderick had pursued her. "Come and have lunch," he
said. "That's the best thing to do. There's another bus in
the afternoon—"

"No," said Sal, trying to speak firmly. "No, thank you,
Roderick. It's very kind of you, but I'd rather—as a matter
of fact, I don't want any lunch. I'll just have a cup of coffee.
There's another bus at two o'clock, and I'll—"

"Come on, Sal," said Roderick, smiling at her. "You're tired
and hungry, that's what's the matter. Give me that damned
basket. Come on, Sal."

She had no strength to argue with him any longer, nor to
resist when he seized the basket out of her hand. He swung
the basket lightly as if it were full of feathers, and grasping Sal's
elbow in his other hand he led her across the square.

"Roderick, I don't want—" she began in a feeble voice.

"I know you don't," he declared. "I know you're fed up
because I made you miss the bus, and you simply hate the idea
of lunching with me. I know *all* that, but I can't help it. I've
got to speak to you, Sal. There's never any chance of speaking
to you at the Vicarage with everybody milling around. D'you
know I haven't spoken to you alone since that first day in the
kitchen when I crept in like a thief in the night to steal Markie's
umbrella? Why d'you always avoid me as if I had the plague—
well, never mind," he added hastily, as they reached the entrance
of the hotel. "Never mind that, now. Go and powder your nose
while I order lunch—and don't be too long about it."

"I'll take the basket," said Sal.

"No, I'll take it," he replied. "You might do a bunk. I'll feel
a lot safer if I have the basket with me."

Sal was obliged to smile. She certainly couldn't "do a bunk" without the precious basket, which contained, among other things, a week's sugar ration for the whole family.

It was early, so the dining room was fairly empty and Roderick had secured a table in the corner near the window. The basket was beside him. He jumped up when he saw Sal approaching and held her chair.

"Drink your cocktail," said Roderick, pointing to it.

"I don't think I want it," replied Sal. She was feeling "contrary." Roderick might have asked her if she wanted a cocktail before ordering one for her.

"It's doctor's orders," he told her, "so it doesn't matter if you've signed the pledge."

"I never signed the pledge," declared Sal indignantly. "And, anyhow, I don't know why you think you have a right to order me about like this."

"You need somebody to order you about."

"I don't!"

"Yes, you do. You think about other people from morning to night; it's time somebody began to think about *you*...We'll have soup," continued Roderick, turning to the waiter who had materialized while he was talking. "Soup first, then beefsteak pie and vegetables, and then chocolate pudding."

"I couldn't possibly eat all that," said Sal.

"You'll need all that before I've finished talking to you," said Roderick firmly.

The waiter went away and there was silence.

"I thought you were going to talk," said Sal rudely.

Roderick leaned his elbows on the table and looked at her. "What's the matter, Sal?" he asked. His voice was quite different now, gentle and deep. So gentle and deep that Sal found it difficult to go on being angry with him.

"What do you mean?" she asked, trying hard to go on being angry. "There isn't anything the matter except that you made me miss the bus and dragged me here when I didn't want to come."

"I must know why you're avoiding me. Sal, I *must* know. You were quite different that first day when I came back to fetch Markie's umbrella—"

"And forgot it again," said Sal, nodding.

"Let's be honest," he said. "I didn't forget it, really. You know I didn't, don't you? I left it so that I should have an excuse to come back and see you again."

"See *me*!" exclaimed Sal.

"You," said Roderick. "You and you and you."

"But—Roderick—" said Sal faintly. She stopped and looked with horror at the plate of soup that had suddenly appeared before her.

"Eat it—or should one say drink it? Go on, Sal, it will do you good. I shan't say another word until we've finished our soup."

They ate (or drank) their soup. It was good soup, and Sal certainly felt the better of it.

"Now," said Roderick. "Now, let's get down to brass tacks. It's *you* I come to see. Every time I come over to Chevis Green, I make up my mind I'm going to talk to *you*, and every time I'm handed over to Liz—all tied up neatly, like a parcel. It's enough to make anyone mad."

The beefsteak pie had appeared and they started to eat it.

"I thought you—liked—Liz," said Sal.

"I do," declared Roderick. "I like Liz immensely (nobody could help liking Liz), but she isn't you."

Sal was silent.

"Why do you do it?" asked Roderick at last.

"Do what?"

"Turn me over to Liz."

"I don't know," began Sal in confusion. "I mean, it—seemed to—to happen naturally."

"It couldn't," he said. "It might happen naturally once or twice, but not every time. There's a sort of conspiracy on—"

"No, no," she cried. "No, Roddy."

"I like you calling me Roddy," said Roderick, smiling. "Nobody has ever called me Roddy before. Funny, isn't it?"

Sal took no notice of this. "There was no conspiracy. It's a horrid thing to say," she declared emphatically.

"There was," he said. "I just couldn't do anything. For instance, what could I do when Liz went to feed the hens and I was told to go and carry the 'heavy pails'? Could I refuse? And another day, when I slunk down the garden hoping to find you there, I was waylaid by Mrs. Mapleton and hauled back to the house."

"Hauled back!" exclaimed Sal in derision.

"Well, you know what I mean," said Roddy earnestly. "She gets hold of you and you simply can't escape. I've even tried being rude to her, but she doesn't seem to mind…but it wasn't only *her*," declared Roderick more earnestly still. "It wasn't only Mrs. Mapleton; you did it, too."

"Did what?"

"Pushed me off with Liz to pick gooseberries," said Roderick with bitter emphasis.

"Only once; I thought you would like it."

"Well, you were wrong," said Roderick firmly. "And that wasn't all, I mean that wasn't the only time. There was the time I came up to the schoolroom and found you there, sewing. You made some sort of feeble excuse and rushed away. There were half a dozen times at least," declared Roderick earnestly.

Sal took a mouthful of beefsteak pie and it tasted like sawdust.

"Sal," said Roderick. "Sal, I hate making you miserable, but we've got to get it straight. I wouldn't talk like this if you gave me half a chance to talk in any other way. There isn't *time* to dillydally. I'm going away on Saturday and I couldn't go away without speaking to you. It's war, Sal. I might be shot off to Burma or anywhere at a moment's notice. I've thought and thought—at last I decided to get hold of you by hook or by crook and tell you exactly what I felt—and here I *am*, telling you."

"Roddy, listen—"

"Afterward I will. You listen first…Oh, here's our chocolate pudding!"

"I couldn't possibly eat it," Sal declared.

"Neither could I," agreed Roderick, pushing the plate away. "I want to tell you, I want to explain how it all happened. It started in church of course. I saw you there, at Archie's wedding, and I thought—I thought." He lowered his voice. "Sal, I thought you were beautiful…and I thought if she's like that *inside*…but of course she is! I seemed to know at once what you were like inside. Then I thought, how can I get to know her?"

He paused. Sal could not speak. She was moved, almost to tears.

"I've always been on my own," continued Roderick. "My father and mother died when I was a child, and I was brought up by an uncle who had a large family; they were all older than me and a bit bored at having a strange kid planted on them. I don't blame them, really. So I just went my own way. I got used to it—to looking out for myself and not depending on other people. When I left school I went into a rubber company and they sent me out to Malaya. I knocked about a good deal, one way and another, but I managed to make a little money. You can, if you're in the know and keep your eyes skinned. So I'm not exactly a pauper. I've got about six thousand pounds," said Roderick in a low voice. He wasn't looking at Sal now; he was drawing little circles with his fork on the tablecloth. "Then," said Roderick. "Then, of course, the war started—the war with Germany, I mean—so I managed to get a passage home and joined up as a private. I was at Dunkirk and got away in a fishing boat. They offered me a commission after that. When the war is over I can go back to Malaya, the company said they would take me back, and there will be plenty to do when they get the Japs turfed out."

"You've had a hard life!" said Sal, not very steadily.

"Not really," replied Roderick. "It's been fun. I've enjoyed being on my own and looking out for myself and being absolutely free. I've had a good time and lots of friends, and I've been in love once or twice—or at least I thought I was in love—but I never wanted to marry anyone before."

Sal did not pretend to misunderstand him. She said, "Oh, Roddy—but you hardly know me—and—and, anyhow, I couldn't—I don't want to—"

"I know I'm not half good enough, but I love you frightfully," Roderick said.

The waiter appeared and asked if they would like coffee, and Sal, looking at her plate, which was being removed, discovered that the chocolate pudding had gone. I must have eaten it, she thought in surprise.

"Coffee?" said Roderick vaguely. "Yes, of course—no—I say, we can't talk here. Let's go out into the garden."

"No coffee," said the waiter in an uninterested voice.

"No, thank you," said Roderick. He seized the basket and made for the door. Sal followed him. The room was full of people now; it was hot and stuffy and noisy. Roderick went downstairs and along a passage and through a swing door that said "private." He seemed to know his way. Sal was tempted to rush madly out of the front door and take the bus to Chevis Green. She could catch the two o'clock bus if she went now, and she wanted to escape, she was so upset and confused; she wanted to get away, to get home, to hide herself in a dark hole. Roderick did not look back at all, perhaps he knew she couldn't escape without the basket—and of course she couldn't. How could she go home without the basket? What would everyone say?

They were in the garden now, the garden at the back of the hotel, which sloped down to the banks of the Wandle. Roderick led the way confidently to a seat screened by a hedge of rhododendron bushes and sat down.

"Roddy, I couldn't," said Sal, sitting down beside him.

"Why not? You don't—actually—dislike me, do you, Sal?"

"No, of course not."

"If you don't like the idea of Malaya we needn't go. I'll chuck it. I can easily get something else, something in this country. I could buy a partnership in a small business and work it up. You don't need to worry. I can look after you, Sal. I don't care what I do as long as we're together. That's all that matters to me."

"It isn't that, Roderick."

"What is it then?"

She hesitated. There were so many things; all little things, but together they made a big thing. She felt it was hopeless to try to explain—hopeless. After a few moments she said, "I never thought you—you were—fond of me."

"You thought I was fond of Liz?"

"Well," began Sal. "Well—"

"But you know, now, that I wasn't," said Roderick sensibly. "I've told you, haven't I? It was you all the time, from the very beginning. You believe me, don't you?"

"Yes," said Sal.

"Well, then," said Roderick, looking at her.

Sal could not say, "But Liz loves you," so she was silent.

"Look here," said Roderick. "I've no intention of marrying Liz, and Liz has no intention of marrying me; you can't make people marry each other, you know."

"No, of course not."

"It's that woman. She's made up her mind that I'm going to marry Liz, but I'm not going to do it just to please *her*."

"No, of course not."

"It's ridiculous, isn't it?"

"Quite ridiculous."

"Liz and I are friends," continued Roderick earnestly. "I like Liz a lot, but—oh, what's the use of going on about it? I've said all this before. Liz doesn't come into it at all, really, so let's rule Liz out, shall we?"

"Yes," said Sal, but she said it doubtfully, for how could she rule Liz out?

"Sal, do be sensible about it," implored Roderick, sensing the doubtfulness. "You don't want me to marry Liz, do you?"

"No," said Sal quickly. "No, Roddy, of course not—if you don't love her."

"I've told you—"

"I know," said Sal, interrupting. "It's just—I can't get used to the idea. Of course I don't want you to—to marry Liz after what you've told me. It wouldn't be right."

"What *do* you want?"

She hesitated.

"Do you love me, Sal?" he asked. "Look at me and tell me honestly."

She looked at him and their eyes met for a moment…then she looked away. "Oh, Roddy!" she said in a trembling voice.

He put his arm around her and kissed her, first on her forehead and then, very gently, on her mouth. "You love me," he said, drawing back and looking at her.

Her eyes were bright with tears.

"Say 'yes,'" he said.

"Yes," said Sal faintly.

"Oh, Sal, you are so beautiful!" said Roderick in a low voice. "You are so sweet and dear. Oh, Sal, I *do* love you so terribly much…Oh, Sal…"

Chapter Fifteen

The four o'clock bus from Wandlebury to Chevis Green was full of women who had been doing their week's shopping. Roderick saw Sal safely in and placed the basket beside her.

"Good old basket!" said Roderick, smiling.

"Don't wait," said Sal. She knew all the women in the bus and was aware that they were interested in Roderick. (She could almost hear what they would say to each other when they got together over a cup of tea.)

"Don't wait," she repeated urgently. "Please, don't wait."

"All right—see you tomorrow afternoon," said Roderick. He saluted smartly and walked away.

Sal watched him walk across the square; he looked strong and confident, sure of his own capacity to deal with any contingency that might arise. He was a real man, thought Sal, loving every inch of him…he turned the corner and was gone. Sal sighed. She would have liked to sit in silence and think about Roddy and try to arrange her thoughts. She still felt bewildered, almost incredulous of all that had happened. She felt tired and excited and slightly hysterical; the least thing would make her laugh—or cry—she wasn't sure which. If only she could sit quietly and think things out…but, of course, she couldn't. Silence and peace to think were denied her; she must pull herself together and join in the conversation or the women would think it odd.

Sal looked around and nodded and smiled to the women.

There was Mrs. Feather, the postman's wife, and young Mrs. Trod, whose husband—a positive giant—was the local blacksmith; there was Mrs. Aleman, Mrs. Element, and nice fat Mrs. Bouse.

Mrs. Element was displaying a pair of stout black shoes she had bought for Bertie. She had stood in the queue for nearly an hour, but they were worth the trouble. "Just look!" said Mrs. Element, passing the shoes down the bus. "You don't see shoes like that very often."

"Not nowadays, you don't," agreed young Mrs. Trod, examining them carefully before passing them on.

"Reel leather," said Mrs. Feather, regarding them with envious eyes. "They'd just about fit Tim. Terrible 'ard on shoes, Tim is."

"Too big," declared Mrs. Bouse. "Bertie's twice the size of Tim; 'e's grown so in the last year I declare I wouldn't know 'im."

This statement was merely rhetorical, of course, for Mrs. Bouse lived next door to the Elements (as we know), and saw Bertie every day of her life.

"I suppose you'll be losing Bertie soon," said Mrs. Feather, whose feathers were slightly ruffled by the belittlement of her son.

"No," replied Mrs. Element. "Miss Sal is writing to 'is mother."

Every eye was immediately focused upon Sal.

"I've written," said Sal, nodding to Mrs. Element. "But of course we don't know what she'll say."

"As long as you've written," said Mrs. Element, with a satisfied air.

"I got onions," declared Mrs. Aleman. "Well, I daresay you can smell them."

"White's had raisins—that seedless kind," put in Mrs. Trod.

"And syrup, too," asserted Mrs. Bouse. She sighed and added, "But it takes such a lot of points."

"Two 'addocks," Mrs. Feather was saying. "Two 'addocks, she got. I'd been standing in the queue for 'alf an hour, and 'e said 'e 'adn't nothin' but smoked cod...then *she* appears an' 'e 'ands out two 'addocks from under the counter. Black market, that's what it is."

"Crule," said Mrs. Bouse sympathetically.

"Where's Miss Bodkin?" asked young Mrs. Trod, looking around the bus.

Mrs. Element smiled in a mysterious way. "Emma Bodkin went 'ome early," she said.

Every eye turned to Mrs. Element (which was what she wanted, of course).

"'ow d'you know?" asked Mrs. Bouse.

"She told me 'erself. 'I'm goin' 'ome early,' she said to me. 'I'm goin' to tea at Chevis Place.' Pleased as punch, she was."

There was silence in the bus. Sal had a feeling that if *she* had not been there, Mrs. Element's piece of news would have roused a good deal of comment, favorable and otherwise.

"Today?" asked Mrs. Bouse, her curiosity getting the better of her.

"Today," nodded Mrs. Element. "That's why she went 'ome early...she'd been buying a new 'at."

Mrs. Feather could not contain herself. She exclaimed, "Emma Bodkin buyin' a new 'at! Whatever next?"

Everybody laughed at that and the tension was eased.

Sal was fond of all these women. They were her friends and usually she enjoyed their conversation and was able to join in it freely, but today, she could not find anything to say and she was thankful when the bus arrived at Chevis Green. The back door of the Vicarage was open. Sal went in and deposited her basket upon the kitchen table. She had expected to find Tilly in the kitchen, preparing supper, but the kitchen was empty... perhaps Tilly was in the scullery? Yes, somebody was there, for she could hear the water running.

"Hallo, Tilly!" she said, looking in at the door.

But it wasn't Tilly, it was William—William with his coat off and his shirtsleeves rolled above his elbows, splashing about at the sink.

"I'm helping," said William, turning his head and smiling at her. "I'm washing the teacups and saucers. Tilly had to go out on her bicycle with a note for Mr. Grace, so I said I would do it."

"You ought to have an apron," said Sal.

"It's there," said William, pointing to it. "Tilly tied it around me, but it was getting rather wet so I took it off."

Sal laughed. It was a cheerful, chuckling laugh; a sound that had not been heard from Sal since the arrival of Aunt Rona.

"I know," said William, smiling. "It *does* sound silly, but it's such a pretty apron and I don't mind about my clothes."

"You *should* mind," said Sal sternly.

William had paused in his self-appointed task and was looking at her curiously. "What happened?" he asked.

"What happened!" echoed Sal, in alarm.

"I mean did something delay you?"

"Oh, I see! Yes, I missed the bus."

"Did you manage to get some lunch in Wandlebury?"

"Yes," said Sal. "As a matter of fact, I had lunch with—with Roderick Herd."

"Good," said William, nodding.

"As a matter of fact, he made me miss the bus," exclaimed Sal. "I mean I met him just as I was crossing the square, so—so

I missed it, you see. So then he asked me to go and have lunch with him at the Apollo and Boot."

"Very natural," said William. "He couldn't do anything else. Did you have a decent meal?"

"Yes...Oh, yes," said Sal vaguely. She stood there, taking off her gloves very slowly, smiling in an abstracted sort of way. She was trying to remember what they had had for lunch... it was rather funny that she couldn't remember...No, she couldn't remember... .

"Have you had tea?" asked William.

"Tea?" said Sal, coming out of her trance. "Oh, *tea*! Yes... no, but I shan't bother." She pulled herself together with a perceptible effort and added in quite a different voice, "Well, this isn't getting us anywhere. I had better go and change and give you a hand. You're getting very domesticated, aren't you, William?"

"I'm learning—a lot," said William gravely.

Chapter Sixteen

The day following Sal's shopping expedition to Wandlebury was Friday, of course. William rose early and was glad to see the sun shining. It was warm and there was a light mist on the hills that promised a lovely summer day. William put on his working clothes (which were even more shabby and shapeless than those he wore for leisure moments), breeches and gaiters, an old brown pullover, and a tweed jacket of nondescript hue. His instruments were ready, neatly packed in a haversack. In everything connected with his work, William was methodical. Breakfast over, William set forth, but when he reached the gate, he heard Sal calling him and turned to see her running after him with a package in her hand.

"Your sandwiches!" cried Sal, a trifle breathlessly. "You left them lying on the table."

"Oh, thank you," said William. "You shouldn't have bothered. You bother about me far too much."

"You're worth it," declared Sal, smiling at him.

William looked at her thoughtfully. She was not only smiling, she was sparkling. Her eyes were bright as stars. It was pleasant to see Sal sparkling, very pleasant indeed, but...

"Perhaps you'll see Liz," said Sal, leaning on the gate.

"Quite likely," replied William. "We often meet on a Friday. Is there any message?"

"Any message?"

"Any message for Liz," William explained.

Sal looked a little taken aback at the question, yet surely it was quite a natural one. She hesitated and then said lightly, "Oh, if you see Liz give her my love."

"I will," said William gravely.

It was quite a long walk to the site where William was working, through fields, over hedges, following a little path through a wood and then breasting the slope of the hill. Sometimes William lingered, watching the birds—he was fond of birds and knew a good deal about them—but today he did not linger, for he wanted to put in a good two hours' work before lunch. There had been heavy dew in the night and the earth smelled good; the grass was very green and full of little flowers. There were sheep on the hill today, hundreds of them, cropping the short sweet turf around the tumbled walls of the camp…clumsy creatures they were, but the lambs were delightfully agile and frisky. It seemed odd to William that such pretty creatures as lambs should grow so quickly into ugly sheep. It seemed wrong, somehow. He wondered what Mr. Grace would have to say on the subject. William had a tremendous respect for Mr. Grace, a respect mingled with very real affection. Like Rona, William had noticed that Mr. Grace worked extremely hard and had very little leisure. He was up at half past seven at least three days in the week, ringing the church bells himself for Early Celebration. He attended meetings, he visited the sick, and was always ready and willing to help when anyone was in trouble. He was so good (thought William). Goodness and kindness flowed from him, so that his mere presence was a benison. William knew that his parishioners were a little apt to take advantage of him and to "spin him a yarn," but that was human nature. Mr. Grace was so sincere, himself, that he believed implicitly what was told him. But, with all that, there was humor in him, too—thought William, smiling. Few men could tell a story better, and still fewer could better enjoy a story against himself.

One night Mr. Grace had been called out very late to see a plowman who lived in a cottage in an extremely out-of-the-way place. The message had been sent by a very small child who arrived at the Vicarage in tears and assured Mr. Grace that his father was dying. When Mr. Grace reached the cottage, he discovered the man sitting in the kitchen smoking his pipe and enjoying a mug of beer. "It's my arm, Passon," said the man. "I slipped on the mat an' give it a sort of twist. It was 'urting something crule, but it's better now." "'E fainted right off," declared his wife. "Give me quite a turn, Passon." Mr. Grace was naturally somewhat annoyed and asked why Dr. Wrench had not been summoned; however, as it was now very late, Mr. Grace consented to look at the arm, and, having profited considerably from first-aid demonstrations, he diagnosed a simple fracture and was able to set it. "Go to the doctor tomorrow," said Mr. Grace as he took his leave. "And, another time, please send for the doctor in the first instance." "You be good enough, Passon," they assured him. "Us 'ud 'ave to pay doctor…"

Mr. Grace loved this story and told it with tremendous gusto. He had told it to William the night before.

Having arrived at his destination William threw off his jacket and started to work, and he was so interested and absorbed in what he was doing that he was oblivious of time. In fact, he "knew no more" till the rumble of wheels announced the approach of Liz.

"I'm late," said Liz, jumping down. "Sorry, William, but it's been one of those days when everything goes wrong and everything takes a little longer than usual. Have you had lunch?"

"No, I forgot the time," replied William.

He spread his coat on a bank and they sat down together. William produced a large bottle of beer and a tin mug.

His companion looked on a trifle enviously. "I suppose you haven't got another mug?" she asked.

"Just one," he replied smiling. "I brought it for you. I'm going to drink out of the bottle."

"Can you, William? If I try to drink out of a bottle my tongue acts like a plug."

"Watch me," said William simply.

Liz watched. There was no doubt about it, William *could*.

"Your tongue must be different," said Liz, with a sigh. "More under control, or something. Father often says my tongue is an unruly member—that proves it, I suppose."

William chuckled. He liked the Graces' manner of joking with a straight face and Liz was a mistress of the art.

"How's it going?" asked Liz, waving her hand to show she meant the work. There was no need to ask how the beer was going.

"Splendidly," he replied. "I'm really excited about it. The measurements show—but I expect you would find it rather dull."

"Tell me about it," said Liz.

He began to tell her. The site was known to archaeologists as a small station or fort on the Roman Road, which ran across the downs; there were dozens of these small forts scattered about the country, but William Single had had a "hunch" that this particular fort was more important than it seemed and had decided to have a look at it.

"Is it important?" asked Liz, looking around in surprise. "There aren't many stones."

"The stones have been taken away," explained William. "Taken to build walls and barns. That has happened practically everywhere."

"Well, how can you prove your point?" Liz wanted to know.

"I measure," said William, who was finding some difficulty in explaining the elements of his craft to the uninitiated.

"What do you measure? How do you know where to begin?"

"We know how the Romans built their forts so—so it isn't really difficult. The first thing to do is to decide on the dimensions of the fort; then I measure and cut a sod where I expect to find a piece of wall—"

"Why buried?"

"Because—because everything gets buried. Darwin said it was worms burrowing in the ground and throwing up their casts—and moles, of course."

Liz nodded, accepting Darwin's word for it. "So you cut a sod and dig down, and find your piece of wall where you expected to find it—and then you know."

"That's roughly the idea," agreed William.

"I don't wonder it's exciting," declared Liz, looking at him with new eyes.

"I can't do much without excavators," he continued. "I never intended to dig seriously; I'm making a plan, with notes. Perhaps, when the war is over, the site may be thoroughly explored. I think it will be," he added thoughtfully. "I think it would be well worthwhile."

"I hope it will be," said Liz.

They were silent after that, munching sandwiches, drinking beer, and enjoying the sunshine. There was no need to talk to William. If you wanted to talk, you talked, and if not, you didn't. The arrangement was a very comfortable one.

"Sal sent you her love," said William when they had finished and were folding up the paper.

"Did she?" asked Liz in some surprise. She and Sal were devoted to each other, of course, but it seemed a little unnecessary to send an affectionate message by William when they would see each other at tea time. "You know," continued Liz in a thoughtful voice. "You know I'm a little worried about Sal. She hasn't been quite herself lately. I think she's badgered to death by Aunt Rona. It's bad enough for me, and I'm out all day; I should go raving mad if I had to put up with that woman from morning to night."

"She's an unpleasant character," agreed William.

"Unpleasant!" cried Liz. "She's absolutely revolting!"

"Why don't you tell her to go away?" asked William in a matter-of-fact voice.

"Me?"

"You're the eldest, Liz."

"And the most outspoken," added Liz, smiling at him. "That's what you meant, wasn't it, William?"

"I think you could do it more easily than the others," admitted William. "But let's get back to Sal. We were talking about Sal, weren't we?"

"We still are," Liz pointed out. "It's all part of the same thing... as a matter of fact, I thought Sal looked better this morning."

"Yes," agreed William.

"So we needn't worry."

"No," agreed William in doubtful tones.

Liz looked at him. "Well, out with it," she said, smiling at him gaily. "What's the mystery? It doesn't suit you a bit to be mysterious, you know."

William drew a long breath. He said, "It's Roderick."

"Roderick! You don't mean Roderick and Sal..."

"Yes," said William.

"Oh, no," cried Liz. "No, William! How funny you are!"

He rose and took a couple of pegs out of his bag and a measuring tape. "I think so," he said gravely. "I think they—understand each other—now." He drove in a peg as he spoke and began to walk away, measuring as he went. He did not look back. When he had measured his distance, he cut some sods and began to dig. He had dug quite a reasonable hole when he found a shadow falling on his work and looked up to see Liz.

"William, are you sure about it?" she asked.

"Nearly," replied William, straightening himself and wiping his forehead with a dirty hand.

"What makes you think…"

He hesitated.

"Please, William," said Liz.

"They met in Wandlebury yesterday—Sal told me."

"Told you?"

"That they had met," he explained. "I was there when she got back and she looked—quite different."

"But that's nothing," objected Liz. "I mean anybody might meet anybody."

"Oh, of course," agreed William.

There was a little silence and then Liz said, in a curiously strained voice, "Why didn't Sal tell me?"

"She will, of course," said William quickly. "She sent you her love. I expect she'll tell you the moment she gets a chance. There aren't many opportunities—"

"No, there aren't," agreed Liz with bitter emphasis. "Nobody has a moment's peace to talk."

"That's why," he told her.

She was silent again, moving the rubble with the toe of her shoe. "Why did you tell me?" she said at last.

"I thought—I thought you'd like me to tell you, that's all."

"Yes," said Liz. "Yes…thank you, William." He watched her walk back to the horse and cart. She walked like a hero, shoulders back, head up. Then he seized his spade and began to dig fiercely.

Chapter Seventeen

Just at this very moment—three o'clock in the afternoon—Sal was standing outside the door of her father's study, trying to make up her mind to go in. Mr. Grace did not usually work in the afternoon; he was working today because tomorrow was the fete at Chevis Place, and he had promised Archie his help. Sal knew this, of course, and hated the thought of disturbing him, but there was no other way.

Sal knocked and opened the door and went in, closing it gently behind her. "Father," said Sal. "Would you mind listening a moment? I want to get married."

"Presently," said Mr. Grace, waving her away and continuing to scribble notes...and then, suddenly, her words got through and he dropped his pen and sat up. "You want..." he began, looking at her over the top of his spectacles. "You want..."

"To get married," said Sal, nodding.

"But you're far too young!" he cried.

She smiled. Her eyes were very bright, shining like stars.

"You're feverish!" cried Mr. Grace in alarm.

"I'm twenty-five," she declared. "That isn't too young."

"Sal, you aren't serious?"

She nodded, her eyes meeting his, very, very bright.

"Have I been blind?" asked Mr. Grace humbly.

"No, darling. It happened very suddenly—like thunder and lightning—yesterday."

"Who?" he asked.

"Roddy. Roderick Herd."

Mr. Grace looked at her in consternation.

"It's all right," declared Sal, putting her arms around him and hugging him fondly. "You mustn't worry like that. You're just surprised, aren't you? You didn't realize I was grown up. It's all right, honestly it is."

"But, Sal, I thought Roderick came over to see Liz."

"I thought so, too. Liz is so marvelous, isn't she? I didn't see how anyone could look at me."

"Wasn't it Liz at all?" asked Mr. Grace, trying to get to the bottom of it.

"It was me all the time."

"I don't like it," said Mr. Grace in concern. "He started by asking for Addie's address and then—"

"No," said Sal, interrupting. "I mean he *did*, but it was all a mistake. He can explain everything. It was me all the time, from the very beginning. You see—"

Mr. Grace did not want explanations, not yet. "What does Liz feel about it?" he asked.

"I haven't told Liz."

"You haven't?"

"No."

Mr. Grace was silent. He wished with all his heart that Mary were here. One felt so helpless, so lost...

"It makes me miserable," said Sal in a very low voice. "I don't know what to do. I wouldn't hurt Liz for worlds. I told Roddy I wouldn't marry him, but it was no use. He said he liked Liz immensely—that was what he said—but..." Her voice died away. She looked at her father anxiously.

"What a muddle!" he exclaimed.

"It makes me miserable," repeated Sal.

"No, no, you mustn't be miserable. It doesn't do any good being miserable. It isn't *your* fault, anyhow."

"It is, really," said Sal. "I was silly about it. I was sure he—liked—Liz. Not the first day, but afterward. And Aunt Rona meddled in it, too. You know what Aunt Rona is like—managing things."

Nobody knew better. Mr. Grace began to relent a little in his attitude to his future son-in-law. "But I should like to be sure he played fair," said Mr. Grace anxiously. "Are you *sure* he played fair?"

"Absolutely," declared Sal, meeting her father's eyes with a frank look.

"And you," said Mr. Grace—it was rather difficult, but he had to know. "Did you feel drawn to Roderick from the very beginning? You spoke of 'the first day,' but you didn't see him the day he came over to look at the rose window."

"Yes, I did," said Sal. "And—yes—I liked him—quite a lot." She blushed and added, "I mean, it's no use saying I didn't."

"You had better tell me the whole story," suggested Mr. Grace.

Sal told him. She didn't make a very good job of it, for it was rather complicated, and she herself was feeling confused and upset, but Mr. Grace, following carefully and asking a question here and there, managed to get the drift of it. Sal made rather a point of the umbrella, stressing the fact that Roderick had returned to fetch the umbrella and forgotten it on purpose after they had met. That showed, didn't it, that Roddy had wanted to see her again?

"You—or Liz," agreed Mr. Grace.

"No," said Sal, who was doing her best as counsel for the defense. "He came back for it after he had seen Liz, because he thought I was Addie, but then, when he found I wasn't Addie, he forgot it on purpose so that he could come back and see me again. That *proves* it," added Sal triumphantly.

Mr. Grace was silent for a few moments, and then asked for the statement to be repeated slowly.

Sal repeated it.

"H'm. I should like to speak to Roderick," said Mr. Grace in doubtful tones.

"Oh, *yes*. Yes, that's what I *want*. He wants it too. We want you to help us. Will you see him now?"

"Now!" echoed Mr. Grace in some alarm. "No, no, it would be much better to wait for a few days before doing anything definite. There's no hurry at all."

"He's going away tomorrow," explained Sal. "He's going to London for some sort of course. Oh, Father, you must see him now!"

"Well—perhaps. Better to get the matter straightened out before he goes."

"I'll fetch him," cried Sal eagerly. She was poised for flight.

"Wait a minute," implored Mr. Grace, holding her arm. "It won't hurt him to wait. I want to be quite sure of your feelings before I see Roderick. You haven't known him long."

"Long enough to be sure."

"I want you to be happy," said Mr. Grace earnestly.

"This is the way," said Sal, meeting his eyes squarely. "We shan't be happy all the time, perhaps, because nobody is, but Roddy needs me and I love him. We understand each other. Even that very first day we understood each other. Then we seemed to lose touch. It was my fault for not being brave, for not being sensible. Roddy says I handed him over to Liz, all tied up, like a parcel."

"Why did you do that, I wonder."

Sal looked thoughtful. "I don't know, really. It just happened like that. I'm not very good at talking to people and Liz knows

I hate talking to strangers, so she does most of the talking—it's a sort of recognized thing. Liz is so friendly and easy, isn't she?"

Mr. Grace nodded.

"And then," said Sal. "Then, when I saw them getting on so well and having jokes together, I thought—well, I thought they liked each other. It seemed *natural* that they should like each other, if you see what I mean."

"Go on," said her father encouragingly.

"Perhaps I was a tiny bit hurt," admitted Sal, with a sigh. "I tried not to be—but—yes, I *was* a tiny bit hurt. That's probably why I turned him over to Liz so—so *completely*."

"And Rona muddled it still more."

"Yes," agreed Sal. "Yes, Aunt Rona seemed so sure. She managed it all…of course if I had been sensible I wouldn't have let her. The whole thing is really my fault," declared Sal.

"It's understandable," said Mr. Grace.

"You *do* understand," said Sal, looking at him anxiously. "You see how it happened, don't you?"

"Yes," said Mr. Grace. "Yes, I see. I don't think it's *all* your fault by any means. I blame myself a good deal."

"Not yours, anyhow!" cried Sal. "Oh, no—what could you have done? But we *do* want you to help us now. We want you to advise us how to put things straight. You *will* help us, won't you?"

"Yes, of course—if you're sure it's the right thing. You've thought it out—"

"I've thought and thought," said Sal earnestly. "I know it's the right thing, Father."

Mr. Grace sighed. "I can trust you, my dear. You aren't a creature of impulse, like Liz. I must say I was thankful when young Coleridge faded out of the picture; he was so very unstable. I should have been sorry if Liz had married Coleridge; she needs someone more human, more understanding."

"You knew about Eric!" cried Sal in amazement.

"I may be shortsighted, but I'm not stone-blind," declared her father. He smiled at her and added, "You've chosen a man, at any rate."

⁓

Roderick was waiting in the schoolroom. First he sat and waited in the big chair near the window, and then he rose and paced up and down like a caged lion. Every few minutes he looked at his watch and held it to his ear to see if it had stopped…Sal had been away *hours*. What were they saying? Was Sal explaining everything? Was she explaining it clearly so that Mr. Grace would understand? Wouldn't it have been better if he had tackled Mr. Grace himself instead of letting Sal prepare the way? For the fiftieth time (at least) Roderick went over the whole sequence of events that had landed him in this muddle… He tried to discover where the fault lay. Could he have acted differently? Once more he threw himself into the chair and gazed out of the window, gazed at the trees, standing so still, their leaves hanging heavily in the blazing sunshine…

Suddenly there were steps on the stair—light, flying footsteps—and Sal burst into the room.

"Sal!" exclaimed Roderick, leaping up to meet her.

"Father understands," said Sal, putting her hands in his. "Father wants to see you."

They stood for a moment holding hands.

"Then—then it's all right!" said Roderick incredulously.

"It *will* be," replied Sal. "Just tell him everything, like you told me. *Everything*, Roddy."

"Everything," agreed Roderick, nodding.

"Explain that you thought I was Addie, and about the umbrella, and about forgetting it on purpose—all that."

"Yes," said Roderick. "Yes, I will." He hesitated, "Well—I suppose I had better go?"

"Yes," agreed Sal.

"Yes? I had better not keep him waiting," said Roderick, without moving.

"No," said Sal.

"I'll see you again afterward, won't I?"

"Yes, of course."

"Because I'm going away tomorrow, you know."

"I know," said Sal.

"Well," said Roderick, taking a deep breath. "Well, here goes!" He dropped her hands, turned, strode to the door, and vanished.

Chapter Eighteen

W hen Archie Chevis-Cobbe decided to do anything, he liked to do it well—and now, of course, he had a wife to help him—so the fete at Chevis Place was going to be something quite out of the ordinary; an absolutely first-rate affair with a band from Wandlebury, an enormous tent for tea, and all sorts of sideshows. There was a Produce Stall, and a Flower Stall, and a Stall for White Elephants; there was a Shooting Gallery and a Fortune-Teller, and a Lucky Dip. You could try your hand at throwing tennis balls into a pail, or rolling pennies down a board, or hurling a piece of wood at poor Aunt Sally. In addition to all this there were prizes; prizes for the best turned-out horse and cart, prizes for the prettiest pony and the cleverest dog—there was also a prize for the neatest ankle. There were pony races and foot races and obstacle races for all ages, and, last but not least, a tug-of-war between Chevis Green and Popham Magna. The village was taking a half holiday and people were coming from all over the county to join in the fun.

The only human beings in the neighborhood who were not looking forward to a happy day were members of the local constabulary, for it seemed pretty certain that a good many otherwise law-abiding people would come in motor cars, burning gas that had been allotted them for domestic purposes only, and the English bobby does not fancy himself in the role of Gestapo official. At dozens of breakfast tables, within a twelve-mile radius of Chevis Green, this very subject was being discussed. Young women who were anxious to attend the fete in summer frocks (unsuitable for bicycling) were trying to persuade their parents that it would be "perfectly all right to go in the car," because there would be a Produce Stall, yielding fruit, fowls, rabbits, and perhaps even butter and eggs, and wasn't that "domestic purpose"? And what was the difference between going in to Chevis Green in the car to fetch the meat at Toop's and going to the Park at Chevis Place to buy rabbits and things? Parents were pretty hard put to it to find any moral difference, but they were aware that in the eyes of the Law the difference might easily be as much as £50—that being the maximum fine imposed upon the citizens of the British Isles for "the improper use of gas."

Fortunately the Vicarage had no such problem.

The party met at breakfast. This was unusual, of course, for on ordinary days Liz was up and away to her work before the others came down; William was often early and Aunt Rona liked breakfast in bed; so breakfast was a "staggered" meal and quite informal. Today everyone appeared at nine o'clock and sat around the table, eating. Tilly looked from one face to the other and wondered what thoughts it concealed. A month ago there would have been no mystery about it, Tilly would have known exactly what everyone was thinking—if not, she would have asked. Now there were strange undercurrents beneath the surface and they were not all due to the presence of Aunt Rona (*not all*, thought Tilly, looking around). Liz was pale and quiet with dark shadows beneath her eyes as if she had not slept. Perhaps she was fretting about Roderick's departure (thought Tilly), or perhaps there was some sort of rift between her and Roderick. Yes, it must be that, because Roderick had come over yesterday afternoon and had gone before Liz came back from the farm. So he had not said good-bye and—as far as Tilly knew—he had left no message for her. Tilly ought to have been glad about this, for she did not want Liz to marry Roderick, but being thoroughly illogical, she was not glad. Damn Roderick, said Tilly to herself, how dare he make Liz miserable! Isn't she good enough for him, or what? Then Sal. Sal was unlike herself, too, this morning. She was talking more than usual. She was chattering gaily about the fete and then suddenly falling silent, so silent that she seemed entranced. There was a sort of suppressed excitement in Sal—surely not due to anticipation of pleasure at the fete! Sal's eyes were very blue today, blue and sparkling. They were often hidden by her long dark lashes, but when she looked up they were very, very blue. Father was distracted; he looked grave and was not saying much—but of course *that* might be due to the fete, for Father did not like the even tenor of his life disturbed. Tilly was aware that he had been cajoled by Archie into an active part in the events; he had promised to direct the Children's Races and was probably regretting it. William was much as usual, if anything a shade more silent. William the Silent, thought Tilly, glancing at him. The last member of the party to receive Tilly's attention was Aunt Rona, and she seemed in very good form. She professed herself as looking forward to the afternoon with delight, and perhaps this was true. At any rate, she would have an opportunity of "dressing up," and clothes were a passion with Aunt Rona.

∞

Two o'clock was the "opening" hour, and by half past one the roads leading to the park at Chevis Place were crowded with all sorts of vehicles and pedestrians. Horses and carts, ponies and traps, cars, vans, prams, and bicycles were all converging upon the scene. Men and women in their Sunday best, men and women in various sorts of uniform, and children in gaily colored dresses were making their way across the fields. The park was an ideal spot for a fete; it was meadowland stretching gently down to the banks of the Wandle and was shaded by some very fine old trees. Beneath these trees, stallholders had erected their booths and spread their wares. At one end of the park a large marquee had been erected and displayed a notice—TEAS 1/6; at the other end was the piece of flat ground where the sports were to take place.

The Vicarage party arrived together, but soon separated to go their different ways. Sal made a beeline for the Produce Stall for she was aware that unless she got there early, everything she wanted would have been sold; already there was a milling crowd around the stall, but fortunately Mrs. Element was helping to sell and had put aside something she thought Sal might like to have.

"You don't need to take them *all*, Miss Sal," said Mrs. Element in conspiratorial tones. "I just put them aside on the chance. I didn't see why strangers from Wandlebury should 'ave my cake—*nor* Mr. Barefoot's 'oney."

"I'll take them *all*," declared Sal recklessly.

Mrs. Element had kept a pound of butter, two rabbits and a fowl, a jar of honey and a cake. I suppose this is Black Market, thought Sal, as she paid for them, but the proceeds were to go to the Red Cross, which made it seem better. Sal had brought a basket of eggs to sell, so she handed these over and stood aside to watch the fun. She had a letter she had brought to show Mrs. Element; a letter from Bertie's mother saying that Bertie was to go home at the end of the month, but she decided that this was neither the time nor the place to produce the letter...let them enjoy today, thought Sal. They were enjoying themselves immensely, that was obvious. Mrs. Element was thoroughly happy, she was feeling important, she was glorying in the bustle and rush, and Bertie was happy too, helping to count out change and doing it a great deal quicker and more competently than his elders. Sal saw the look of pride and affection upon Mrs. Element's face as she glanced at Bertie, and she saw Bertie return the look with a cheerful, mischievous grin. It mustn't happen, thought Sal. It shan't happen if I can prevent it…perhaps if I went and saw Mrs. Pike I might manage to persuade her to leave Bertie here. The letter was in Sal's pocket and it seemed to weigh her down; it was a heartless letter, completely lacking in human feeling, completely selfish. Mrs. Pike did not want Bertie for his own sake, she just wanted a boy, somebody who would be "useful." Sal remembered the very words. "There are all sorts of jobs he could do out of school hours, and he is mine so why should that Mrs. Element have him now he is an age to be useful." I'll go, thought Sal. I'll ask Father if I can go to London and see her. I could stay the night at Addie's flat.

Sal left her purchases with Mrs. Element and wandered on. She had lost the others, of course, but she would find them later; meantime it was very pleasant to be alone in the crowd. The sun was golden and it was getting warmer every moment; it would be grilling soon, but Sal liked heat, and she was comfortably aware that her smooth, white skin would remain smooth and white under the most trying conditions. I suppose it would be like this in Malaya, thought Sal, suddenly…and that made her think of Roddy. Of course she had been thinking of Roddy "at the back of her mind" all the time, but now she allowed her thoughts to dwell on him. He was in London now; perhaps he was doing a little shopping before presenting himself at the barracks where he had been posted for the course. He would shop well, Sal thought, for he knew exactly what he wanted, he would be polite and firm and quick. Sal wished she could see him walking smartly along Piccadilly in the brilliant sunshine—yes, it was lovely to think of Roddy, but unfortunately when she thought of Roddy she could not help thinking of Liz, and thinking of Liz made her feel wretched. Mr. Grace had decided that nobody was to be told of the engagement for at least a month. Roderick was going away, and a month would give everyone time to settle down. Sal would have time to think it over (it was the greatest mistake to rush into matrimony without a period of reflection), and if, at the end of a month, Sal and Roderick were still of the same mind, Liz could be told and the engagement made public. Thus said Mr. Grace, and Roderick had agreed, though somewhat reluctantly. Sal had been forced to fall in with the plan, though all her instincts were against it. She wanted Liz to be told at once. She and Liz had always told each other everything; it would be impossible to hide this enormous secret from Liz for a whole month. Besides, Liz had a right to know, and to know immediately. Surely it was better to *know*, than to go on thinking about Roddy and wondering why he did not write, wondering why he had gone without saying good-bye to her.

Sal was pushing her way through the crowd when suddenly she came face-to-face with Joan, and of course Joan was wearing the blue frock.

"It's lovely," said Joan, smiling. "It fits me a treat. Makes you 'appy to feel you look nice, don't it?"

"You look very nice indeed," said Sal with perfect truth.

By this time it was getting on for four o'clock so Sal made her way to the Flower Stall. Mrs. Chevis-Cobbe had chosen her site with care and the tables had been placed beneath the leafy branches of a fine old chestnut tree. The flowers were magnificent and were beautifully arranged. They were in pails, the smaller flowers in front and the larger, such as lupins, delphiniums and hollyhocks, behind. The effect was that of a high semicircular bank of gorgeous coloring.

Mrs. Chevis-Cobbe was busy selling. She had chosen to wear a perfectly plain frock of black charmeuse that molded her pretty figure and showed it to advantage. Black was absolutely right against that gorgeous mass of color—she looked marvelous, thought Sal, and Archie (who was standing near) obviously thought the same. Miss Bodkin was helping to sell; her choice of garments was less felicitous. Her bright-pink silk frock was scarcely more vivid than her face, and, like her face, was shiny. The pink hat (which she had bought in Wandlebury) was just the wrong shade; it was high in the crown and narrow in the brim, and her carroty hair straggled from beneath it. She was wearing pink stockings and pale tan shoes with straps across the instep. To complete the mess Miss Bodkin had donned a small apron of yellow muslin with little black spots; rather a pretty apron taken upon its own merits, but an unsuitable adjunct to her costume. However, it did not matter, for Miss Bodkin was completely happy and completely oblivious of her extraordinary appearance.

"Delphiniums?" said Miss Bodkin to an inquiring customer. "Yes, certainly, two and sixpence a bunch. They're from Chevis Place garden, of course. Lovely, aren't they? I don't think I've ever seen such beauties before...and so fresh. Two bunches? Oh, thank you; that will be five shillings, won't it?"

"I say, Sal," said Archie, seizing Sal's arm. "I say, you're going to take over and let Jane have some tea, aren't you? Thank heaven for that. She's simply wearing herself out with those damn flowers. What do you think of my Jane? Isn't she absolutely marvelous?"

"Marvelous," agreed Sal, looking up at him with her frank blue eyes.

Archie squeezed her arm. "And she's tremendously taken with you."

"Really?"

"Yes. I did hope—I mean I do want her to have friends here, and I was sure you two would get on like a house on fire. You both like books and all that sort of thing. So do go on with it, won't you? Come up to Chevis Place whenever you can—as often as you possibly can. You will, won't you?"

"Yes, I will," said Sal, nodding.

"Grand!" said Archie. "And now for goodness' sake, get hold of Jane and make her come and have tea. I've got to go and judge competitions at five, so unless she comes now—"

"Are you going to judge the ankle competition?" Sal inquired with a slightly mischievous look.

"Are you going in for it?" inquired Archie, closing one eye.

They both laughed.

At this moment Mrs. Chevis-Cobbe saw Sal and beckoned to her. "So good of you!" exclaimed Mrs. Chevis-Cobbe. "Archie is getting restive so I had better go. Look, this is the list of prices."

Sal took it and examined it. She said in a low voice, "Congratulations on Miss Bodkin."

"It was too easy," replied Mrs. Chevis-Cobbe out of the side of her mouth. "We're bosom friends now. I want to ask you more about her later." Aloud she said, "If you get muddled about the prices just ask Miss Bodkin. She'll keep you right."

"Just ask *me*," said Miss Bodkin, bustling forward. "You'll soon get into the way of it. This is the cash box, here, on the table. We've made over twenty pounds already."

Chapter Nineteen

L iz was helping at the tea tent. She was extremely busy but she did not mind, for being busy helped to take her mind off her troubles. She had spent all night thinking of Roderick and trying to remember all he had said, and she had been forced to admit to herself (for she was extremely honest with herself) that Roderick had never said anything the whole world might not have heard. He had been friendly, that was all, and, if it had not been for Aunt Rona, Liz would have accepted him as a friend and nothing more. Aunt Rona had not *said* much, but she had *looked* a great deal, and she had so managed things that Liz and Roderick were constantly being paired off, constantly finding themselves in each other's company. She had managed it with consummate tact and guile, just as she managed everything and everybody at the Vicarage. (What a fool I have been! exclaimed Liz, tossing and turning on her bed.)

It was all the more galling because Liz had known from the very beginning that Aunt Rona was a dangerous person and not to be trusted; so why—why on earth—had she allowed Aunt Rona to meddle in her affairs? Why had she allowed the hints and innuendos to affect her feelings? She had accepted the "managing" and gone off with Roderick and all the time Roderick was longing to be with Sal—hating me, thought Liz.

But, no, that was not fair. Roderick didn't hate her. In fact, Liz was pretty certain Roderick liked her quite a lot. He didn't hate her—but he didn't love her. He loved Sal. Well, that wasn't surprising. Sal was a darling. Sal was a far finer person than herself.

Now that William had opened her eyes, the whole thing was perfectly plain to Liz, and the more she thought about it the plainer it became; Liz couldn't imagine for the life of her why she hadn't seen it for herself. "Blind!" said Liz aloud. "Stone-blind." And she raised herself and turned her pillow for the fifth time. Why hadn't she seen? Was it because she was used to receiving attention, because she was used to being admired? (Rather a nasty thought, that.) But let's be fair, thought Liz. I'm used to being in the limelight because Sal and Tilly prefer the shadow. They don't like talking to strangers and I do. Somebody has to talk and entertain people who come to the house. This reflection—which was perfectly justified—comforted her a little, but it did not comfort her for long. She felt angry and sore, and very humble. Everybody knew. William knew, of course, and how thankful she was that William had told her. It really was very considerate of him, but William was considerate to a surprising degree; surprising that such a big, clumsy creature should have so much delicacy of feeling. She remembered their conversation in detail, his remarks about Aunt Rona, for instance: "An unpleasant character," William had said. "Why don't you tell her to go away?" Well, why don't I? thought Liz. She *must* go before she does any more mischief in the Grace family. Having settled the fate of Aunt Rona, in her own mind, Liz began to think of Roderick again. She had been angry with Roderick at first, but, now that she was getting things clear, her anger had evaporated. It wasn't Roderick's fault. She must dismiss from her heart all angry feelings about Roderick...she must dismiss from her heart *all* feelings for Roderick. Well, that wasn't going to be easy...

So the night had passed and here was Liz in the tea tent, much too busy to do any more serious thinking, but not too busy to be conscious of an aching heart.

"Miss Grace, your table is asking for milk," said Mrs. Bouse, ambling past with a plate of buns in each hand.

"Oh, sorry!" exclaimed Liz, and she seized a milk jug and flew for her life...for your heart might be broken into fragments, but a table that asked for milk must not be denied. But how ridiculous—a table—asking for milk! It was the sort of silly joke the Graces adored (or *had* adored before the advent of Aunt Rona) and Liz actually found herself giggling as she thought of the manner in which she would present the joke to Sal and Tilly. "Can I have some milk, please?" she would say in a creaking voice, the sort of voice you would expect from a table...and then she thought, but my heart isn't broken, not really; I'm not absolutely shattered as I was when Eric went away. I'm upset, of course, and I feel horribly degraded, but—

"Could we 'ave some more sandwiches, miss?"

"Yes, of course," said Liz.

"May I have a second cup of tea?"

"Will you bring some more hot water?"

"Are there any chocolate biscuits?"

"Could we have a table for three?"

"Yes," said Liz. "Yes, certainly. Yes, of course. No, I'm afraid not. No, not at the moment, but this table will be free soon."

~∞~

Mr. Grace was superintending the children's races. It was extremely hot in the field near the river and there was no shade, so he was very glad that he had flouted his daughters' wishes and put on his panama hat. It was an old hat, yellowed and shapeless, but that did not worry Mr. Grace.

"The girls would like me to get sunstroke, of course," said Mr. Grace, explaining the matter to Toop, who was helping him to marshal the children at the starting line. And Toop, instead of being horrified at this frightful injustice to Mr. Grace's devoted daughters, nodded quite cheerfully and said, "That's right, sir. Women be all for show."

"It's a perfectly *good* hat," continued Mr. Grace, tugging it down over his ears so that it looked like a very shabby halo around his kindly, rubicund face.

"So it be, so it be," agreed Toop, who was so attached to his vicar that he would have agreed with equal alacrity that black was white.

By this time Mr. Grace had explained his plan of campaign to his helpers, who consisted of William, Jos Barefoot, and Toop. William and Jos were dispatched to the winning post, Toop was to fire the gun. So far so good, the difficulty was to get the children into line, and to keep them standing behind the white line until the moment came to start. They hopped about with excitement; they shrieked with joy and dug each other in the ribs; some of them stood on their hands, kicking their legs in the air, and seemed oblivious to the fact that this was an unorthodox manner of starting the hundred yards. Fond mothers broke through the ropes and rushed at their offspring to tie up shoelaces or hair ribbons or make other small adjustments of dress, and were chivvied away by Toop waving the starting gun in a threatening manner. Mr. Grace was aware that it was essential to obtain a "good start" not so much for the sake of the children as the parents. The parents were watching with the closest attention to see that justice was done and it might cause quite a lot of trouble in the village if any of them had cause to complain. They would complain, of course, whatever happened, but Mr. Grace was determined they should have no just cause, so he went up and down the line putting the children in place, explaining exactly what they were to do and exhorting patience.

"One, two, three," said Mr. Grace loudly. Toop fired and away they went…it was a charming sight. The boys were in gray or blue flannel shorts and white shirts; the girls in gaily colored frocks. Away they went, their hair flying in the breeze of their passage, fat legs and thin legs, long legs and short legs, all twinkling and scurrying and galloping down the meadow. Mr. Grace watched them, smiling. It was indeed a charming sight.

"George," said a voice behind him.

Mr. Grace's smile faded. He turned reluctantly.

("Dashed, that's what 'e was," said Toop, retailing the incident later to his great crony, Jos Barefoot. "You could see all the 'appiness leakin' out of 'im like a sieve. Why does 'e bear it, that's what I want to know?" "'E be a mild-mannered man," replied Jos, removing his pipe and spitting into a flowerpot with uncanny accuracy. "Why does 'e bear it?" repeated Toop thoughtfully. "You got to bear things from a wife—badgering an' what not—but she ain't 'is wife, nor won't be neither." "I b'ain't so sure," said Jos in his squeaky voice. "She be after Passon, she be. 'E don't get no peace, not in 'is own garding nor nowhere. She be after 'im all day. 'Jawge,' she bellers. 'Jawge, where are you? Where are you, Jawge!'" [Toop smiled—he could not help it; Jos Barefoot's rendering of Rona's "Oxford accent" was extremely funny.] "Ar' she be a proper ow'd vixen," added Jos, shaking his head.)

"George," said Rona. "George, haven't you finished here? I've been waiting at least twenty minutes. I should like to meet Mrs. Chevis-Cobbe."

"She's over at the Flower Stall."

"I know. I saw her there. I think it would be the right thing for you to introduce us."

"Get Liz," said Mr. Grace. "I must find out from William who won."

William was walking toward him, smiling and holding a child firmly by each hand. "Timothy Feather first, Lizzie Aleman second," said William, showing them off with pride.

Timothy was scowling with bashfulness in the sudden limelight, but Lizzie was all smiles. She was a young sister of Joan's—there were dozens of little Alemans—and as she spent a good deal of her spare time at the Vicarage she was in no awe of its master.

"I was second!" cried Lizzie, running up to Mr. Grace and taking his hand. "I come in just after Tim. The gentleman saw I did."

"She'd 'ave won," declared Mr. Aleman, who had been watching his daughter's progress with the keenest interest, and now approached to do battle upon her behalf. "She'd 'ave won outright if that young varmint 'adn't rode 'er off. Rode 'er off, that's what 'e did," said Mr. Aleman bitterly.

"No, 'e didn't, then," cried Mrs. Feather, bustling up behind him. "It was 'er pushed 'im—right at the start—put out 'er 'and an' shoved. I saw it with my own eyes, there now."

"I don't think so," said Mr. Grace gravely. "I was watching very closely and the race seemed perfectly fair."

"'E rode 'er off," repeated Mr. Aleman.

"She shoved 'im—didn't she, Tim?" said Mrs. Feather.

Tim scowled horribly. He stood first on one leg and then on the other. "Nobody didn't shove me an' I didn't shove nobody," said Tim gruffly.

"Splendid," exclaimed Mr. Grace. "Nobody—er—shoved—er—anybody. It was a grand race, a magnificent race…and perfectly fair. You agree, don't you, William?"

"Perfectly fair, and very well run," said William solemnly.

Mr. Grace wrote down the names of the winners in his little book, and the crowd, which had gathered to see the fun, melted away reluctantly.

This was the last race, and Mr. Grace was just turning away when he was accosted by a very pretty woman, beautifully and fashionably dressed.

"You're Mr. Grace, aren't you? Will you come and have your fortune told?"

"Yes," replied Mr. Grace, smiling at her. "Yes, I'll come. Are you the sibyl?"

"I'm Mrs. Smith," she replied, missing the allusion.

"Of course! You've come to live at The Beeches! My daughters would have called before this, but we're a very large household at the moment and that keeps them busy."

"Oh, calling is a bore," declared Mrs. Smith. "It would be much nicer if they could drop in some evening about seven for a drink…and you, too, of course, if you don't think it very wicked."

"I see nothing very wicked in it," said Mr. Grace in surprise.

She smiled. "Oh, I'm so glad you're broad-minded. I hope you're broad-minded in *every* way."

"No," said Mr. Grace.

"No?" she exclaimed in amazement.

"Not in the sense you mean, I'm afraid," said Mr. Grace firmly. "I have noticed that nowadays when people speak of being broad-minded they really mean muddleheaded, or lacking in principles—or possibly lacking the strength to stand up for any principles they may have. Nowadays people are anxious to appear worse than they are," said Mr. Grace, smiling. "It's a queer sort of inverted hypocrisy, Mrs. Smith…but I must apologize for sermonizing."

"Not at all," replied Mrs. Smith. "I always think it's so interesting to hear people talking shop."

Mr. Grace was a trifle taken aback at this description of his calling. He was silent.

They had been walking toward the fortune-teller's tent,

and now they were there. It was a small bell tent, wonderfully decorated with cabalistic signs cut out of black paper. Mr. Grace fished in his pocket for half a crown and prepared to go in, but Mrs. Smith had not done with him; she caught him by the arm and said, "I suppose you believe in Jonah and the whale, and all that?"

Mr. Grace was annoyed. This seemed to him the wrong time and place for a theological discussion, so he did not take up the challenge.

Mrs. Smith waited for a few moments for a reply and as none was forthcoming, she continued, "I don't. You see a whale's throat is very small so it would be quite impossible for it to swallow a man. Perhaps you didn't know that."

"My dear young lady," said Mr. Grace. "I don't think it matters in the least whether or not you believe the whale swallowed Jonah. Many deeply religious people are not prepared to take the story literally." It was rather a neat reply, and Mr. Grace was pleased with it. He was also rather pleased with himself for having denied himself the obvious joke. It had been an effort not to tell Mrs. Smith she need not swallow the whale, but it had been right to abstain.

"We aren't religious, Wilfred and I," declared Mrs. Smith. "In fact, we don't believe in *anything*."

Mr. Grace looked at her sternly. This was too much. He was really angry. Was she trying to rouse him, trying to drag him into a discussion, here and now, in the middle of this holiday-making crowd, or was she merely making the position of herself and her husband perfectly clear, or, thirdly, was she just an absolute fool? He was inclined to the third alternative.

"So you see how it is," said Mrs. Smith. "And if you would rather your daughters did not come to The Beeches—"

"Oh, I *see*," said Mr. Grace, interrupting her. "I *see* your point—but of course they can come. One of the principal duties of a Christian is to visit the heathen." He smiled at her and, raising his battered hat, turned to go into the fortune-teller's tent.

Mr. Grace was going into the tent and Tilly was coming out; father and daughter almost bumped into each other in the narrow entrance.

"Father!" exclaimed Tilly in delight. "Oh, Father, you're the very person I wanted to see. Do you believe in it?"

"No," replied Mr. Grace. "I am going in to spend half a crown in an extremely good cause."

Tilly was a trifle dashed. "Oh!" she said. "Oh, I can't help believing there's *something* in it, you know. She's so *weird*. She's got such a marvelous deep voice…she says I've got an absolutely marvelous fortune. I'm born under Leo, which makes me terribly brave, and I'm going to have seven children."

"You will need courage for that," said Mr. Grace gravely. "I find four children rather more than I can manage comfortably."

"My husband will be tall," continued Tilly. "Tall and dark—and he will love me passionately. I can't remember any more at the moment."

"You have remembered quite enough to go on with," said Mr. Grace.

Chapter Twenty

After her interview with the sibyl, Tilly made her way to the other end of the park where the competitions were taking place, where dogs and ponies and horses and carts were being paraded and judged for prizes. She was not particularly interested in ponies or dogs, for she had never possessed either, but she did possess a pair of ankles, which, although not considered by her sisters to be of any great merit, she herself considered fairly presentable. It would be rather fun, thought Tilly, if she should win a prize—that would show them, wouldn't it—and of course if she didn't win a prize there would be no need to mention the subject. All the afternoon Tilly had been ankle-conscious to a marked degree. She had seen thick ankles and thin ankles walking about the place, ankles that were "beef to the heel," ankles that were like broomsticks. She had seen bulgy ankles, and ankles with painful-looking knobs sticking out at the sides, a sight that made one shudder, but nowhere (to be perfectly honest) had Tilly seen a pair of ankles to match her own for shapeliness.

Arrived at the enclosure where this interesting competition was taking place, Tilly stood and watched for a few minutes, trying to make up her mind to take the plunge. She saw that the competitors were being judged by two young men who were seated upon two chairs in front of a large white sheet. The bottom of the sheet hung about eighteen inches from the ground and the competitors stood behind the sheet with only their feet and ankles visible, so that no beauty of face or figure should influence the verdict of the judges. That was fair, thought Tilly; it was also reassuring. The ordeal would not be nearly so alarming as she had expected.

The young men were strangers to Tilly and therefore strangers to Chevis Green. They looked rather nice, rather interesting, but, as one was tall and fair and the other short and dark, neither of them was the future husband who would love her passionately and help in the production of her family.

Tilly watched five competitors before she managed to summon up sufficient courage to go forward herself (none of the five had ankles worth looking at). Then she paid her shilling and walked behind the sheet and stood there, awaiting judgment. She couldn't see her judges, but she could hear them talking to each other in low voices, she could hear all they said. They did not know this, of course. They were obviously under the impression that their conversation was inaudible to their victim…but Tilly had sharp ears.

"Pretty nifty," said one young man after a short silence. "I rather like this ankle, Ted. How do you feel about it?"

"You don't think it's a bit on the plump side, Wilfred?"

"I don't," replied Wilfred firmly. "To tell you the truth I'm a bit sick of these skinny ankles, they give me the willies." He raised his voice, quite unnecessarily, and said, "Will the competitor turn around slowly, please?"

The competitor turned around slowly.

"No, Ted," said Wilfred. "It is not too plump. The more I look at this ankle the more I like it. Look at the charming way it swells into the calf."

"The calf is no business of yours," declared his friend.

"And the instep, Ted. You must admit the instep is quite adorable. I wonder what sort of face this ankle has."

"Like the back of a bus, most likely."

"I don't agree," said Wilfred. "I bet you she's a peach. I bet you she's a flyer. Look here, Ted, I bet you ten bob she's an absolute flyer. Will you take me?"

"All right—but I've got to judge for myself. I mean if I say she's no flyer, you've lost. I suppose we give her the ankle prize, do we?"

"We do, my lad," declared Wilfred. "We look at a few more, just for eye wash, and then we close and have a drink. How's that?"

"Suits *me*," replied Ted cheerfully.

Wilfred raised his voice and said, "That's all, thank you. Please give your name to the attendant and wait."

Tilly gave her name to the attendant, who wrote it carefully on a small blue card and presented it to her with a grin. "Looks as if you'd won," he said cheekily.

Tilly knew she had won, but she did not feel as elated as she had expected. She had been nervous before, now she was feeling worse; she was feeling positively ill with fright. If it had not been for Leo and the courage with which he had endowed her, she would have taken to her heels and fled. Leo helped a good deal. It was Leo who suggested she should take out her powder compact and remove the shine from her nose… it would be a pity (whispered Leo) if Wilfred lost his bet; Wilfred was much the nicer.

Fortunately there was not long to wait. The attendant put up a notice saying, "Competition Now Closed," and the two judges came out. They had no sooner emerged from the enclosure than they were set upon by a very smart young woman in a pale gray silk coat and skirt and a scarlet halo hat.

"Wilfred!" she exclaimed, seizing his arm. "I've been looking everywhere for you. I've been talking to the Padre, the most quaint creature, straight from Dickens, with the funniest hat you ever saw."

"It was Trollope," said Wilfred, shaking off her hand in a casual way. "I mean it was Trollope, not Dickens, who wrote about comic parsons. Wasn't it, Ted?"

"What does it matter!" said the young woman crossly. "I wish you'd come home. I'm dead tired. I couldn't think where you had got to."

"Why on earth did you wait?" he retorted. "Surely you're capable of walking home by yourself if you want to."

"What *have* you been doing?" she inquired.

"As a matter of fact," said Wilfred in an offhand way. "As a matter of fact, Ted and I have been judging a competition. Chevis-Cobbe asked us if we'd take it on."

"It's been pretty hard work," declared Ted.

"Hard, but interesting," agreed Wilfred.

"Do come home, Wilfred. If you want a drink, you can have it at home—"

"Presently. You buzz off."

The young woman showed no inclination to "buzz off." She waited impatiently.

"Where's the winner?" asked Ted, looking around.

The attendant pushed Tilly forward and she presented the little blue card. She was aware that the two young men were regarding her with interest and felt herself blushing beneath their scrutiny. ("Leo," said Tilly firmly to herself.)

"Oh!" said Wilfred. "Oh, yes—er—you've won. Hasn't she, Ted?"

"Definitely," said Ted. "Er—congratulations."

"Good show, wasn't it?" said Wilfred.

"Awfully good show," agreed Ted.

Tilly had a feeling that the gentlemen would have said a

good deal more if Mrs. Wilfred had not been standing by. The young woman in gray was obviously married to Wilfred; he had treated her as his wife, thought Tilly (with cynicism deplorable in one so young).

"Oh, by the way," said Ted. "Look here, Wilfred, old man, I owe you ten bob, don't I?"

"Most definitely you do, old man."

The money changed hands.

"A horse, I suppose," said Mrs. Wilfred contemptuously. "I can't see the fun of betting on horses."

"A filly," said Ted casually.

"An absolute flyer. Eh, Ted?" inquired Wilfred.

"You've said it, old man," replied Ted.

"Oh!" said Wilfred. "Oh, look here, Miss Grace! You keep this card and hand it in when the prizes are being presented. I hope you get a good one."

"A pair of silk stockings," suggested Ted. "That would be about right, I should think."

"Artistically correct," agreed Wilfred.

Mr. Grace emerged from the dim shadow of the fortune-teller's tent into the blazing sunshine. He felt rather pleased with himself. Of course it was all absolute nonsense, merely a dodge to get half a crown out of your pocket for the Red Cross, but, still, it was rather pleasant to be told pleasant things about your constitution. Mr. Grace's constitution was "finely balanced"; it was "powerful yet delicate"; it was "extremely sensitive to beauty." He had been warned that he had "a decided tendency to overwork the body, intellectually or physically." Aries (the ram) ruled his head and the sibyl had assured him that further investigation of this sign of the Zodiac would yield excellent results. She had added that his lucky day was Saturday.

Sensitive to beauty, thought Mr. Grace, looking around. That, at least, was true. He felt extraordinarily sensitive to the beauty of this charming and typically English scene—the bright golden sunshine and blue sky, the tall shady trees, the green grass, and the brilliantly colored dresses, groups of which formed and scattered and reformed before his eyes so that the whole effect resembled a kaleidoscope…Mr. Grace was delighted with it all.

Mr. Grace was so delighted with the scene and with his own reaction to the beauty of it that he felt at peace with the world, so, when he saw Rona making her way toward him, he went forward to meet her cheerfully, and being ultrasensitively-minded he noticed what an air she had and how well her clothes became her.

"Well, Rona, are you enjoying yourself?" he inquired.

"Yes, indeed. Who wouldn't be on a day like this? Your lines are laid in pleasant places, George."

Mr. Grace agreed that they were.

"I introduced myself to Mrs. Chevis-Cobbe," continued Rona. "I went straight up to her and told her who I was. She was *most* kind. I was drawn to her at once and I'm certain she had the same feeling about me. I hope we shall become great friends."

"Yes," said Mr. Grace, but not with any great enthusiasm, for it sounded as if Rona intended to stay on indefinitely at Chevis Green.

"It is most important that we should be on friendly terms with the Chevis-Cobbes."

"We always have been," replied Mr. Grace. "Archie is an excellent fellow and a very good landlord—"

"I know," interrupted Rona. "But it is quite different now he is married. The social side of it comes into the picture. We must make certain that if there are parties at Chevis Place the girls will be asked; we must be not only on friendly but on *intimate* terms."

"I don't like that implication very much," said Mr. Grace. "As a matter of fact, Sal has met Mrs. Chevis-Cobbe and likes her immensely—"

"Really? I shouldn't have thought—" Rona paused, and then continued, "You are so busy, George, you haven't time to attend to the social side…The girls do their best, of course, but they're too young and inexperienced to understand the importance of social contacts with the big houses, with the county people. Social contacts *are* important, George, not only important to yourself, but to the parish as a whole. The fact is," said Rona archly. "The fact is you need a wife."

Mr. Grace was no fool, he had seen the point for which Rona was making and he had decided that this time he would not evade the issue, but would meet it fair and square. It was therefore without the slightest hesitation and in an unexpectedly resolute voice that he replied, "I am married, Rona."

"You are married!" Rona exclaimed in horror-stricken tones.

"To Mary," said Mr. Grace. "Mary and I took each other for better or for worse, and death has not parted us."

"But that's nonsense!" cried Rona.

"It isn't nonsense to me," returned Mr. Grace, smiling. He was able to smile, for he had gained the initiative and intended to use it freely. "It isn't nonsense to me. Mary is with me constantly; her presence is very real; she guides me and gives me help and counsel in my life, in my parish, and in all problems connected with the girls."

Mr. Grace felt perfectly happy now. The cloud that had cast its shadow upon his spirit had lifted, the sun was shining again. He was amazed at the sudden transformation of his feelings, absolutely amazed. It just shows you should always take the bull by the horns, thought Mr. Grace.

"But, George," began Rona, pulling herself together. "But, George—"

Mr. Grace looked the bull squarely in the eyes. "I have no intention of committing bigamy," he said.

"Bigamy!" echoed the bull in a strangled voice.

"Bigamy," repeated Mr. Grace cheerfully. "You said I needed another wife..."

The conversation, though reasonably consecutive, had been interrupted several times by passersby; people were moving about all the time, laughing and talking and calling to one another, but the conversation had been so all absorbing that neither Mr. Grace nor Rona had taken much heed of the crowd. Now, however, a child appeared, carrying a large doll, and, forcing herself between them, inquired if they would take tickets for the raffle. Mr. Grace took four tickets, one for each of his daughters, and by the time the transaction had been completed, Rona had recovered a little from the shock. She had recovered sufficiently to find her voice and suggest to George that they should go and have some tea.

"Not for me, thank you," said Mr. Grace briskly. "I'm on my way down to the field to see the pony races." He raised his hat and left her.

Chapter Twenty-One

It was now after five and Rona had lunched early; she had received a severe setback; she felt that she simply must sit down quietly and revive herself with tea. If she could find nobody to have tea with her she must have it by herself.

The tea tent was fairly empty by this time and Liz was not so busy; she spotted Aunt Rona and waved. Elizabeth was the best of the bunch, thought Rona, as she made her way between the tables toward her niece by marriage. Her heart warmed toward Elizabeth and warmed all the more when Elizabeth found her a secluded table and brought her tea and a plate of sandwiches and cakes.

"I'll have some, too," said Elizabeth, sitting down beside her. "The rush is over and I've earned my tea. The others can carry on quite well now."

Yes, Elizabeth was much the best—and much the prettiest. Rona decided that when Elizabeth was married and Roderick went abroad (as he was certain to do) she would have Elizabeth to stay with her in London and give her a good time. Properly dressed, Elizabeth would be really beautiful and would make quite a sensation…Rona imagined herself presenting her to her friends. "My niece," she would say. "My niece, Elizabeth Herd…"

They sipped their tea and thought their thoughts. Suddenly it occurred to Rona that Elizabeth was very silent. Rona looked at her, watching her closely. Twice Elizabeth leaned forward, as though about to speak, and twice she seemed to change her mind and leaned back. The third time she got a little bit further. "Aunt Rona," she said—and then stopped.

"Yes, Elizabeth?" said Rona encouragingly.

"Nothing," said Liz, becoming rather pink in the face.

"I think there *is* something," said Rona, smiling archly. "I think you're going to tell me something, aren't you, Elizabeth?"

"Yes," said Liz. "Yes—well—as a matter of fact—I was."

"Something *very* interesting," said Rona. "I *wonder* what it can be. Do you know, Elizabeth, I *believe* I can guess."

"I don't think you can," replied Liz in a perfectly ordinary voice.

"You're going to tell me something about you—*and Roderick*," said Rona, smiling more archly than before.

"Yes," said Liz, "I was going to tell you that there's nothing at all between me and Roderick. We're friends, that's all. So would you mind not—not going on about us—as you do?"

"My dear! You've had a little misunderstanding. You mustn't take it too seriously. People often have little tiffs—"

"No," said Liz steadily. "We understand each other perfectly. We're good friends. We always have been good friends. That's all."

"Not on Roderick's side," declared Rona. "I've had a great deal of experience in these matters, and I can assure you—"

"Roderick is engaged to somebody else," said Liz firmly.

"Elizabeth!" exclaimed Rona in horrified accents. "How unfair of him to treat you like this!"

"He hasn't," declared Liz. "I mean he has been perfectly fair. He comes over to see us because he likes us. Why shouldn't he come? It was you who kept on—kept on throwing us together—making something out of nothing."

"My dear girl, I could see—"

"No!" cried Liz. "No, you couldn't see anything, because there was nothing to see. You could only *imagine* there was something."

Liz had hoped that Aunt Rona would be offended by this plain speaking, that she would be annoyed and lose her composure. It would be so much easier to go on and say all the other things she intended to say if Aunt Rona "lost her hair"; for the other things were definitely rude, and it is easier to be definitely rude to somebody who hits back. But Aunt Rona was unmoved. Aunt Rona was armored with the skin of a rhinoceros.

"I wish," continued Liz earnestly. "I *do* wish you had not interfered. You made things uncomfortable for everyone."

"Ah, now *you* are imagining things," objected Aunt Rona in a friendly manner. "I certainly never interfered in any way with you and Roderick. It seemed to me, I must admit, that he was fond of your society."

"Just as a friend," said Liz quickly.

Aunt Rona took out her powder compact and proceeded to powder her face, peering into the little mirror and restoring her complexion with the greatest care. "I still maintain," said Aunt Rona, dabbing her nose assiduously. "I still maintain that Roderick showed you marked attention."

Liz laughed—in fact, she gave her usual explosive snort of laughter. "Oh, Aunt Rona!" she cried. "How absolutely Jane Austenish that sounds! You'll be saying in a minute that Father should have asked him his intentions."

"Jane Austenish!" exclaimed Rona, pricked at last.

"Yes," said Liz, nodding, for now she had found the chink in Aunt Rona's armor. "Yes, *absolutely*. All that has gone out of fashion years ago."

Rona's eyes flashed. "Nobody has ever accused me of being old-fashioned—*nobody*. I'm extremely modern in my ideas, and extremely broad-minded. I know the world a great deal better than you do. I have friends in London who defy every convention, they know they can depend upon me to understand; I have several *very* great friends who—who—"

"Who live in sin, I suppose," said Liz, helping her out. "Well, to be perfectly frank, that wouldn't appeal to me, but of course if you like them that's your business. I shouldn't dream of meddling in your business, so please don't meddle in mine."

"I don't understand you at all," declared Rona, in a voice that shook with rage.

"No, you don't," agreed Liz. "You don't understand any of us. That's why I think you should go away."

Rona was stunned to silence.

"We don't need you," continued Liz, warming to her task. (It was undoubtedly one of those occasions on which plain speaking ceases to be a duty and becomes a pleasure.) "We're—well, I daresay we're a funny sort of family, but we got on much better by ourselves. In fact, we're very happy indeed together and it bothers us and worries us to have people staying in the house— people like you, who don't understand our ways. You think we're dull, I know—but you're wrong. We have plenty to say to each other when *you* aren't there, talking incessantly about all your grand friends and giving nobody else a chance. So you see, it will be very much better if you go away—" Liz paused for breath. She had said more than she intended, but she wasn't sorry.

"You certainly are a most extraordinary family," cried Rona furiously. "I think *you* must be *mad*. I suppose it's living in this frightful, god-forsaken place. I should go raving mad if I had to live here much longer."

"You needn't," Liz pointed out. "You have hundreds of friends. Why don't you go and stay with them?"

Rona gasped. She said thickly, "Don't worry, I wouldn't stay here a moment longer if you paid me. It may interest you to know I've already arranged to leave here on Tuesday."

(A lie, thought Liz, looking at her, but never mind, as long as she goes…and she'll have to go after this.)

"*Tuesday*," repeated Rona viciously. "I suppose you're glad."

"Well—yes," said Liz. "It wouldn't be much good saying I was sorry, would it?"

Rona rose. She stood for a moment, her hand on the back of the chair, looking at Liz with blazing eyes. "You shall pay for this, Elizabeth," said Rona threateningly. Then she turned and went away.

"Whew!" said Liz, whistling through her teeth in a very unladylike manner. "Whew! Likewise golly!" She took a cigarette out of her bag and lighted it—she had earned a cigarette, she felt.

"It *is* 'ot," said Mrs. Bouse, coming over to the table. "I saw you were feeling the 'eat a bit. Gets stuffy in a tent, don't it? I think you should just go 'ome, now, Miss Liz. Elsie Trod and me can easily finish…by the way, did that lady you was 'aving tea with pay for 'er tea?"

"No," said Liz…and then suddenly laughed. "As a matter of fact, she said I should have to pay!"

"Well, there now," said Mrs. Bouse doubtfully, for it seemed a little queer. "Perhaps it was a joke, was it?"

"I don't think so," replied Liz. She took one and sixpence out of her purse and gave it to Mrs. Bouse. "I wonder if that will be all I shall have to pay," she said thoughtfully.

"Why, of course!" exclaimed Mrs. Bouse, looking at her in alarm. "*You* get your tea free, being a 'elper. One and six is all it costs, no matter 'ow much you eat. You know that as well as I do, Miss Liz. You just finish up your tea and 'ave your cigarette quietlike, and then go 'ome. That's the best thing to do."

"Do I look awful?" asked Liz, touched at the solicitude.

"Not awful—just a bit flushed," said Mrs. Bouse, nodding kindly. "It's the 'eat, that's what."

And I feel flushed, thought Liz, as she watched the kind,

fat woman bustle away, but I'm flushed with victory, not with heat, and it was fairly easygoing once I got started. I just told her the truth straight out—that was all—and the only pity is I didn't do it before. And now there's Sal (thought Liz), and I shall just go straight up to Sal and say I'm very glad about her and Roderick. Liz frowned a little at this point in her meditations, for unfortunately that would not be true. She couldn't feel glad about Sal and Roderick—not yet—but perhaps it soon would be true; for, if you make up your mind firmly enough, there is very little you cannot accomplish—so Liz had found.

⁓

In spite of Mrs. Bouse's injunctions, Liz stayed on at the tea tent and helped to clear up the mess, and then sat down with the others and helped to eat up the remains, so it was quite late when eventually she got home, and she found she was the last member of the family to arrive. The others were sitting in the drawing room—all except Aunt Rona—and discussing the day's doings in the desultory, inconsecutive manner of the very tired, but in spite of their exhaustion they looked happy—there was a festive feeling in the air.

"Liz, she's going!" cried Tilly. "She's leaving for good on Tuesday. Somebody must have done something, we think."

"I took the bull by the horns," said Liz.

"Liz!" cried her two sisters with one voice.

"Somebody had to," explained Liz. She glanced at William as she spoke and found William was looking his approbation.

"What did you say?" cried Tilly.

"What did she say?" cried Sal.

Liz flung herself into a chair. "It wasn't very difficult. In fact, once I got a grip of the horns it was surprisingly easy. The bull isn't as strong as she looks."

"You must have been rough; the bull has gone to bed with a bad headache," said Tilly, giggling.

Mr. Grace looked up from his paper. "Bull?" he said reprovingly. "I don't think you should call Aunt Rona a bull." (He had thought of her as one, but that seemed different.)

"No, darling, neither do I," agreed Liz. "I can think of a much more suitable name beginning with the same letter."

"Really, Liz—"

"Darling," interrupted Liz, going over to him and sitting down beside him on a low stool. "Darling, you aren't sorry, are you? You didn't *want* her to stay?"

"No," replied Mr. Grace. "She has been here long enough, but for the next two days—the remaining period of her stay—I think we should all be particularly kind and thoughtful. She has received a severe shock."

"If we're too kind, she'll stay on," objected Tilly.

"No, Tilly," said her father. "She is aware, now, that there is no reason to stay on at Chevis Green, so we need not be apprehensive on that score." Mr. Grace hesitated. He was uncomfortably aware that his daughters were looking at him with interest. He took up the paper and began to read.

There was a short silence. It was broken by Liz, whose eyes had fallen upon Tilly's stockings.

"Silk!" she exclaimed, pointing to them.

"Yes, real silk," agreed Tilly, holding up one leg and regarding it with affection.

"Tilly, how come?"

"Oh, well," said Tilly, blushing. "They were a prize, really. I won it. A prize for the nicest ankles." She had been aware that this moment would come and had gone out to meet it, half in fear and half in gleeful anticipation. She had known her sisters would fall upon her like a ton of bricks—and they did.

"*Your* ankles!" cried Liz, in horrified tones.

"They're too fat!" cried Sal. "They're *much* too fat."

"Mine are far neater!" cried Liz and Sal in unison.

"You haven't won a prize, anyhow," Tilly pointed out, stroking one ankle in its new silken covering with a complacent air. "Neither of you has *ever* won a prize."

"Neither of us has *ever* gone in for a competition," retorted Liz.

"Why didn't you?" inquired Tilly innocently. "Anybody could go in for it."

"If we had, you wouldn't have won," said Sal firmly.

"I'm not so sure," said Tilly in a thoughtful voice. "As a matter of fact, Wilfred would probably have thought your ankles much too thin. He said thin ankles gave him the willies—whatever that means."

"Who—is—Wilfred?" asked Liz, regarding her young sister with a stern eye.

"I don't know."

"You don't know?"

"I don't know their other names," explained Tilly, and then she shut her mouth firmly for she had decided that the rest of the story was unsuitable for the ears of her family.

Mr. Grace looked up from his paper. "There were more than one, I gather?"

"Two," said Tilly reluctantly. "Wilfred and Ted, that was what they called each other. They were *very* nice." She caught her father's eye and added hastily, "Neither of them was tall and dark."

Mr. Grace chuckled. His daughters were a perfect nuisance. They worried him to death, turned his hair prematurely gray, and caused him intense anxiety, but they also caused him intense amusement—so perhaps it evened out.

"We still don't know who Wilfred is," Liz remarked in a pointed manner.

"Probably Wilfred Smith," said Mr. Grace. "It seems unlikely that there should be two young men called Wilfred in Chevis Green."

"The new people at The Beeches?"

"Yes," said Mr. Grace, looking at his daughters over the tops of his spectacles. "Yes, Smith is the name. I met Mrs. Smith this afternoon and she wants you all to go and have—er—refreshments at seven o'clock some evening."

"Supper?" asked Liz. "All of us? That seems a large order."

"Drinks—that's what she said. I imagine the Smiths must have dinner at eight."

"How?" asked Tilly. "They haven't a cook for one thing. Their advertisement is in the *Wandlebury Times* again this week—screeching for a cook and offering her the earth."

"Custom dies hard," said Mr. Grace.

Liz hugged her knees and looked thoughtful. "I don't think I want to go," she declared. "Mrs. Bouse says Mrs. Feather says when the Smiths get together, they rage furiously at each other all the time."

"How funny!" exclaimed Sal, thinking of herself and Roddy (and of how much more profitably they could spend their leisure hours).

"Funny?" echoed Mr. Grace.

"Sal means funny peculiar, not funny ha-ha," said Liz, smiling.

"Ah!" said Mr. Grace, accepting the explanation, but it did not seem funny peculiar to him, for in the days of David, the sweet singer, the heathen had behaved in exactly the same way.

Chapter Twenty-Two

I t was a cloudy afternoon. The Serpentine was pale silver in
the subdued light and so still that every tree was mirrored on
its surface. Mirrored on its surface, also, were the people upon
the opposite bank, children in bright summer dresses, dabbling
in the water.

Sal walked slowly, taking everything in. She had felt reluctant
to come to London (only a stern sense of duty had made her
come—that and Mrs. Element's tears) but now she was here
she had a very pleasurable sense of freedom, and she was loving
London as she always did. London was a friendly place even if
you knew nobody; it was not the people who were friendly, it
was London itself, the very stones. You felt, somehow, that the
place belonged to you; it was the hub of the nation of which you
were a part. Walking across the park, Sal looked at all the people;
there were people everywhere, people hurrying, dawdling,
talking, sitting on seats. There were people who looked full
of business, full of cares, and people who looked as if they had
nothing to do and were merely waiting for time to pass. There
were hundreds of children running and shouting, or sitting on
the grass in listless attitudes; there were hundreds of soldiers—
soldiers belonging to every allied nation; there were girls in
uniform and girls in summer frocks…Sal found it enthralling.

The streets were noisy and seemed full of traffic—it was slightly alarming to a country cousin like Sal—but as she was in no hurry, it was easy enough to wait at the crossings and cross with a group of more experienced traffic dodgers. The shops were fascinating, of course. Sal did some window gazing and bought a few things she wanted: a smart blue hat with white flowers in it, which sat on her head in a perky manner and went rather well with her navy blue coat and skirt, a blue silk scarf, and two pairs of thin, artificial silk stockings.

Addie's flat was in a mews not far from Hyde Park Corner. She lived there with another girl—a school friend who was working in the same office as herself. Neither of them would be there, of course, because they did not get back till late, but Sal had been told to ask for the key at a greengrocer's shop and to make herself at home. She found the shop with some little difficulty; it was very small (tucked away in a narrow lane blocked by a brewer's dray). It seemed odd that anybody could make a living out of a shop like this, so small and poor and empty. The mews was cobbled and narrow and rather dirty; it smelled of gas fumes instead of horses, but when Sal climbed the stairs and opened the door of the flat, she was agreeably surprised. The girls had made a home out of the little flat...Yes, it had quite a homey atmosphere. Of course this might be due in part to the fact that at least half the furniture had come from the Vicarage...that comfortable chair, for instance (how odd to see it here!), and the small bookcase, and the well-worn carpet on the sitting room floor...Sal knew them all quite well, she had looked them out for Addie when Addie moved into the flat. Besides the sitting room there was a small kitchen and a bathroom and two bedrooms, one of which had a double bed. This was Addie's room, and tonight Sal would be sharing the bed with Addie (and Addie had put clean sheets on the bed in honor of her guest, which was really rather decent of her, thought Sal). The flat was very small but clean and bright. It gave Sal a curious insight into the character of her youngest sister to see the way she had arranged it all. Addie was capable and artistic and in addition she liked to be comfortable…the flat showed all this and more.

Sal took off her hat and gloves and made herself a cup of tea; then she washed up and put everything back where she had found it. She had decided to go and see Mrs. Pike tomorrow morning; there was just a chance she might see Roddy tonight. She had sent Roddy a wire telling him she would be here, but there had been no time to get his answer. She sat down on the window seat and waited (she had left the door ajar, for the bell was out of order, and she was afraid Roddy might come while she was busy and go away again). It was very quiet in this little back lane—incredibly quiet—in the distance you could hear the roar of traffic, the voice of London, but you could easily imagine it was the voice of the sea. Sal sat there, imagining it. Now and then you heard somebody shouting, or a sudden grinding of brakes. The lane was empty save for an occasional passerby (an errand boy with a basket; an old woman, ragged and dirty, shuffling past; a lean ginger cat nosing among some garbage in the gutter); it was so narrow that Sal had to press her forehead against the window pane to see the street at all…she had to crane her neck to see the sky.

The sky had been so blue, but now clouds were gathering; there was a growl of thunder in the distance and presently it began to rain. Big drops fell upon the windowsill, making splashes in the dust. Roddy wasn't coming—that was certain. It was too wet, or perhaps he hadn't gotten the wire, or he might be busy at the course and unable to get away. She was almost glad he wasn't coming. She would have a quiet evening, alone with a book. She peered out…was that Roddy? No, it was a man with a barrow of coal. Life is queer, thought Sal; here I am waiting for Roddy, and two months ago I didn't know him. Two months ago I thought my life would go on forever just the same, and now everything has changed. Two months ago I thought nothing would ever happen and now *this* has happened. She sighed; it was horrible waiting, not knowing whether he would come; not knowing, really, whether she wanted him to come. She wished she had not sent him the wire and told him she would be here. She had been buoyed up with excitement, but the excitement was all ebbing away. She felt sick. She was aware that her cheeks must be deathly pale...nice for Roddy to arrive and find her looking like a ghost!

Sal ran into Addie's room and gazed into the mirror...yes, a ghost! She found some rouge in one of the drawers and dabbed it on. Was that better? No... (Heavens, I look awful! thought Sal. I look like a tart. I look—awful.) She seized some cotton wool and rubbed it all off. Her cheeks were burning now, they were even pinker than before...powder was the answer.

Sal was powdering her cheeks when she heard footsteps in the lane (firm footsteps, quite different from the patter of the errand boy and the shuffling tread of the dirty old woman). She ran back to the sitting room and pressed her face against the window... yes, it was Roddy! He came along the lane looking at each door, looking at the numbers; he stopped just below the window. Sal could see only the top of his head now, only his beret. She had meant to run down and meet him at the door but her heart was beating so violently that she couldn't move...she waited...a few moments later he came in.

He was just the same; brown, tough, wiry, very sure of himself. "Well, here I am," he said, smiling at her.

She rose as he came forward and he put his hands under her elbows and looked at her.

"Afraid?" he asked.

"A little."

"Why?"

"Because…"

"To be afraid gives people an advantage over you, Sal."

"I can't help it."

"But you can trust me—always," said Roddy, and he kissed her gently.

It was all right. She loved him dearly, completely…and he loved her. It was all right.

"Darling," said Roddy. (They were sitting together on the window seat.) "Darling, I haven't seen you for a year."

"A week," said Sal, smiling.

"A year," declared Roddy. "As a matter of fact, I've known lots of years pass quicker. Have we really got to wait three more weeks—years, I mean—before we can be properly engaged?"

"That's what Father said, and you agreed."

"I didn't know it would be like this," said Roddy, with a sigh. He took out a little box and opened it and took out a ring. "Try it on," he said.

"Oh, Roddy!" exclaimed Sal. "It's far too good!"

"You like it?"

"Oh, Roddy!"

He slipped it onto her finger and they both looked at it. He had chosen a large dark blue sapphire set in platinum—a beautiful ring. "Yes," he said, nodding. "Yes, it's right. I knew it was your ring the moment I saw it. The sapphire matches your eyes."

Sal took it off, regretfully.

"Keep it on, *please*," said Roddy. "Please, Sal, just for tonight. I'm going to take you out to dinner, and I *do* want you to wear it."

She hesitated…but how could she refuse? "Well, just for tonight," she said. "And, Roddy, I do *love* it."

"Now," said Roddy, when they had finished discussing the ring. "Now tell me about everything. How is Liz?"

"Very well indeed," replied Sal. "She congratulated me, and said she hoped we would be very happy. She sent you her love."

"There!" exclaimed Roddy. "What did I tell you! She doesn't care a pin for me—except as a friend. I knew it all the time. All that fuss for nothing!"

"I know," agreed Sal. "I was very silly about it." She had made up her mind to say this, and it had come out quite naturally, she thought. Roddy must never know Liz cared for him; the least she could do for Liz was to keep her secret. Now she had *that* off her chest she went on to tell Roddy about all that had happened since he left Chevis Green, and it really was rather amazing how much had happened in a week. William had guessed that they were engaged (said Sal), though how he had managed it nobody knew. He had told Liz, and Liz—not knowing it was supposed to be a dead secret—had met Miss Bodkin and told *her*, and Miss Bodkin had met Mrs. Chevis-Cobbe and told *her*, and Mrs. Chevis-Cobbe had rushed up to the Vicarage to congratulate Sal, and had assured her that marriage was absolutely marvelous (having been married for exactly two months, she was, of course, an authority on the subject). Meantime, Miss Bodkin had careered wildly all over the village, spreading the news far and wide.

"Good," said Roddy. "Splendid! Good old Miss Bodkin!"

"Father was annoyed, but he couldn't say much. It wasn't anybody's fault, you see."

"Nobody's fault," agreed Roddy cheerfully. "Go on, Sal. What else happened?"

"Aunt Rona left on Tuesday," said Sal, smiling at the recollection. "She left with great ceremony, kissing us all and shaking hands with Father. I believe she would have kissed Father if he had given her half a chance. She thanked us all for our kindness and said she had enjoyed herself immensely and she gave me quite a lot of instructions and hints about how I was to do the flowers. After she'd gone, Joan and I went upstairs to take the sheets off the bed, and there on the dressing table was…What do you think?"

"Her false teeth," suggested Roddy.

"Oh, Roddy, you *are* naughty. Of course it wasn't her false teeth (as a matter of fact, I believe her teeth are all real), it was half a crown. She had left it there for Joan."

"Stingy old b-brute," said Roddy.

"Joan took it up and looked at it. Then she opened the window and threw it out…into the pond!"

"No!"

"Yes, she did. I didn't blame her, either. Aunt Rona was beastly to Joan."

It was now seven o'clock, time to go out and have a spot of dinner, Roddy thought. It had stopped raining and the sun was shining again so Sal fetched her new hat and put it on, and asked Roddy how he liked it.

"I do and I don't," said Roddy thoughtfully. "I mean you look simply marvelous and exactly right to come out to dinner at the Savoy, but to tell you the truth I like you better in your old clothes; I like that blue overall you were wearing the day I saw you in the kitchen."

"It's a pity I didn't bring it," said Sal, arranging the hat most carefully in front of the mirror and giving it the slightest bit more of a tilt over her right eyebrow. "If I'd known you liked it so much I could easily have brought it. I'm sure it would have caused quite a sensation if I'd worn it to go to dinner at the Savoy."

"Cheek," said Roddy, and he tucked his hand through her arm and they went downstairs together.

∽≫

They went downstairs arm in arm and as they went, Sal said to herself, I'm happy. I'm enjoying every single moment. It's fun. It was fun being with Roddy and walking by his side through the London streets—not arm in arm, of course—and seeing all the soldiers saluting and Roddy returning the salutes. Roddy knew his way about. The traffic had no terrors for him and no terrors for Sal either, with Roddy's hand at her elbow. And, when at last they reached the crowded restaurant and Roddy asked for the table he had engaged, it was fun to see the air of confidence with which he spoke to the somewhat alarming head waiter, and the instant service that confidence evoked. When they had decided what to eat, Sal looked around, and that was fun, too. What a lot of people, what chatter, what laughter, what brightness and movement there was!

Sal leaned across the table, and said, "Roddy, I'm happy."

"Oh, Sal, I've never been so happy in all my life," said Roddy earnestly. "You're the most marvelous person in the world. I adore you."

The waiter, who had just brought their soup, was a good deal younger than the waiter at the Apollo and Boot and seemed more human. He looked sympathetic and interested and Sal had a horrible suspicion that he had heard Roddy's words. She sat back in her chair and tried to look bored and *blasé*, but she couldn't manage it for long. This dinner reminded Sal of the lunch at the Apollo and Boot: in some ways it was the same, and in other ways different. It was like in so much as they were here together, talking earnestly, and being interrupted every few minutes by the arrival of food. It was unlike because the surroundings were so different; because Sal had no wish to escape from Roddy, but every wish to remain in his company as long as she could; because she knew she was looking her best, with a new hat on her head and a new engagement ring on her finger, and because she was feeling on top of the world. Sal was about to communicate these interesting reflections to her companion when he leaned forward and said, "Where's the basket? I rather liked that basket. Will you give it to me for a wedding present?"

"You don't need it," she told him.

He saw the implication at once. "Shan't I *ever* need it?" he inquired.

"Never," said Sal confidently.

His eyes said all sorts of things. His voice said, "Everybody is looking at you; everybody is thinking what a frightfully lucky fellow I am. Oh, Sal, it was *dear* of you to come up to town and see me."

"I didn't," replied Sal, dimpling at him. "I came up to see Mrs. Pike. You're just a sideshow."

"Who the dickens is Mrs. Pike?" asked Roddy in amazement.

Sal told him about Bertie and the Elements, and was delighted to find he shared her views on the subject. He was so interested and asked so many questions that she produced Mrs. Pike's letter from her handbag and showed it to him.

He read it carefully. "It's a horrible, selfish letter," he declared. "She's a nasty woman. You mustn't go and see her, Sal."

"I came up to London on purpose to see her," Sal pointed out.

"I know, but you mustn't go."

"She can't eat me."

"She could be very unpleasant. I can't bear to think of her being unpleasant to you."

"I'm not exactly looking forward to it—"

"Well, then," said Roddy earnestly. "You don't want to go and I don't want you to go. That settles it."

"Oh, no, it doesn't."

"I say you're *not* to go."

"But I must go," said Sal, smiling.

Roddy was surprised. He had found Sal so amenable, he had

found her not exactly soft, but certainly very gentle. He had made up his mind that she needed someone to look after her, and, of course, he was the person to do it.

"Nonsense," said Roddy. "You aren't going. That's all."

She smiled obdurately.

"I shall be very angry if you go," declared Roddy.

"That *will* be a pity," she replied.

He looked at her. She sat there smiling, defying his wishes, so soft and gentle and pretty—and so damned obstinate. "It's your chin," said Roddy suddenly. "I never really noticed your chin before."

Sal laughed.

"Little wretch!" exclaimed Roddy. "I'm going to have trouble with you—bags of trouble."

"If you want a doormat—"

"I want you," declared Roddy, suddenly grave. "Just you—always."

They danced a little, and then they went and sat in a corner of the lounge because Roddy wanted to talk.

"Sal," said Roddy. "We've got to think about the future. I shall be here at this course for another month, and then I shall get twenty-eight days' leave; after that it's Burma. Not just at once, perhaps, but any time. The twenty-eight days is embarkation leave, of course."

"Burma!" exclaimed Sal in horror.

"I thought you realized I should have to go sooner or later."

"Yes—but—"

"You wouldn't like a fellow who stayed safely at home and let other fellows go and fight for him, would you?"

Sal was sure she would like Roddy just as much if he stayed at home, so she said nothing.

"You know," continued Roddy. "If it weren't for you I should be glad about it. I mean I'm pretty sick of training. It isn't much use training unless you're going to fight. Burma is the obvious destination for *me*, because I know the east. We'll be in Malaya before very long, and I could be useful there. And another thing: I can speak Japanese fairly decently. So you see…"

Sal saw, but was not convinced.

"Couldn't we be married soon?" asked Roddy anxiously.

"Wouldn't it be better to wait?" said Sal in a low voice. "I mean it can't go on much longer—the war with Japan. Father wants us to wait."

"The Japs are queer devils. I don't see them giving in," replied Roddy thoughtfully. "They'll go on fighting long after they're beaten—at least that's my opinion. It's about time I had a crack at the Japs."

"Oh, Roddy!" said Sal. Suddenly, from being gorgeously happy, Sal had fallen into misery. Life—the whole living world—seemed to her insane and war the maddest part of the insanity. And Roddy shared this madness; he was looking forward to having "a crack at the Japs."

"Couldn't we be married soon?" asked Roddy again. "It would mean an awful lot to me. You see, I've never had anybody belonging to me—never since I can remember. I've always been on my own. It's difficult for you to understand that, I know."

It was difficult. She tried to imagine what it would be like to be absolutely alone, to have nobody at all who really cared what happened to you, to have no home to go back to when you wanted comfort and quietness. And because she loved him so truly she began to understand a little of what it meant to be Roddy. He seemed self-sufficient and master of his fate—the circumstances of his life had made him so—but beneath that outside crust he was just a little boy, needing love and sympathy. She was aware that other women had given him love (he had told her so), but they had not given him all she could give him, not friendship and understanding and the companionship of shared thoughts. She must give him all this and give it now. She wanted to.

Roddy had been silent, watching her face. It was very expressive. He said, "You're everything I've always wanted, Sal. You understand, don't you?"

"Yes," said Sal. "Yes…and I want to marry you soon."

"Sal!" cried Roddy. "Oh, darling—but what will your father say?"

"Father will understand," she declared. She must make Father understand. It might not be easy, of course.

"How soon?" inquired Roddy eagerly. "I mean there isn't much time, is there? But of course you'll have to ask Mr. Grace. Will you ask him the moment you get home, and ring me up? How soon do you think it could possibly be?"

"In a fortnight," said Sal, smiling at him. "A fortnight from today. Will that do?"

"Will it do," repeated Roddy in amazement. "A fortnight today! But what about Mr. Grace? He said we weren't to be engaged for another three weeks, so—"

"We're engaged now," replied Sal, turning the ring on her finger and looking at it affectionately.

"Good Lord!" exclaimed Roddy. "This is absolutely staggering! For heaven's sake, let's get out of this place so that I can kiss you…"

Chapter Twenty-Three

Sal was sitting up in bed watching Addie cream her face. It was a lengthy business and quite interesting, but did it really do any good? All the Graces had beautiful skins, and Sal could not see that Addie's was any better, or for that matter any worse, than it ever had been.

"What happened about Aunt Rona?" asked Addie suddenly.

"Oh, well—" said Sal and then stopped.

"It was rather mean of you," said Addie. "I think you might have been decent to her. The poor old thing is back at her flat now."

Sal chuckled. "Poor old thing!" she exclaimed. "If Aunt Rona could *hear* you!"

"I'm sorry for her," declared Addie. "There she is, living in a sort of gloomy twilight with all the windows boarded up. It isn't very cheerful for her."

"But, Addie, she has hundreds of friends—"

"Oh, yes, she knows hundreds of people, but none of them seem keen to have her. She's a bit of a bore."

"More than a bit."

"You needn't listen."

"Listen!" cried Sal. "You'd have to be stone-deaf!"

"I don't mind, really," said Addie. "Of course I know

some people *do*. Betty says she wants to stand on the table and scream."

"Exactly my reaction," said Sal, nodding.

"Oh, well, you might have stuck it a bit longer. She's been very decent to me; she gives me lots of things and she's very useful, really. I mean if I meet anyone and want to ask him out, I can always ask him *there*. She's always quite pleased to do anything like that for me, so I thought if you had her at Chevis Green, it would be paying her back a little."

Sal smiled at Addie's idea of repaying kindness. "You might pay your own debts in future," she suggested.

"Pay my own debts? Oh, I see…But how could I?"

"You might have asked her here."

"Be your age!" exclaimed Addie contemptuously.

There was a short silence. Addie was now engaged in twisting little strands of hair into rings and pinning them carefully.

"Wouldn't *one* of the hundreds of people have her?" inquired Sal. "Hundreds of people with an average of fourteen bedrooms each—and not one available for Aunt Rona!"

"She's written to some of them," said Addie. "But there's nothing doing so far. Of course she does exaggerate a bit. I mean she goes up to a person and says I knew your mother at Montreux, or I met your uncle in Rome, and the person can't escape. As a matter of fact, I've seen people pop into shops when they see her coming. It's quite amusing sometimes."

"It must be," said Sal dryly.

"She collects people like postage stamps—it's her hobby," Addie explained.

"She sticks pins into them like butterflies," amended Sal. "She's a human entomologist, that's what she is."

"Well, I don't mind her, and she likes me because I take her advice—or at least pretend to take it. By the way, what happened, exactly? She came back with a long tale about Liz being practically engaged to a man and then finding he was engaged to somebody else."

"It isn't true."

"There must have been something in it," objected Addie. "She couldn't have dreamt the whole thing. Who was the man, and what did he do?"

Sal had expected these questions. She said, "Roderick Herd. He came over from the camp at Ganthorne quite often and Aunt Rona got it into her head he was fond of Liz."

"And he's engaged to somebody else?"

"Yes, to me," said Sal.

Addie turned and look at her. "Heavens!" she exclaimed. "That was a bit of a slipup for Aunt Rona!"

"People who talk most see least," said Sal sententiously.

"So you're engaged! The first of the Graces! Sal tell me about it. Is it a secret?"

"Not really," replied Sal. "At least it was supposed to be a secret, but we're going to be married in a fortnight."

"How exciting! At Chevis Green, I suppose?"

"I suppose so," said Sal.

"You suppose so?"

"It all depends," explained Sal. "I mean Father may want us to wait."

"Then it isn't fixed," said Addie, somewhat disappointed. "I mean if it's fixed I could see about leave, couldn't I?"

"The date is fixed," replied Sal firmly.

"Goodness!" cried Addie, looking at her in surprise tinged with respect and admiration. "It's like that, is it? I shouldn't have thought it of *you*. I mean I should have thought Liz might kick over the traces, but not good little Sal."

"I know it's the right thing," said Sal in a very thoughtful voice. "I *know* it's right. I'm twenty-five. If Father won't marry us, someone else will."

"My hat!" exclaimed Addie inelegantly.

✦

The Pikes lived in Bloomsbury. It was a street of tall, narrow houses, respectable and dreary. Mr. Pike worked on the railway and Mrs. Pike took lodgers—very respectable lodgers, of course. Sal had found her way to the house without difficulty; she had asked the policeman at Hyde Park Corner and he had told her exactly what to do. Now she had arrived, she stood on the doorstep for a few moments before she rang the bell, going over in her mind all she would say. Then she rang and Mrs. Pike appeared: a tall, big-boned woman with protruding teeth and pale blue eyes and curlers in her hair. She was not in the least the sort of woman Sal had expected to see, not sinister, not even very alarming. Indeed she smiled quite pleasantly when she saw Sal and led the way into the dining room where the remains of the lodgers' breakfasts were still upon the table and the odor of kippers was still in the air.

"I'm all be'ind this morning," announced Mrs. Pike in apologetic tones.

"I expect it's difficult to get help," said Sal sympathetically.

"Difficult ain't the word. And I'm full up, too—but you're in luck. The second floor back will be leaving tomorrow. It's a nice room, and quiet. I'll let you see it in a minute. Two-pound-ten a week, is my terms—take it or leave it. Bed an' breakfast, and if you want a bite of supper I don't mind cooking it for you if *you* bring it 'ome. You keep your room, of course, an' laundry's extra. Breakfast's at nine. If you want it sooner you get it yourself, that's my rule an' I don't alter it for nobody, not for the queen, I wouldn't. Most of the lodgers is out all day. That suits me best."

Mrs. Pike had rattled it all off at a terrific rate, and now she paused for breath.

"I don't want a room, thank you," said Sal. "As a matter of fact—"

"Oh," said Mrs. Pike suspiciously. "You're collecting, I suppose. I don't give to nothing excep' the Red Cross, an' that was larst week."

"It's about Bertie. I live at Chevis Green, you see, and—"

"Bertie's coming 'ome. I wrote an' said so. I've a right to my own child, I suppose."

"Yes, of course. I just wondered if you had thought it out."

"Thought what out?" inquired Mrs. Pike suspiciously.

"I wondered if you would have time to look after him, that's all."

"'E'll be away at school all day so what looking after will 'e need? And 'e could 'elp, too. There's more to do in this 'ouse than one pair of 'ands can manage. A boy would be useful; 'e could run errands an' help wash the dishes, couldn't 'e?"

"I wonder," said Sal thoughtfully. "He isn't eleven yet, is he? Boys of that age take a good deal of looking after. And what about his meals?"

"'E'll get 'is dinner at school. I've fixed that."

"What about his breakfast?"

"Breakfast?" said Mrs. Pike doubtfully. "Breakfast's at nine in this 'ouse."

"School is at nine, isn't it?" inquired Sal, seeking information.

"At nine, is it?"

"At nine—usually," said Sal, nodding. "That means he'll have to have his breakfast at eight. Then he'll be back at five for tea, of course."

"I don't know who'd give it him," said Mrs. Pike thoughtfully.

Sal was silent. It was really very lucky indeed that Mrs. Pike had mistaken her for a prospective lodger.

"Well, I don't know," said Mrs. Pike at last. "'E could be

useful—the trouble I 'ave with girls nowadays! I daresay it would work out all right. It was you wrote to me, I suppose. You want Bertie to stay on with that Mrs. Element."

"I want what's best for Bertie—*and for you*," declared Sal, smiling at her in a friendly way for, thank goodness, it was true. Sal had come expecting to dislike Mrs. Pike, but there was something likeable about her. She was selfish, of course, but she was perfectly honest about it. There was no hypocrisy in her. She worked hard, and her house, though gloomy, was clean. That must take a bit of doing.

"Well," said Mrs. Pike thoughtfully. "Well, I'll 'ave to talk to 'is father. It's the breakfast worries *me*. The morning's a bit of a rush as it is, an' I ain't a good riser, never was. Breakfast's at nine in this 'ouse an' I don't fancy getting up at cockcrow an' giving Bertie 'is breakfast at eight…an' tea at five wouldn't be easy, neither. It's the only time I 'ave to myself to do a bit of washing an' such like. Looks as if young Bertie might be more trouble than 'e's worth."

Sal said nothing.

"You ain't leading me up the garden?" inquired Mrs. Pike, with a return of suspicion.

Sal shook her head. "I just thought things out," she said. "You could ask at the school what time the boys have to be there. They would tell you. It would be a pity if you sent for Bertie and then found you couldn't manage."

"That Mrs. Element would 'ave 'im back, wouldn't she?"

"I don't know," said Sal. This was the only lie she had told, and she hated telling it.

"You don't think she would," said Mrs. Pike, mistaking the cause of Sal's embarrassment. "Well, that would be a nice thing, I must say. If I found I couldn't manage an' Mrs. Element wouldn't 'ave 'im back. Where would 'e go?"

Sal could offer no suggestions.

Mrs. Pike deliberated for about a minute. It seemed a long time to Sal.

"What about 'er?" asked Mrs. Pike at last. "*She* wants to stick to Bertie. What's Bertie doing for '*er* that she's so set on 'aving 'im stay?"

Sal hesitated. It was a difficult question to answer, for she had decided it would be a mistake to speak of the affection that existed between Bertie and his foster mother. Jealousy was a queer thing and unpredictable in its effects. "It's quite different in the country," said Sal. "Mr. Element works in a garage and has to be there early, so they all have breakfast together in plenty of time for school—and of course Mrs. Element isn't nearly as busy as you are. It's a different sort of life." Sal rose as she spoke. "I won't keep you," she said. "I'm afraid I've kept you back as it is."

"I'll think about it," said Mrs. Pike. "I won't pay nothing for 'im to be kept. That's flat."

"I daresay that could be arranged," said Sal hopefully.

They were at the door now. Sal held out her hand.

"Good-bye," said Mrs. Pike. "I'm glad you came. I'll speak to 'is father, see?"

"Good-bye," said Sal.

They shook hands solemnly on the doorstep.

Chapter Twenty-Four

*"The voice that breathed o'er Eden,
That earliest wedding day..."*

Tilly Grace was playing the well-known hymn for the second time in three months, but this time she was not humming the words, for she did not feel like humming. As a matter of fact, she felt so wretched, so upset and altogether miserable that she did not care whether she played well or ill; she did not care whether the wedding went off with a swing or not. If by suddenly going on strike and ceasing to provide music for the ceremony Tilly could have stopped the wedding, she would have done so—that was the sort of mood she was in—would prevent Sal from marrying Roderick, and marrying him today. Sal had overcome worse obstacles than the strike of an organist to attain her end, and she had overcome them by sheer dogged determination—and, having gotten over or under or around or through every obstacle in her path, here she was at her goal, standing at the altar steps beside Roderick, calm and composed with not a hair out of place.

Tilly had not wanted Roderick to marry Liz, but this was a worse disaster; for Tilly had discovered quite unexpectedly that she loved Sal best (better than anybody in the world, better even than Father), and Sal was so much more vulnerable than Liz, so easily hurt, so tenderhearted…and Tilly didn't trust Roderick a yard. If he isn't kind to Sal, I shall kill him, thought Tilly, grinding out "The Voice That Breathed o'er Eden" with clenched teeth.

Roderick was not nearly good enough for Sal…in fact (thought Tilly), in fact, he was not "good" at all. He had a Past—Tilly was sure of that—and even if he had no Past worthy of a capital letter before he appeared at Chevis Green (to see the rose window, of which he knew nothing and cared less) he had a Past *now*. First he had fancied Addie and had wheedled her address out of Tilly…and what a pity he hadn't stuck to Addie, for Addie would have been a match for him… and then he had dropped Addie and fallen for Liz…and now he was marrying Sal!

What about me? said Tilly to herself with frightful cynicism. Why was I left out of everything? He saw me first, didn't he? It's a pity he isn't a Mormon, so that he could have us all!

Archie's wedding had taken place at the end of May, so the church had been decorated with the flowers of spring, but now it was early August and the church was full of roses. Mrs. Chevis-Cobbe had brought the roses from Chevis Place— cartloads of them—and had decorated the church with her own hands, aided and abetted by Miss Bodkin, who was now her faithful slave. There were roses everywhere, white and pink and red roses; the scent of them drifted up to Tilly in the organ gallery and made her feel sick. She would never enjoy the scent of a rose again, that much was certain. And what right had Mrs. Chevis-Cobbe to decorate the church for Sal's wedding? What right had *she* to interfere? Sal wasn't *her* sister. *She* wasn't losing the person she loved best in all the world.

(Yes, Tilly was in one of her moods. She had been in that uncomfortable condition for a whole fortnight; in fact, ever since Sal's return from London with Roderick's ring upon her finger and the fixed determination to marry him without delay.)

The church was crowded. There were quite as many people here today as there had been at the Chevis-Cobbe wedding; the congregation comprised practically the whole population of Chevis Green (there had been no time to invite outsiders, because Sal did not want them). Tilly, peering through the grille, saw Liz and Addie—not in the Vicarage pew today, but in the front pew, which looked odd and wrong and was all just a part of the oddness and wrongness of the whole affair. Behind them sat the Chevis-Cobbes, Dr. Wrench, and Miss Bodkin, and behind them Mr. and Mrs. Toop and Jos Barefoot. Jos Barefoot did not attend weddings, as a rule, but he had come to Sal's. Tilly's eye strayed further. She saw Joan, looking very pretty in Sal's blue frock, and she saw the Alemans—a whole pewful of them—and she saw the Bouses and the Feathers with all their progeny, and she saw Mr. Element. There was no sign of Mrs. Element nor of Bertie, which seemed queer. (Ungrateful pigs not to come after all Sal had done for them!) It was the bridegroom's side of the church that, today, was empty of relations; Miss Marks was the only person in the front pew on Roderick's side, and she—as Tilly knew—was no relation but probably had come out of good nature because Roderick had nobody else.

Tilly had been so busy looking at the congregation and thinking her own thoughts that she had not paid much attention to the service, but now, suddenly, she realized it was time for her to play her part, so she swung around hastily.

Liz and Addie had arrived at the church much too early and it was not until they were seated in the front pew without hope of escape that Liz realized what a mistake they had made. It was *her* mistake, really, because of course it did not matter to Addie how long they sat there, the cynosure of every eye, until the arrival of the bride. Addie was quite pleased to know that people were staring at her. In fact, she turned and stared back and smiled at her friends in a cheerful manner, and she stared at the flowers and thought how lovely they were. She decided that, if possible, *she* would be married in rose time; no other flower was so sweet, and no other flower had the same symbolic meaning. "Roses, roses all the way," said Addie to herself...

Addie was the only member of the Grace family whose reaction to this wedding was cheerful and natural. She had arrived at the Vicarage last night for a fortnight's leave, bubbling over with excitement, eager to know all that was to be known, eager to help in all the arrangements, but (being Addie) most eager of all to display her new and extremely becoming hat and frock to her less dress-conscious sisters. Although all this had jarred a little on people who were not feeling the same enthusiasm, her presence had helped to make things easier, and the fact that (being Addie) she was completely oblivious of any strain helped still more. Sal was especially glad to see her, not only because of her excitement and enthusiasm (so lacking in the other Graces), but also because within five minutes of her arrival she had solved one of Sal's most pressing problems by offering her the flat. Sal and Roderick could have the flat for the remaining fortnight of Roderick's course; Addie would be on leave and Betty was "rooming" with another girl during her absence, so the flat was "absolutely available" as Addie put it. Could anything have fitted in more beautifully? Nothing, declared Sal with fervent gratitude. It would be far nicer than living in a hotel, which was the only alternative. They would have the place to themselves and Sal could cook the most succulent meals for Roddy...Having made the offer (which, to be perfectly honest, was not entirely altruistic, for naturally Roderick would insist on paying rent), Addie proceeded to bask in the sunshine of Sal's gratitude, all the more abundant because this was the only fruit that had fallen into Sal's lap. Everything else connected with the wedding had been won by perseverance, with blood and tears. The flat was Sal's reward.

I must smile, thought Liz, as she sat in the front pew with Addie, awaiting the arrival of the bride. I must smile, but not too brightly, not like the Cheshire cat. The worst of trying to smile, when you didn't feel like smiling, was that your face got stiff, as it did when you were having your photograph taken. Liz remembered having her photograph taken by the man at Wandlebury when she was about eight years old. Father had decided that he wanted a photograph of Liz—goodness knew why—and had escorted her to the studio in much the same spirit as he escorted her to the dentist, but dressed in her best blue silk frock, which was different, of course. Liz had been proud of the honor and anxious to behave exactly as Father wanted. "Oh, what a pretty little girl!" said the man—foul creature. "But *rather* a sad expression." "Smile," said Father, nodding at her. Liz had done her best to produce a smile. "A little brighter," said the man encouragingly. "A *little* brighter, please…too bright, too bright. Moisten the lips and start again." The result of this appalling experience still hung in Father's study, enlarged and tinted. Father liked it and often displayed it to his swans. Fortunately, it was unrecognizable and the swans looked at it vaguely and said, "How nice!" One of them had asked in reverent tones if it were a representation of St. Celia when a child.

All this passed through the mind of Liz as she sat beside Addie waiting for Sal to come…and, now, here was Roderick, coming out of the vestry attended and supported by Jimmy Howe. They both looked grave and anxious. Roderick looked as if he would like to run away…and that made it easier for Liz to smile at him. She smiled.

The bride had arrived and here she was, coming up the

aisle leaning on William's arm—for William was giving her away. Liz looked around (everybody looked around) and saw Sal. She was wearing a pale blue frock and a tiny pale blue hat with a pink rose in it. How pretty she was! How brave she was, thought Liz. She looked fragile, but there was strength in her. She had been quietly but absolutely determined to marry Roderick *now*. Quietly but resolutely she had gone her way, arranging everything. Being away from home all day, Liz had been unable to follow in detail the sequence of events, but she knew that Father wanted them to wait. Father, who was a very determined person and whom they all obeyed, had said quite definitely that the wedding would take place when the war with Japan was over…and now, here was Father, marrying them. Liz often "stood up" to Father. She teased him and "pulled his leg," but she was doubtful if she would have had the moral courage to run counter to his wishes—as Sal had done. Sal must have been awfully sure, thought Liz, looking at her. Would Liz herself have been as sure as that—as sure of Roderick? So sure that she would have fought for him, even against Father? Quite honestly she decided she wouldn't…and that decision suddenly made all the difference; it made Liz see that Sal had more right to Roderick…for, if you couldn't be *certain sure* in your own mind, you hadn't any right to complain if somebody else *was*. This thought released Liz; it opened something that had been shut…and when she knelt and joined in the singing of "Oh, Perfect Love," she felt tears on her cheeks, but they weren't bitter tears, they were cleansing and healing.

William was giving Sal away. Sal had asked him to undertake this onerous task and he had agreed, though a trifle reluctantly. He was quite willing to do anything for the Graces but he distrusted himself, for he was aware that if he became nervous or flustered he was liable to make a mess of things. He pointed this out to Sal and reminded her of the circumstances of their first meeting. "Oh, I know," Sal had replied, smiling at him. "But you don't do things like that now. Look at how clever you are at washing up! You never break things *now*!" "I'm used to it," William had replied. "I'm used to family life now, so I don't get flustered…I should be extremely nervous, giving you away." But there was nobody else available, so, after a little more persuasion, William consented. He wrote to Oxford for his best suit, which he had not worn for years, and proceeded to study the marriage service. Everybody coached William; he was so thoroughly coached that when the day came, he was thoroughly muddled; he was, also, even more nervous than he had anticipated, bowed with the heavy responsibility laid upon his shoulders. In spite of this, all went well. William was ready in plenty of time and looked extremely nice in his well-cut lounge suit, with his hair neatly brushed and a rose in his buttonhole. He walked steadily up the aisle with Sal's hand on his arm and stood beside her at the altar steps looking like a rock, but feeling like a man of straw. The flowers, the music, the consciousness that everybody in the building was gazing at his back—all this increased his discomposure. He could not follow the service at all; he forgot everything he had learned.

"Who giveth this woman to be married to this man?" inquired Mr. Grace.

William awoke from his trance and replied immediately in a loud voice—a voice that startled even William himself by its unexpectedly stentorian tones, "I, William Single."

Mr. Grace hesitated. He was in such a very emotional state of mind that the unlooked-for response put him out of his stride (in fact, Mr. Grace might easily have married his daughter to the wrong man, for of course, it was now the moment for Mr. Grace to "prompt" the young couple and it was on the tip of his tongue to say, "I, William Single, do take thee, Sarah Mary…"). Fortunately, however, the bridegroom, who had studied the marriage service with meticulous care and had learned all the important bits by heart so that there should be no possible mistake, saved the situation by taking Sal's hand and pronouncing in audible, though not stentorian, tones, "I, Roderick James, do take thee, Sarah Mary, to be my wedded wife." And he smiled so sweetly and proudly and confidently at his almost-father-in-law as he said the words (unprompted) that his almost-father-in-law was comforted and reassured and was able to continue the service in the conventional manner.

And now it was over, and Tilly was playing the Wedding March: "Tum, tum, te tum tum tum tum *tum, tum*, te te *tum*," but playing it mechanically and quite without the verve and expression with which she had rolled it out at the Chevis-Cobbe wedding, and the congregation was streaming out, first two by two, and then in a flood as if a dam had burst…and Tilly could hear the chatter of voices outside the church door where people were standing about in the blazing August sunshine. They would stand there and chatter for quite a bit, because most of them were merely onlookers—not guests—so they had no further goal and would just stand and talk and then go home to tea.

Only close friends had been invited to tea at the Vicarage, only the Chevis-Cobbes, Dr. Wrench, Miss Marks, Jimmy Howe, and Miss Bodkin, and a few other near neighbors who have not appeared in this veracious chronicle of the Grace family, and who, like the flowers of spring, have nothing to do with the case. There had been some doubt in Sal's mind whether or not to ask Miss Bodkin, for if one asked Miss Bodkin it might cause a little jealousy in the village, and, although Sal would have been charmed to ask the whole village, it just wasn't possible. But Mrs. Chevis-Cobbe had solved the problem. "Ask her, poor soul," said Mrs. Chevis-Cobbe. "She'd love to be asked—she needn't come if she doesn't want to—and, after all, it's her affair if the others are jealous." So Miss Bodkin had been asked and had accepted rapturously, and when Tilly came out of the side door, there she was walking across the churchyard to the Vicarage in her pink dress and hat (but, of course, not wearing the yellow muslin apron with the little black spots). The others were drifting toward the Vicarage, too. Sal and Roderick first, arm in arm, and seemingly oblivious that anybody else existed; Addie with Timmy Howe and, following them, a little group composed of Liz, Dr. Wrench, William, and the Chevis-Cobbes. Miss Marks was alone. Tilly came upon her standing before the memorial to the victims of the Black Death.

"How delightful to see you again!" exclaimed Miss Marks. "I hope you remembered to dust the organ today. It would have been most unfortunate if you had got dust upon that very charming dress."

"Yes, I remembered," replied Tilly, not very graciously, for of course the blame for the whole affair was directly attributable to Miss Marks and her umbrella (she even had it with her *today!*).

"Such a pretty dress, and so becoming," added Miss Marks, with a friendly smile.

"Oh, I'm glad you like it," replied Tilly, relenting a little. "You're coming to tea, aren't you? I think I'd better run on…"

Tilly had taken very little interest in the arrangements for tea, which was horrid of her, of course (she knew it was horrid), but, now, seeing all these people converging upon her home, her domestic instincts got the better of her horridness. Who was getting the tea, wondered Tilly, racing across the churchyard like a mountain goat. Not Joan, because Joan was in the church, not Liz nor Addie, because they were strolling idly and talking to the guests, and it was obvious that Sal's thoughts were not engaged with domestic affairs. Tilly rushed into the kitchen with the belated intention of putting on kettles, and trying to find something for the guests to eat—and so preventing an absolute fiasco—and there, to her amazement, she found Mrs. Element and Bertie busily engaged in filling teapots with boiling water from a magnificent array of kettles bubbling and hissing merrily upon the stove...and it was obvious that teapots and kettles from all over the village had found their way to the Vicarage kitchen to play their part in the celebrations.

"It's all ready, nearly. There's the trays," said Mrs. Element, pointing to the trays of cups and saucers set out upon the kitchen table. "I'd be grateful if you'd just carry them in, Miss Tilly. I don't 'ardly like to trust Bertie and I ain't too keen on appearing myself. All those people makes me 'ot and bothered, so if you just take in the trays..."

"This is kind of you!" said Tilly.

"Kind!" exclaimed Mrs. Element. "Look what Miss Sal's done for Bertie and me! Bertie and me would do a good deal more than that for Miss Sal—Mrs. 'Erd, I *should* say."

"Mrs. Herd?" cried Tilly. "Oh, yes...Mrs. Herd."

"It'll take a bit of getting used to," agreed Mrs. Element, smiling.

Put to shame by Mrs. Element (for what, after all, had Sal done for Mrs. Element compared with her endless kindnesses to her own family?), Tilly seized a tray and bore it into the drawing room where the guests were congregating and where there was such a storm of conversation already raging that there might have been a hundred people in the room instead of about a score. The newly married couple were standing in front of the fireplace, which was banked with flowers, and were receiving the congratulations of their friends with the blend of happiness and embarrassment usual under the circumstances.

There was a lull in the noise when Tilly appeared and the male element in the company rushed forward from all directions, converging upon the tray bearer and embarrassing her a good deal in its eagerness to be of service. Jimmy Howe was the successful competitor for the tray, and having obtained it he stood there holding it tightly with a strained expression upon his face.

"Where?" he inquired anxiously.

"Over there, I should think," replied Tilly, pointing to a table in the window that was spread with a white lace cloth and was laden with cakes.

"Oh, yes, of course," said Jimmy Howe.

The tray having arrived at its destination in safety, Tilly was free to look at the cakes that, as far as she was concerned, were as manna, fallen from the skies. The *pièce de résistance* was a large iced cake bearing the inscription "Happiness and Good Fortune" done in pink sugar upon the top. On closer inspection Tilly decided the cakes must have come from the village, for she recognized the gingerbread as being of Mrs. Feather's baking, and the sponge was identical with the sponge Mrs. Bouse had made for the Women's Institute. Miss Bodkin, who was standing near the table, cleared up the mystery of the iced cake by remarking to Tilly in a low, anxious voice, "The icing is just a *little* soft, I'm afraid, but it's better than being too hard, isn't it?"

"Much better," agreed Tilly. "It looks a marvelous cake. Sal had better cut it, hadn't she?"

The party followed a natural course; people talked and laughed: healths were drunk in tea and a few of the waggishly inclined made waggish speeches. Long before anyone had expected, the station taxi arrived from Wandlebury to convey the married couple to the station. There was no time for long-drawn-out farewells. Sal hugged everybody she could lay hands on—including Miss Bodkin—and the next moment had vanished from the scene, and the climax having been reached the party broke up rather quickly and the guests departed.

"It went off very well," said Mr. Grace; he had said exactly the same after the Chevis-Cobbe wedding, but this time he said it differently, not cheerfully, not rubbing his hands together with satisfaction, but in a somewhat forlorn tone of voice.

And Liz, instead of replying—as she had done before—that weddings always *did* go off well and that she, for one, had never heard of a wedding that *didn't*, replied quite soberly that she thought it *had*, and at any rate Sal had looked perfectly sweet.

Chapter Twenty-Five

Jane Chevis-Cobbe walked down to the five-acre field with a large basket on her arm. The field was being harvested today—Archie had told her so at breakfast—and as it was a perfectly lovely day, fine and warm with just a suspicion of a breeze to keep it from being sultry, she had decided to take tea down to the field for Archie and herself. She intended to ask Liz to have it with them for Sal had asked her to keep an eye on Liz and cheer her up. Jane did not feel quite so drawn toward Liz—Sal was more her kind of person—but she realized that Liz must be feeling a little flat and this was a good way to keep an eye on her. Jane was disappointed when she got to the field to find no Archie, but Liz was there, helping to load up the last two wagons with the sweet-smelling sheaves of corn. Liz was a marvelous-looking creature, decided Jane, watching her at work, watching her gathering the sheaves and forking them onto the wagons. With her long legs and her straight back she looked like a Greek boy—yet not like a boy, either. The sun shone on her golden hair and her fair skin was tanned to a beautiful smooth brown.

Liz saw Jane and waved, and a few minutes later she came over to the hedge in the shade of which Jane had sat down.

"Archie's gone," said Liz. "He had to go down to the garage

to see Element about one of the tractors that wasn't behaving nicely. He asked me to tell you."

"Perhaps you'd like some tea," suggested Jane.

Liz sat down at once. "That's very nice of you, Mrs. Chevis-Cobbe. I was hoping you might have enough for me," admitted Liz, smiling. "The fact is this sort of work agrees with me so well that I'm always hungry and thirsty. I don't know why I don't get fat."

Jane thought the reason pretty obvious. "You work too hard," she said. She hesitated and then added, "Sal calls me Jane. I'd rather, really. It seems funny when you call Archie, 'Archie.'"

"We've known Archie such ages," said Liz hastily. "But— yes, it *is* rather silly. I'd like to."

"Good," said Jane, taking out a Thermos flask and unscrewing the top.

"I wanted to thank you for decorating the church. It was lovely."

"Sal was lovely. She's very happy, you know. I think you're a little worried about her, aren't you?"

"Just selfish," declared Liz. "I'm missing her so horribly. We all are."

"She'll miss you," said Jane thoughtfully. "Oh, yes, she will. I'm terribly happy with Archie, but I miss my sister quite a lot. There are all sorts of things you share with a sister—silly little things that you wouldn't think of talking to a husband about."

"I thought you had no relations!" exclaimed Liz. "She wasn't at the wedding—"

"We quarreled. She didn't want me to marry Archie...there was a reason, of course."

Liz was interested. She had always sensed a mystery about Archie's wife, and as Liz was a forthright person she voiced her feelings at once. "A reason? What sort of reason?" inquired Liz eagerly.

Jane hesitated. She had very nearly told Sal her unusual

history—that day when they were sitting on the seat in the middle of Chevis Green—but Sal had shown no curiosity and the moment had passed. Now, here was Liz, thirsting for information, and Jane felt inclined to give it to her. "I'll tell you if you're interested," said Jane slowly. "I don't want other people to know—you'll soon see why."

This mysterious utterance made Liz more anxious to know than ever. She promised the strictest secrecy and prepared herself to listen to the tale.

"Helen and I were very badly off," said Jane, offering Liz a sandwich. "It was quite horrible. We lived in lodgings and scrimped and scraped, and then, quite suddenly, I found I could write stories, and the *extraordinary* thing was that the stories were accepted by a publisher and people bought them and read them."

"Why extraordinary?" inquired Liz, who was under the impression that this was the natural sequence of events.

"Because they were so terribly bad," explained their author in a matter-of-fact voice.

"Bad!"

"Oh, not *wicked*," said Jane smiling. "They were silly, and soppy, and untrue to life and the characters were puppets."

Liz was dumb. She gazed at her companion with wide blue eyes, her sandwich halfway to her mouth.

"But in spite of that," continued Jane, "or perhaps because of that, thousands of people liked them, so all at once Helen and I found ourselves quite well off. We bought a very pleasant house and settled down comfortably—and of course I went on writing and the stories went on selling like mad. Everything in the garden was lovely; I liked writing and I liked getting letters from people all over the world. I was most horribly complacent and pleased with myself," said Jane, nodding gravely. "I was as smug as a tabby—quite disgusting. *Then* I met two young airmen at tea one day, and one of them told me straight out exactly what he thought of my books."

"He didn't like them?" asked Liz.

"Definitely not," replied Jane, smiling at the recollection. "But I wasn't angry, I was interested, because really and truly in my inmost heart I had begun to feel bored with them myself. I had begun to realize what rubbish they were; he was only putting into words—and pretty hard words—exactly what I had been feeling. That finished it," said Jane, with a shudder at the recollection. "That absolutely put the lid on—as Archie would say. I tried to go on writing but I couldn't. The whole thing revolted me. Helen was furious, of course, and I didn't blame her, really, because the books were our bread and butter, and also because she had helped a good deal in building up the publicity. I won't go into details, it would just bore you, but the end of it was I ran away and went to Ganthorne Lodge as a P.G. and there I met Archie."

Jane stopped. She was obviously under the impression that the story—her own story—was finished. Liz thought otherwise.

"How interesting!" exclaimed Liz. "It's just like a novel, isn't it? Do go on and tell me more."

"There isn't any more to tell."*

"Are you still writing?"

"No, indeed!" cried Jane. "And I never will—not *that* sort of story."

"I wonder if I have read any of your books?"

"Quite likely," said the author casually.

"Tell me some of their names," urged Liz.

"Oh, there were dozens of them. I called myself Janetta Walters."

Liz was amazed. "Janetta Walters!" she cried. "Oh, but how exciting! I *love* her books! I thought you said they were

---

*Further details of Jane's history are available in *The Two Mrs. Abbotts*.

frightful—and there's one just out—all about Cornwall. It isn't quite as good as the others, of course; I like *Her Prince at Last* the best, and I like—"

"I wish I hadn't told you!" exclaimed Jane.

Liz was no fool. "Oh, don't say that," said Liz, full of remorse. "I mean, of course, if you're sick of them, you hate them. I understand that."

"Yes, I hate them," nodded Jane.

"But think of the pleasure they give other people," urged Liz. "Surely you must feel proud of that—and pleased. Archie likes them. Archie has a whole set."

"I know," said Archie's wife.

Liz sighed. "It seems so *sad*. No more Janetta Walters! Couldn't you go on writing when you've had a good rest?"

"No, I couldn't," replied Jane, smiling at her. "But you needn't worry; there will be plenty of Janetta stories to read. Helen is writing them now…but of course that's a secret."

"Helen is writing them? But—"

"Anybody could write them if they had enough time and patience, if they sat down at a desk with plenty of foolscap paper and a good solid pen."

"I don't believe it," said Liz frankly.

"It's quite true. Helen wrote the new one, about Cornwall."

"I told you it wasn't so good!"

Jane laughed. She said, "Yes, you did. I couldn't help being a little bit pleased about it, which is very illogical."

"Why illogical?"

"Think it out," said Jane, laughing quite cheerfully.

They were silent, drinking tea and eating buns. It was warm and pleasant; the sky was blue and cloudless, the stubble of the cut field glittered like millions of little spears in the sunshine. Jane looked about for another topic of conversation, for she did not want to answer any more questions about Janetta Walters.

"What are you reading?" asked Jane, pointing to a large, thick, shabby volume lying beside Liz's coat. She felt quite safe in asking the question for even at this distance, she could see the book was not one of her own.

"Oh, that!" said Liz. "As a matter of fact, I got it from the librarian at Wandlebury. I'm going to read every word of it."

Jane was intrigued. Liz had announced her intention with resolute determination—almost with defiance—and the book certainly looked pretty heavy reading. If Liz liked the Janetta type of book, *that* shabby volume was obviously not her meat. Should she inquire further or not, wondered Jane, glancing at her companion…Liz was gazing in the other direction and looked so like an oyster that Jane decided not.

Jane was right, of course. The book was not the kind of literature Liz enjoyed, but she had not borrowed it for the purpose of enjoyment, nor had she borrowed it with the object of improving her mind. She had borrowed it because she needed something to *occupy* her mind. You had to have something to occupy your mind (so Liz had found). If you had decided not to think about Roderick—who was now your sister's husband—you had to have something else to think about. You couldn't just not think about Roderick, there had to be some positive alternative, so that when you found yourself beginning to think about Roderick you could immediately switch over. The problem was *what* positive alternative should you choose. Looking about for something, Liz's eye fell upon William, whose enthrallment with the Romans and everything to do with Roman civilization was obvious to the meanest intelligence. There must be something in it, thought Liz. The Romans must be interesting—if you knew about them. Liz wasted no time. She went to Wandlebury, sought out the custodian of the public library, and informed him that she wanted a book about Roman remains. He produced several books for her inspection and Liz chose the thickest (it was *A History of the Romans Under the Empire*, Vol. VIII, by Charles Merivale). I shall read every word of it, said Liz to herself as she tucked it under her arm. It was pretty heavy going, of course, but she set her teeth and stuck to it. She took the book to the fields with her and read it while she ate her lunch, and she took it to bed with her—it certainly had the merit of sending her to sleep. The experiment was taking a good deal of courage and determination, but nobody, not her worst enemy, could question the courage of Liz. Her judgment was sometimes faulty and she had a habit of leaping before she looked, but for sheer moral courage and determination it would have been hard to find her match.

"There's Archie!" exclaimed Jane, and she stood up and signaled to him with a Thermos flask.

❦

Liz had been born upon the first of September and it was a habit of the Graces to have a picnic upon that auspicious day. This year, of course, Liz would be busy at the farm unless she asked for a special holiday.

"I think you *should*," said Tilly. (It was the thirty-first of August; they were all having supper together in the kitchen, because it was Thursday and therefore Joan's day out.)

"I see no reason why you shouldn't," agreed Mr. Grace.

"You work hard enough," added William, helping himself to raspberry jam.

"I see lots of reasons why I shouldn't," replied Liz firmly. "Archie would give me a holiday for my birthday if I asked him—he'd give it because I'm me—but what would he say if Nat Bouse asked for a day off because it was his birthday? Archie would think he had gone mad...Yes, it's silly, isn't it?" agreed Liz, surveying the laughter of her family with complete gravity. "It's silly if it's Nat; so it's silly if it's me. There's no difference at all between me and Nat except that he can milk three cows to my two. We're both farmhands, working for a weekly wage—what's the difference between us?"

"He has a red mustache," replied Tilly, giggling.

With a lightning transition from the sublime to the ridiculous, Liz dipped her finger in the remains of the raspberry jam and the next moment was like Nat in this respect also.

"Crazy girl!" exclaimed Mr. Grace, laughing immoderately.

Perhaps the Fates were pleased with Liz for her devotion to duty; at any rate they provided a lovely day for her birthday. The morning had just the faintest tang of September when Liz let herself out of the back door of the Vicarage; she sniffed the air appreciatively and, throwing one long leg over her bicycle, rode off to work.

A lovely day for her birthday and there were more pleasures in store; for Polly—one of the huge Clydesdales of which Archie was so proud—was considerate enough to cast a shoe that very morning, and Archie called Liz away from cleaning the pigsties and asked her to take Polly to the blacksmith at Chevis Green.

"Take Toby, too," said Archie. "Take them both. Trod may as well have a look at Toby while he's about it."

"Honestly, Archie?" asked Liz, scarcely able to credit her good fortune.

Archie waved and strode away.

It was still quite early so Liz finished the pigsties, as a sop to her uncomfortably sensitive conscience, then off she went with the two big gentle creatures, sitting sideways on Toby's back and leading Polly in true plowboy style, joggle, joggle—joggle, joggle, through lanes smelling deliriously of damp earth drying in the warm September sun. It was a real birthday treat, and Liz enjoyed it all the more because she had just begun to enjoy life again with her old zest. The Romans had done their job and ousted Roderick. The odd thing was that now, when there was no longer any need to pursue her labors and immerse herself in their affairs, the Romans had become interesting to Liz on their own account, so, instead of throwing up her studies and exchanging *Romans Under the Empire*, Vol. VIII, for a thinner and less weighty tome, in the Janetta Walters *genre* (which was a pleasure Liz had promised herself and to which she had been looking forward with eager anticipation), Liz had exchanged Merivale for another equally thick and no less weighty volume, which she intended to peruse from start to finish.

The forge was at the other end of Chevis Green, so Liz had to ride through the village to reach her goal, and this pleased her enormously for she was proud of her job and delighted that her friends should see her perched upon Toby's back. Mr. Toop was the first to see her; he came to the door of his shop in his blue-striped apron and told her she was a proper plowboy and no mistake. Jane Chevis-Cobbe, coming out of the post office, saw her and waved frantically. Mrs. Element saw her and rushed out of her cottage to see her better, calling shrilly to Mrs. Bouse. Mrs. Bouse waddled to her door with her youngest in her arms, and entreated the infant to "Look at Miss Liz on the big 'orsie, then!" All this was extremely pleasant to Liz.

Reuben Trod was hard at work when Liz arrived at the forge, she could hear the clang of his hammer as she approached; he came to the doorway attired in his leather apron, with his shirt sleeves rolled up and his huge hairy arms black with coal dust.

His face broke into a broad smile when he saw Liz. "Well, there now, look at that!" he exclaimed. "You be a proper farm lad. 'Tis a pity Passon can't see you!"

"I can wait if you're busy, Reuben," said Liz, sliding from her perch.

"I'll take 'em now," declared Reuben. "I'll take the mare first. You'll get a surprise when you see my new 'prentice."

"Where's Jim Aleman?" asked Liz, with interest. "Why has Jim left and who have you got instead?"

Reuben was chuckling delightedly—there was some joke on, thought Liz, as she followed him into the big open shed.

"There 'e be!" said Reuben, shaking with laughter. "There be my new 'prentice. I tell 'im 'e be too strong for a smith—nearly blew the fire clean out, so 'e did."

Liz looked at this prodigy of strength who was "too strong for a smith," and was amazed to see William Single standing beside the fire with an enormous pair of bellows in his hand. He had taken off his coat and rolled up his sleeves, and his arms were every bit as thick and sinewy as Reuben's own—though not as hairy.

"William!" exclaimed Liz.

"Yes," said William, looking a trifle sheepish. "I just—er—dropped in to see Trod about something, and, as Aleman was out getting his dinner, I just—er—"

"Nonsense," said Liz sternly. "You needn't try to take me in."

"We'll 'ave to make a clean breast of it," declared Reuben, still chuckling. "We be caught out good an' proper, Mr. Single."

"Oh, well," agreed William. "It's nearly finished, anyway."

"What's nearly finished?" demanded Liz.

"'Tis a secret, Miss Liz," explained Reuben. "Mr. Single an' me be making a little present for Passon. 'Tis for the church, so it be. We be putting our 'eads together over it—an' our 'ands, too."

Liz promised discretion and was shown the work; it was a lectern of wrought iron, and was decorated with vine leaves and delicately curling tendrils to match the grille of the organ gallery. Reuben obviously was proud of his work, and he had every reason to be proud, for it was a beautiful thing. He pointed out its merits to Liz and explained that Mr. Single had made the design, copying it from the grille and drawing it to scale, and he himself had been working at it for some weeks in his spare time.

"Father *will* be pleased," said Liz. "It's lovely. The design is beautiful and so is the workmanship. A lectern is just what we need."

"I know," said William, nodding. "It was Roderick who gave me the idea; he said you were going to get up a subscription for a new lectern after the war."

"How on earth did Roderick know?" wondered Liz.

The lectern was now put aside for the more urgent business of shoeing Polly, and Liz, leaning against the wooden pillar of the shed, watched the process with interest. She had always loved the forge and had spent hours here when she was a child, watching Reuben's father at work, but today the experience was even more enthralling, perhaps because she was in such a very receptive frame of mind.

Reuben sized the piece of metal with his tongs and thrust it into the heart of the glowing embers. "Blow," he said to William. "Blow 'er up, Mr. Single...gently, now...you be blowing too 'ard, you'll be blowing me out of my own forge in 'alf a minute. That's better...that's right, blow 'er up."

William was intent upon his job, his face grave with responsibility, red with the glow from the fire.

The iron was glowing now; Reuben threw it upon the anvil and, seizing his hammer, began to shape it quickly and neatly with strong, deft blows. The hammer rose and fell, the sparks flew...it was thus men had worked for thousands of years, heating iron and shaping it to their needs; it was an old, old trade and there was magic in it. Liz was enthralled.

The shoe was ready for fitting when Jim Aleman returned from his dinner. He was somewhat surprised to find his place filled by a stranger.

"See now," said Reuben gravely. "You be out of a job, young Jim. Better be looking out for a new job so you don't want to be on the dole."

Young Jim fell in with the jest. "I be gettin' along, then, Reuben, so be you don't want me," he replied.

They sparred at each other gravely while Tim took off his coat and hung it on a nail, then William surrendered the bellows and came over to talk to Liz.

"Do you think he'll approve of it?" inquired William anxiously. "Will he think it good enough for the church?"

"He'll simply love it," declared Liz. "Father always likes original things, made by people's hands, and he'll like this all the more because it has been made by one of his own people. You couldn't have thought of anything that would please him better."

"Good," said William, nodding. "I wanted to give something to Chevis Green—something in return for all I've received."

William was standing in the entrance to the forge, half in shadow and half in sunlight. He was hot and dirty and his face was smeared with dust, but somehow he looked right. There was a dignity about him. Without his clumsy shapeless coat he seemed a different man. Liz had a sudden feeling that this sort of work was William's birthright. His tremendous strength had not been given him for nothing—in another, earlier, more natural civilization, William would have been a smith. Like Jove he would have fashioned thunderbolts, thought Liz, looking at him.

"Is my face dirty?" inquired William, smearing it still more.

"Yes, but it doesn't matter," replied Liz. "What *does* matter is your clothes. Why don't you take more interest in the fit of your clothes, William?"

"I don't know," said William, somewhat surprised at the urgency of her tone. "I suppose I should, really. This coat *is* rather old. I'll order a new one when I go back to Oxford."

Liz sighed. "I suppose you must go back to Oxford?"

He turned his head and looked down at her. There were not many people who could look down at Liz. "Why—yes—" he said in surprise.

"Shall you be glad or sorry?"

"Sorry...and glad," said William slowly. "Of course I enjoy my work..."

"I know!" cried Liz. "I know exactly how you feel. It was like that at the end of the holidays when I went back to school. I hated leaving home, but I loved school."

She waited for a few moments but William said nothing. He was gazing out over the sunlit country. He looked rather forlorn.

"You'll come back," said Liz comfortingly.

Chapter Twenty-Six

It was a wet Saturday afternoon in October. Liz was spending it in the schoolroom, curled up in a big chair with her long legs tucked beneath her, reading a book. The volume that was engaging attention was not concerned with Roman Britain, but with Roman Rome, and in some ways it appealed to Liz even more than its predecessors. The writer of this particular book had a vivid imagination and therefore was able to arouse the imagination of his reader; so when Liz raised her eyes she saw, not the shabby schoolroom, familiar since infancy, but the dirty, narrow, cobble-paved streets of bygone Rome, and she heard, not the sounds of wind in the chimney and rain pattering rhythmically upon the jutting gable outside the window, but the creaking of axles, the crack of whips, iron wheels grinding over the stones, and all the noisy clamor of a jostling, shouting, virile crowd. Smelly, dirty, noisy, that was Rome; that was the cradle of the race whose sons had come to Britain more than two thousand years ago, and left their mark on Britain's soil and shaped her destiny.

So interested and absorbed was Liz that it was with some surprise she noticed the time—after four already—and she rose to switch on the electric kettle for tea. It had always been Sal's job to prepare tea when they had it in the schoolroom; now it was anybody's job, which was not a satisfactory arrangement. Both Liz and Tilly had been astounded to find how many little jobs remained undone after Sal's departure.

"Oh!" cried Tilly, coming in and slumping into a chair. "Oh, goodness, how tired I am! Why isn't tea ready?"

"It will be in a minute," replied Liz in conciliatory tones. She was aware that Tilly had far too much to do. This afternoon, for instance, Tilly had been all around the village collecting for the Red Cross Penny-a-Week Fund.

"It's too much for one person," continued Tilly. "We'll have to get Mrs. Feather or somebody to help with the cooking. I've got the hens to do and shopping, and collecting and the choir practices and the work party, and teaching Sal's Sunday school. It wasn't quite so bad when William was here; he helped a good deal in various ways. I miss William frightfully. I wish he hadn't had to go back to Oxford."

She rather expected Liz to voice the same sentiments, but Liz was silent.

"Damn Cleopatra's nose!" added Tilly venomously.

"Cleopatra's nose?" inquired Liz, pausing, teapot in hand.

"If it had been shorter the whole history of the world would have been different—so Miss Marks said—I don't know why, really."

"Antony wouldn't have loved her so much," suggested Liz thoughtfully. "He must have liked long noses, I suppose, but what has that got to do with William?"

"Nothing at all. I was thinking of Sal."

"Sal hasn't got a long nose."

"Goodness, how stupid you are!" exclaimed Tilly with sisterly candor. "It all began at Archie's wedding. My duster was Cleopatra's nose and if I hadn't forgotten it, the whole history of the Grace family would have been different. If I had dusted the organ, I shouldn't have got my frock dirty, so I shouldn't have stayed behind when you all went on to the reception. I shouldn't have met Miss Marks and Miss Marks wouldn't have come to tea and forgotten her umbrella, and Roderick wouldn't have met Sal and—"

"And the pig won't get over the stile, and I'll never get home tonight," said Liz, smiling.

Tilly had to smile, too, because it *did* sound rather like the nursery classic Father used to say to them when they were little. "But all the same…" said Tilly, and left it at that.

There was a little silence. The two Graces were both thinking the same thoughts, regretting the fact that Cleopatra's nose had been so long.

"Perhaps Sal will come home when Roderick goes to Burma," said Liz at last.

"Perhaps she won't," retorted Tilly. "She never *says* so. To tell you the truth I feel as if Sal were a hundred million miles away."

Liz had the same feeling. It was because Sal was married, of course. Sal wasn't just Sal anymore; she was Mrs. Herd. Even her letters were Mrs. Herdish, thought Liz, who had had one that very morning, and found it colorless and unsatisfactory.

"I feel as if Sal were a *thousand* million miles away," amended Tilly with bitter emphasis…and at that very moment the door opened and Sal walked in.

Liz and Tilly gazed at her as if she were a visitant from another sphere—and as a matter of fact, she looked like the ghost of Sarah Grace. She stood for a moment in the middle of the room without speaking and then sat down in a chair and burst into tears.

"Sal!" cried Tilly, rushing at her. "Sal, darling! What's the matter? Oh, goodness! Oh, Sal, *don't*! What's happened? What *has* happened?"

"N-nothing," said Sal between her sobs. "I mean he's gone, that's all. I saw him off—this morning—I came straight home."

"Of course you did!" cried Tilly, hugging her. "It's lovely to have you—lovely. Don't cry anymore."

Liz was not as vocal but quite as solicitous. She pressed a clean handkerchief into Sal's hand. "Take this," she said huskily. She could think of nothing else to do or say. It upset Liz frightfully to see Sal cry, for Sal was not a crying sort of person. Tilly and Addie sometimes indulged in tears, but never Sal—even when she was very small and had fallen out of the swing and broken her arm she hadn't cried.

"My own hankie is quite dry, thank you," said Sal, refusing the offer. "I wanted to get here before I started—and I did."

"Tea," said Tilly, patting her gently on the back. "Tea will do you good. Liz, *tea*."

"Tea—of course!" cried Liz, dashing for the teapot, thankful there was something she could do.

Tea is a most refreshing and reviving beverage and after two cups Sal felt a good deal better. She sat up and ran her fingers through her hair and began to take notice of her surroundings. "Everything just the same!" she said in surprise.

"Well, of course," said Liz. "What did you expect?"

"I don't know," said Sal slowly. "I mean of course I expected everything to be exactly the same, and I should have been frightfully disappointed to find anything different, but it seems so awfully odd to think that all this has been here all the time, and you having tea here every afternoon. I can't believe it, somehow. Either this is real and the other is a dream, or else I'm dreaming now."

"This is real," said Tilly firmly. She much preferred that Roderick should be the dream.

"I feel as if I had been a thousand miles away," added the wanderer.

"So do we," said Liz.

"And William has gone back to Oxford."

"Yes," said Tilly. "We miss him frightfully and he says in his letters that he misses *us*. He's coming down to see us sometime soon, but he doesn't say when."

"He wouldn't," smiled Sal, thinking of William's unannounced first arrival at the Vicarage.

"It's a pity he isn't here today," said Tilly.

Sal didn't think so. "Oh, no," she said. "It's nice to be just ourselves."

"Just ourselves," agreed Liz cheerfully. "Not even dear Aunt Rona!"

"I wonder where Aunt Rona is now," put in Tilly.

Liz smiled mischievously. "Wherever she may be she's the center of attraction, the life and soul of the party, keeping everyone merry and bright."

"That goes without saying," nodded Sal.

"*Dear* Aunt Rona," said Liz. "Perhaps she's staying with the Earl of Elephant and Castle. You know him, of course. He and the Countess are in Essex at the moment, enjoying a well-earned rest after the London season. Their Essex property is *so* delightful," declared Liz, imitating the well-remembered drawl. "It's just a *cottage*, of course, there are only sixteen bedrooms, but so comfortable and quiet. Mildred Mildew is there, too, another *intimate* friend, and quite the best-dressed woman in London when I'm not there myself. Have you never met Mildred?...What a pity! I picked up her nephew at the Grand Hotel in Mentone, he tripped over my feet in the lounge. It was a little unfortunate, of course, because he upset his coffee over a Russian lady who was sitting beside me on the sofa and she made rather a fuss...but Marmaduke Mildew apologized *so* gracefully that I quite lost my heart to the dear fellow and we became friends for life in exactly five minutes. His sister married a brother of poor Titus—Titus Dunderhead, who died of drink, you know. He was usually as tight as a drum. You mustn't confuse them with the Dunderheads of Scatterbrain, of course. That is quite a different family. Euthanasia Dunderhead is *not* out of the top drawer. I'm afraid Titus picked her up on the pier at Brighton, when he was half-seas over."

Sal and Tilly were laughing uncontrollably, but Liz remained grave. "Then there's Drusilla Dunderhead, of course. I met her at a wedding. I knew who she *was*, of course, so I went straight up and made my number to her. I managed to pin her into a corner so she couldn't escape. Drusilla is the *most* delightful creature, absolutely out of the top drawer—in fact, practically off the mantelpiece—and so interesting in spite of the impediment in her speech. She was a Hickup before she married. I expect you've heard of Lord Hickup, Sarah."

"Don't," cried Sal hysterically. "Don't, Liz. It hurts…"

Liz took no notice. She continued in reproachful tones. "I can't understand how you haven't *heard* of Lord Hickup, Sarah. He was a most distinguished man, and such an unusual character. Some people found him a little *difficile*, of course—he was apt to throw the ornaments about when anything annoyed him—but he was always delightful to *me*. I remember on one occasion when I went to stay at Hickup Castle; we were having drinks on the terrace when Egbert Hickup came in. 'Hallo, Rona, here again!' he exclaimed and threw his cocktail at me in *such* a playful manner—he was always good company. Shortly after that he fell ill with *delirium tremens* and passed on, and they laid him to rest in the mausoleum below the castle walls. I have often felt that if Egbert had lived, the friendship between us might have deepened into something very beautiful."

Tilly, weak with laughter, besought her to stop. "I've got it," gasped Tilly. "I've—*hick*—got the Egbert Hick—Hickup. Please—*hick*—Liz, stop."

Liz had begun to laugh herself, so she could not go on.

"Hold your breath, Tilly," said Sal, mopping her streaming eyes. "Drink some tea and hold your breath…"

They were all three still laughing weakly and spasmodically when Mr. Grace came in.

Chapter Twenty-Seven

N ow that Sal was home she settled down into the old ways and took over her usual jobs, and things began to run smoothly again, as they had done before her departure, but Tilly noticed a difference in Sal. Sal was married; she had stepped out of spinsterhood into the married state and left her sisters behind (when she thought of it, Tilly was just a tiny bit shy of Sal). She was prettier, Tilly thought; there was a new dignity about her and, in spite of the fact that she worried about Roderick, a new serenity. Sal never mentioned the fact that she was worried; she laughed and talked much as usual, but for all that Tilly knew. For one thing, Sal was always at the gate to meet the postman, though it seemed unlikely that the postman would have anything to give her…and then one day she received a bulky letter and disappeared for at least an hour (secluding herself in her bedroom while she digested its contents), after which she emerged looking a little dazed but with starry eyes. So when Liz said, "She's *just* the same; not Mrs. Herdish at *all*," Tilly gave a very doubtful affirmative. Of course Liz was away all day so she didn't see Sal waiting for her letter at the gate, returning without it, walking like an old woman without any spring in her step, and of course Liz was a bit vague herself, these days, cheerful as a cricket one moment and lost in dreams the next.

Mr. Grace, like Tilly, saw a difference in Sal. In a way his dream had come true, for here was Sal home again, and although her stay was only temporary (only to be enjoyed until Roderick came back from the East), that fact did not prevent Mr. Grace from enjoying it to the full. To him all life was temporary. "This transitory life," as the prayer book puts it, was but a road upon which he was moving toward eternal life. He was in no hurry to reach the end of the road; for the road, though sorrowful at times, was intensely interesting (there was so much to see and to learn and so many things to do; he would be sorry when he came to the last mile), but still it was as a road that Mr. Grace looked upon it.

One Sunday afternoon when Sal had been home about a fortnight, Mr. Grace was walking up and down the terrace after lunch. Sal came out from the house and, pushing her hand through his arm, walked up and down with him in comfortable friendly silence. My dream! thought Mr. Grace. It was almost his dream. He loved her dearly; she was first in his heart (he realized that now), but of course he was second in hers. It was right that he should be; he would not have had it otherwise. He, like Tilly, thought his married daughter was prettier than ever, but he was a little worried about her. She looked fragile, he thought. She looked delicate (she had never been very strong and she was fretting about Roderick). She was more like Mary than ever, closer to him than ever before, they understood each other better...

Sal put his thought into words. "I love you better because I love Roddy," she said. "More, not less. That's funny, isn't it?"

They walked the length of the terrace before he replied. "Love is like that," said Mr. Grace. "The more you divide it the bigger it grows."

"Like shallots," said Sal, with a little chuckle.

"Just like shallots," agreed Mr. Grace, smiling.

"We'll have to divide it again," Sal told him. "You'd like a grandson, wouldn't you?"

So that was the explanation! He pressed her hand against his side. "Either," he said. "A boy in the family would be a change, but girls are *very* satisfactory."

⌀

It was now time for Mr. Grace to collect his notes for the children's service, which was at three o'clock. He was going to talk to the children about the Prodigal Son, and especially about the joy of the Father when he saw his long-lost child. Mr. Grace understood this joy a good deal better than before, not that Sal had wasted her substance, nor eaten husks, but simply because she had been away and was now returned. On entering his study Mr. Grace was somewhat surprised to find his eldest daughter there, browsing among his books...Liz did not, as a rule, worry herself about literary matters.

"Can I help you?" he inquired politely.

"Er—no, it's all right," said Liz. "I was just looking for something."

"You found it, I hope?" he asked, gathering his notes together.

"No, but it doesn't matter. It's just—nothing much—a quotation, really." She hesitated, blushing furiously, and then mumbled, "'When half gods go the gods arrive.'"

Mr. Grace had heard the quotation, but could not remember where, nor in what connection; he suggested that Liz should ask Sal.

"No," said Liz quickly. "No, I'd rather not—it doesn't matter a bit—don't bother. I think perhaps I'll go up the hill and have a quiet afternoon instead of going to church. You don't mind, do you?"

She withdrew in disorder, leaving her father bewildered and

anxious. Her behavior had been so queer. "When half gods go the gods arrive." What did Liz want with the quotation? What meaning did she attach to the words? She could not be thinking of Sal's arrival, could she? No, for she had blushed. Who were the half gods? Not Rona, surely—nor William. She had blushed... Who were the gods?

Really his daughters were a worry to Mr. Grace.

Meantime Liz was on her way to the hill where she intended to spend her quiet afternoon. She was taking with her a basket containing a Thermos flask and a good supply of sandwiches, for it was no part of her intention to fast, and she was also taking the book about Rome just in case she got tired of her own thoughts and needed food for her brain. Arrived at the Roman camp, where William had dug and measured, Liz climbed still farther and sat down upon the hillside to think things out. There was a great deal to think about. What a lot had happened to the Grace family in a few short months, what changes had taken place! Life was like that, thought Liz. You drifted on for years and years—then, suddenly, everything happened at once and all the things that had seemed so stable dissolved and disintegrated before your eyes...and life was new.

"When half gods go the gods arrive," murmured Liz. It was a pity she hadn't been able to find the quotation and so learn the context, but perhaps it was just as well because the context might spoil it. As it was, Liz could attach her own meaning to the words and apply them to the condition of her own heart... Liz was in love again.

Liz wouldn't have put it like that, of course. She would have said she was in love—or perhaps she might have said she was in love for the first time (the other times paled into the insignificance of passing fancies). This was real love. This was deep and high and broad; it filled the whole of her being with magnificence. This love had grown slowly and naturally, had

developed from respect and liking into affection and so had
become love…and this love made her happy, filled her with
unutterable joy, for she knew it was returned in full measure.
She knew he loved her—had known it for months—and then
she had found her heart turning to him. Now she adored him,
and who wouldn't? He was a real man, whole, splendid, worthy
of the best that life could give; worthy of a far better fate than
herself…but no other girl could love him so dearly, that was
certain, and no other girl could understand him so well, could
give him so much tenderness and care… "When half gods go
the gods arrive."

The sun was warm. It was very quiet up here. Below were
the ruins of the Roman fort sleeping in the sunshine as they had
slept for hundreds and hundreds of years. Liz lay back against
the bank and presently closed her eyes…she began to dream.

It was a very curious dream, muddled and inconsecutive
as dreams are apt to be. She was sitting on the hill, the sun
was warm, the sky was blue, one little white cloud floated
in it serenely; below her lay the Roman fort, a curious squat
building, surrounded by earthworks, but Liz was not interested
in the fort, it seemed to her (in her dream) too familiar to be
interesting, she was more interested in the Roman soldier who
was standing on the hill with his back to her, gazing out over
the sunlit landscape. He was a centurion in full armor that glittered in the sun; he was tall and broad shouldered, his limbs
were strong and shapely.

Somehow or other—this was the curious part—Liz knew he
was standing here for the last time. She knew that he had done
his tour of duty and was going back to Rome. He was thinking
of Rome, of his life there, of his friends and his family…but he
was not as glad as he should have been at the prospect of seeing
them again. The centurion was going home, but he was leaving
his heart behind him. All this was vague to Liz in her dream; the

centurion's thoughts passed through her mind like a cloud, like a whiff of perfume caught on a summer breeze. She watched him closely and saw him stretch his arms. She heard him sigh. Then he sat down on the green turf, leaning forward over his bent knees in an attitude of dejection.

Liz awoke slowly, so slowly that she scarcely was aware of the moment of her awakening, so gradually that she scarcely knew she had been asleep. Everything looked exactly the same as it had looked in her dream: the bright sun, the green grass, the slowly moving cloud in the clear, blue sky. The centurion had vanished, of course, but in his stead was William Single... and he sat in exactly the same place, in exactly the same position (shoulders hunched, hands dangling between raised knees), and his expression was exactly the same, dejected, forlorn.

"William Single," said Liz softly. "Why don't you ask me to marry you?"

He turned. "Oh, Liz, because I'm too old, too clumsy and stupid and slow."

"You certainly are very slow," said Liz, with her little snort of laughter.

He came toward her and took her outstretched hand, and she drew him down until he was sitting beside her on the bank.

"Oh, Liz," he said. "But you couldn't...I mean why...why *me*?"

"Because you're you," said Liz. "You're you and I'm me. That's all that matters. If you think I'm going to let you go back to Oxford and live there without me—like the Roman soldier—"

"Like the Roman soldier!"

"The centurion," explained Liz. "It wasn't fair of him. He should have told her, you know. He should have taken her with him to Rome—"

"Is it a story?" asked William, taking her hand and kissing the fingers very gently.

"Not my hand, silly," said Liz, putting up her face.

She was somewhat surprised at the effect of her words, but pleased too. After a few breathless moments she slipped from his grasp and her hands went to her hair, pushing it behind her ears. "Goodness!" she said.

He was chuckling now; he was sitting back with his hands around his knees, laughing at her.

"Well, I asked for it," admitted Liz, smiling.

"That's nothing," declared William. "Ask for something else. Ask for the moon. Ask for the stars." His eyes were shining like stars as he spoke.

"Oh, William!" she cried. "Do you really feel like that?"

"I feel like a god," said William Single.

Continue reading for an excerpt from
Miss Buncle's Book

Chapter One
Breakfast Rolls

O ne fine summer's morning the sun peeped over the hills and looked down upon the valley of Silverstream. It was so early that there was really very little for him to see except the cows belonging to Twelve-Trees Farm in the meadows by the river. They were going slowly up to the farm to be milked. Their shadows were still quite black, weird, and ungainly, like pictures of prehistoric monsters moving over the lush grass. The farm stirred and a slow spiral of smoke rose from the kitchen chimney.

In the village of Silverstream (which lay further down the valley) the bakery woke up first, for there were the breakfast rolls to be made and baked. Mrs. Goldsmith saw to the details of the bakery herself and prided herself upon the punctuality of her deliveries. She bustled round, wakening her daughters with small ceremony, kneading the dough for the rolls, directing the stoking of the ovens, and listening with one ear for the arrival of Tommy Hobday who delivered the rolls to Silverstream before he went to school.

Tommy had been late once or twice lately; she had informed his mother that if he were late again she would have to find another boy. She did not think Tommy would be late again, but, if he were, she must try and find another boy, it was so important for the rolls to be out early. Colonel Weatherhead (retired) was one of her best customers and he was an early breakfaster. He lived in a gray stone house down near the bridge—The Bridge House—just opposite to Mrs. Bold at Cozy Neuk. Mrs. Bold was a widow. She had nothing to drag her out of bed in the morning, and, therefore, like a sensible woman, she breakfasted late. It was inconvenient from the point of view of breakfast rolls that two such near neighbors should want their rolls at different hours. Then, at the other end of the village, there was the Vicar. Quite new, he was, and addicted to early services on the birthdays of Saints. Not only the usual Saints that everybody knew about, but all sorts of strange Saints that nobody in Silverstream had ever heard of before; so you never knew when the Vicarage would be early astir. In Mr. Dunn's time it used to slumber peacefully until its rolls arrived, but now, instead of being the last house on Tommy's list, it had to be moved up quite near the top. Very awkward it was, because that end of the village, where the old gray sixteenth-century church rested so peacefully among the tombstones, had been all late breakfasters and therefore safe to be left until the end of Tommy's round. Miss Buncle, at Tanglewood Cottage, for instance, had breakfast at nine o'clock, and old Mrs. Carter and the Bulmers were all late.

The hill was a problem too, for there were six houses on the hill and in them dwelt Mrs. Featherstone Hogg (there was a Mr. Featherstone Hogg too, of course, but he didn't count, nobody ever thought of him except as Mrs. Featherstone Hogg's husband) and Mrs. Greensleeves, and Mr. Snowdon and his two daughters, and two officers from the camp, Captain Sandeman and Major Shearer, and Mrs. Dick who took in gentlemen paying guests, all clamoring for their rolls early—except, of course, Mrs. Greensleeves, who breakfasted in bed about ten o'clock, if what Milly Spikes said could be believed.

Mrs. Goldsmith shoved her trays of neatly made rolls into